TRUTH
STAINED
LIES

Books by Terri Blackstock

The Moonlighters Series

1 Truth Stained Lies
2 Distortion
3 Twisted Innocence

The Restoration Series

1 Last Light
2 Night Light
3 True Light
4 Dawn's Light

The Intervention Series

1 Intervention
2 Vicious Cycle
3 Downfall

The Cape Refuge Series

1 Cape Refuge
2 Southern Storm
3 River's Edge
4 Breaker's Reef

Newpointe 911

1 Private Justice
2 Shadow of Doubt
3 Word of Honor
4 Trial by Fire
5 Line of Duty

The Sun Coast Chronicles

1 Evidence of Mercy
2 Justifiable Means
3 Ulterior Motives
4 Presumption of Guilt

Second Chances

1 Never Again Good-bye
2 When Dreams Cross
3 Blind Trust
4 Broken Wings

With Beverly LaHaye

1 Seasons Under Heaven
2 Showers in Season
3 Times and Seasons
4 Season of Blessing

Novella

Seaside

Other Books

Shadow in Serenity
Predator
Double Minds
Soul Restoration
Emerald Windows
Miracles (The Listener/
The Gifted)
The Heart Reader
of Franklin High
The Gifted Sophomores
Covenant Child
Sweet Delights

TERRI BLACKSTOCK

New York Times Bestselling Author

TRUTH
STAINED
LIES

☾MOONLIGHTERS SERIES

ZONDERVAN

Truth Stained Lies
Copyright © 2012 by Terri Blackstock

This title is also available as a Zondervan ebook.
Visit www.zondervan.com/ebooks.

This title is also available in a Zondervan audio edition.
Visit www.zondervan.fm.

Requests for information should be addressed to:

Zondervan, *Grand Rapids, Michigan 49530*

Library of Congress Cataloging-in-Publication Data

Blackstock, Terri.
Truth-stained lies / Terri Blackstock.
p.   cm. (Moonlighters series; bk. 1)
ISBN 978-0-310-33156-8 (hardcover, jacketed)
1. Sisters—Fiction. 2. Women private investigators—Fiction.
3. Murder—Investigation—Fiction. I. Title.
PS3552.L34285T79—2013
813'.54—dc232012027197

Scripture quotations are taken from the New American Standard Bible®.
Copyright © 1960, 1962, 1963, 1968, 1971, 1972, 1973, 1975, 1977, 1995 by The
Lockman Foundation. Used by permission. (www.Lockman.org). Also from the
Holy Bible, New Living Translation. © 1996, 2004, 2007, 2013 by Tyndale House
Foundation. Used by permission of Tyndale House Publishers, Inc., Carol Stream,
Illinois 60188. All rights reserved.

Any Internet addresses (websites, blogs, etc.) and telephone numbers in this book
are offered as a resource. They are not intended in any way to be or imply an
endorsement by Zondervan, nor does Zondervan vouch for the content of these
sites and numbers for the life of this book.

Published in association with the literary agency of Alive Communications,
Inc., 7680 Goddard Street, Suite 200, Colorado Springs, CO 80920. www.
alivecommunications.com

Cover design: James Hall
Cover photography: Ken Kochey/Getty Images®
Interior design: Michelle Espinoza

ISBN: 978-0-7180-7744-0 (mass market)

Printed in the United States of America

15 16 17 18 /OPM/ 13 14 13 12 11 10 9 0 7 6 5 4 3 2 1

This book is lovingly dedicated
to the Nazarene

CHAPTER 1

The email from Jay's wife clearly demonstrated that miracles happen. He hadn't expected her to ever speak cordially to him again, even though the custody battle was tearing their child apart. When he read her letter on his office computer, his jaw dropped. The civility in her tone and the plea for him to ditch his attorney's advice and come to her house to talk shocked him.

Hope budded where it had all but shriveled. Dropping everything, he wrote a quick note back:

I'll be right over leaving now.

Yes, it was a miracle. Annalee hadn't spoken to him in almost a year. Every visitation had been arranged through their attorneys. He had longed for the chance to talk to her face-to-face and tell her of his concerns for Jackson if she won full custody. Every other weekend and Wednesday night visitations—the deal most fathers got under this judge—would not cut it. He had wanted to remind her how desperately the child needed his dad. To remind her that children who had their father ripped out of their lives often grew up with voids they tried to fill through self-destructive choices. He'd wanted to appeal to her as an adult and a parent, to get past this bickering and put Jackson first.

Now he had an invitation to do just that.

It wouldn't be an easy conversation. He'd have to put aside his bitterness over her string of affairs and the influence some of her boyfriends had on his five-year-old son. He'd tread carefully, so as not to set her off.

He realized as he drove that he was almost out of gas. Why hadn't he filled up this morning? He pulled into a gas station and hurriedly put in ten dollars' worth, then headed to her neighborhood.

He turned onto her street, wondering if Jackson was home from kindergarten yet. If so, he would run to Jay yelling, "Daddeeeee!" Or was he still at day care? Usually, Annalee worked until seven or eight in her home office, taking tech support calls for the software company she worked for. She often had to work late, since she had to be available for those on the west coast as well as those in the Eastern time zone. Her long hours were the main reason Jay had tried to get custody during the week. There was no reason for Jackson to spend twelve or thirteen hours a day with a babysitter when his own father could be with him part of that time.

Jay slowed as he reached the neighborhood. The houses sat on five-acre wooded lots, so they were spaced far apart. He remembered the day he and Annalee had closed escrow on their lot. They'd been giddy with excitement and had pitched a tent and spent the night there.

It seemed like an eternity ago, back when they were still in love.

Then came Jackson, and the joys and exhaustion of parenthood. After that they'd entered the house-building phase, and the stress tamped their romance. Annalee wanted more than they could afford, running the cost higher with every decision. Their head-butting became more and more frequent. By the time they'd moved in, their love had grown lukewarm. It was probably around that time that she'd had her first affair.

But there was no sense in thinking about that now. He passed the stretch of woods separating their house from the others. As he rounded the curve, the house came into view.

A white pickup truck was parked at the curb in front of the house. Annalee's latest boyfriend drove a silver Jaguar, but according to her Facebook posts, they had broken up weeks ago. As far as Jay knew, she wasn't seeing anyone now. So who was visiting when she knew he was coming over?

As Jay pulled into the driveway, the front door swung open. He shifted into PARK as a clown bounced out. Jay did a double-take. *A clown?*

The man wore a wig with a bald head on top and red curly hair on the sides, and was dressed in a red costume with yellow, white, and green polka-dots. His face was painted in full clown makeup, so it was diffi-cult to tell if he was smiling or if that was just the effect of the red lips curving up on his face. The clown lifted his gloved hand in a wave to Jay as he went to the truck, his big yellow shoes flopping across the lawn.

Jay waved back. Maybe Annalee was hiring a clown for Jackson's birthday next month. But that wasn't like her. She rarely spent money on anyone but herself.

Was she turning over a new leaf?

He got out of the car and went to the front steps. A year ago he would have used his key and gone in, but she had made it clear that he was no longer welcome to walk in like part of the family, even though his name was still on the deed. He knocked, then rang the bell. Its chime rose over the wind, ostentatious and irritating. He'd always hated that bell, but she'd insisted on it.

She didn't answer, so he knocked again. Was this all a joke? Had she set him up to dash his hopes?

He pulled out his cell phone and called her, but it went straight to voice mail. Now what?

Maybe she was in the back of the house and couldn't hear the doorbell. He thought of leaving and chalking it up to her mood swings, but this was important. They were going to talk!

He pulled his key ring out of his pocket, found the house key, and unlocked the door, hoping the violation didn't send her into a rage.

He opened it and stepped inside. "Annalee!" he shouted. "It's me. Where are you?"

There was no answer. The front room was immaculate, just as her designer friend had left it. She only went in there to dust. He went through the front rooms and into the study where she usually worked. "Annalee?"

Still no answer. Her computer was on, her Arabesque screensaver dotting across the black screen. Her desk phone began ringing . . . once . . . twice . . . three times. Where could she be?

Then he heard water running . . . upstairs. Was she showering?

It was just like her. Luring him over, then changing her mind. Toying with him like he was some idiot. "Annalee!"

Still no answer. Getting angry, he bolted upstairs and looked in the open door of the master bedroom, where the two of them had slept for years. The bed was made up as neatly as always. Jackson's room was orderly too. His son wasn't here. Jay went to the hall bathroom where he could hear the running water, pounded on the locked door.

"Annalee? I'm here! Do you want to talk or not?"

Nothing. "Annalee!" he shouted, pounding again. "Answer me!"

Water began seeping out from under the door. What was going on? Was she in there with the water running over?

Sudden fear burst through him. Something wasn't right. He pounded again, and when there was still no answer, he backed up and kicked the door, his foot landing just below the doorknob.

Wood splintered, and he kicked it again, twice more, until the door broke and flew open.

And there she was.

His wife . . . fully dressed and motionless in the bathtub . . . pink water running over . . .

For an eternity of seconds he stood frozen, staring at the scene, unable to take it in. Then reality shook him.

"Annalee!" He ran to the tub and turned the water off, got his arms under her, lifted her out, water sloshing over the side of the tub.

She was fully clothed and wearing shoes, but her white blouse was stained and torn . . .

Horror pounding through him, he realized it wasn't torn. The hole in the cloth burned into a wound on her chest. Heart racing, he laid her on the wet floor and tried to revive her. "Annalee, wake up! Please . . . God . . . don't let her die!" She was limp and her face was gray, her lips colorless. Her eyes were partially open, vacant.

Jay groped for his phone with wet hands, couldn't find it. The other pocket . . . he pulled it out, punched in 911.

The dispatcher answered, "911, what is your emergency?"

"My wife . . . I think she's dead . . ."

"You think your wife is dead?" the dispatcher repeated. "Sir, what's wrong with her?"

"She was in the bathtub . . . shot, I think . . . she's not breathing."

"You think she was shot?"

Why did she keep repeating his words? "Yes . . . I don't know . . . looks like a bullet hole. Please, send an ambulance!" He gave her the address.

"They're on their way, sir. Stay on the phone with me. Do you know CPR?"

He tried to think. Chest compressions . . . "Yes. I think so."

"Sir, can you feel a pulse?"

He almost dropped the phone as he touched the carotid artery on the side of her neck, praying for a pulse.

There wasn't one.

"No! I don't feel one. You have to hurry!"

"Sir, I need you to put the heel of one hand on her chest and pump it with your other hand."

Trembling, he put the phone on the commode lid. What about her wound? He put his hands next to it, over her heart, and started pumping, praying her heart would start. The hole was to the right of center. Maybe it had missed the organ. If the paramedics came in time . . .

"Sir, is she responding?" The voice sounded distant. He reached up and set it to speakerphone.

"No, not yet," he said, breathless. "When will they be here?"

"In a few minutes. Is the door unlocked?"

He tried to think. "Yes, I left it unlocked. Tell them we're upstairs." He kept pumping as he talked, Annalee's body jerking with the force of his weight. But nothing changed. Sweat dripped into his eyes.

"She's not responding!"

"You said she was in the tub?"

"Yes, with her clothes on," he said, breathless. "Soaking wet."

"Sir, keep pumping."

"Yes." He pumped, praying, but there was still nothing. Jackson . . . his mother . . .

This wasn't what he wanted. Despite all the fighting, part of him still loved her.

"Annalee, please!" he shouted. "Wake up! Jackson needs you!"

But she didn't move.

He heard the sirens coming—loud, spiral sounds in front of the house. They could save her. They'd give her oxygen, blood, defibrillate her, bring her back.

He heard the door downstairs, the thunder of footsteps coming up the stairs. "I'm in here!" he shouted. "The bathroom!"

Two firemen appeared at the door, dressed in firefighting gear. "No!" he shouted. "I need an ambulance, not a fireman!"

They stepped aside as a paramedic burst in and knelt across from him. "Sir, move away and let me," the medic said.

"Please . . . I've been doing CPR . . . she's not responding." Jay moved back as the paramedic examined her. "You have to revive her. We have a little boy."

"She's been shot," the medic called to someone. "Exit wound on her back."

The firemen pulled Jay out of the bathroom and into the hall. Only then did he notice that his pant legs and shoes were wet. His arms were soaked and stained pink.

Police were waiting for him on the staircase. They introduced themselves as Officers Shelton and Blake. "Sir, do you know who shot her?"

He started to shake his head, then remembered the

clown. "There . . . there was a guy when I got here. He was coming out the front door. He was dressed like a clown."

The eyebrows of one of the cops shot up. "A clown?"

"Yes. Big curly red wig and his face all painted up. He got into a white truck and drove east."

"Did you see the tag number?"

"No. His truck was facing me when I pulled in. It didn't occur to me to check his tag. I didn't know anything was wrong."

The cop named Shelton tipped his head. "So let me get this straight. You're saying a clown shot your wife?"

"I don't know if he shot her! I just saw him!"

Shelton sent the other one a look. "A clown."

"Yes."

They didn't believe him. He looked toward the bathroom. "There was water running out under the door, and the door was locked. I kicked it in."

Someone near the bathroom called up the hall. "Shelton . . . you need to see something."

Shelton left them and walked over to stand at the bathroom door. Jay watched, breath held. He heard the word "gun," then Shelton stepped into the bathroom.

After a moment, he came back out. "Get some pictures, document how we found it. I'll notify Homicide."

"Homicide?" Jay asked. "No . . . you have to keep trying!"

Shelton shot Jay a harder look as he came back toward him. "Mr. Cramer, do you own a gun?"

Jay tried to shift his thoughts. A gun? "No . . . I mean, yes, I did. I left it with Annalee when I moved out."

"What kind of gun is it?"

"A .38 revolver. It's registered. I think she keeps it in her bed table drawer."

The men exchanged looks.

"Are they still working on her? Are they trying?" He had barely gotten the words out when he saw the first paramedic coming out of the bathroom, no longer hurried.

"Is she gonna be okay?" Jay asked, tears burning his eyes.

The paramedic shook his head. "No sir, I'm sorry."

Jay bolted forward, and the cops grabbed him, pulling him back. "No, she can't be dead. We have a five-year-old. He can't lose his mother!"

But he could see from their faces that it was too late. There was nothing they could do.

CHAPTER 2

Cathy Cramer couldn't wait for a recess. She'd sat on the hard wooden bench for four hours with only one ten-minute break, watching the drama play out in the murder trial. Her bones ached from being still, and she was only thirty-two. The older reporter sitting next to her was probably suffering. She could hear his joints cracking when he crossed his legs. Each time they broke for recess, he'd raced to the bathroom as if a kidney might burst out of his side and stumble to the bathroom itself.

The pretty young defendant showed no signs of cracking, even after three weeks of sitting under the world's scrutiny, her hair slicked back in a severe bun each day. She was probably glad to be out of her cell this whole time, though Cathy would have been much happier to be hidden away if the same sorts of accusations had been hurled about her.

The accused child-killer was definitely guilty. Surely the jury saw it. Cathy's own readers of her investigative blog *Cat's Curious* saw it clearly, even though they relied on what Cathy's blog and the rest of the media interpreted into the court testimony.

The case, which was being tried right here in Cathy's home town of Panama City, Florida, had doubled her readership in the last few months and netted her some heavy advertisers for her blog. Her past as an attorney, her deep intuition about these cases after her own experiences with murder, and her fearless way of nailing the truth, kept her fans reading.

If people ever stopped killing each other, she supposed she'd be out of work. She could always switch to debunking urban myths or exposing corporate crimes, if she couldn't force herself to go back to practicing law. But until sociopaths developed consciences, Cathy was happy to do her part in championing the victims and dissecting the crimes for all to see.

At last, the judge called a recess until tomorrow. As the jury was led out of the room, Cathy locked onto the defendant's face. Sara Chesney's emotionless facade melted away, and she smiled at her attorney and gave him a wink.

Perfect. Cathy hoped no one else had seen that. Max, the reporter next to her, was focused on his notes. The TV camera had already cut off. The other reporters on the second row seemed to be watching the jurors' faces. Maybe Cathy was the only one who'd caught it. If not, she could at least be the first to report it. She'd write about it this afternoon. What could it mean? That Sara felt the defense had pulled off their latest subliminal suggestions to the jury? That she and her attorney had a thing going?

Or was it just that the defendant was relieved to be

out from under the judging eyes of those jurors and that camera?

Sara was handcuffed and led out, her pastel button-down shirt more wrinkled than it had been this morning. Cathy wondered if the woman had ever worn a button-down in her life before now. The pictures of her before her niece's death showed that she preferred outfits that exposed skin and were at least a size too small. The schoolmarm image wasn't fooling anyone.

When the judge left the room, Max mowed through the spectators to get to the restroom. Cathy stepped out quietly, checking over her notes. She made a quick pit stop by the ladies' room, listening to the conversations among the spectators. They all seemed to have the same impression of today's testimony that she had— that the defendant's husband was lying, that the best friend was telling the truth . . .

Cathy's instincts were rarely wrong.

She stepped out on the front steps of the courthouse. Media lined the sidewalk out front, some of them already broadcasting about the last few hours in the trial. She trotted past the television vans and hurried to the parking garage. Her Miata sat in a parking space on the top level, baking in the hot sun.

She slipped in and pushed the button to put the top down. As it retreated over her head, she saw an envelope stuck under her windshield wiper. What now? She opened the door and reached to grab it.

The flap was tucked inside the envelope and her

name—Cat Cramer—was typed on the center of it. No return address.

She turned on her engine and sat idling as she pulled the typed note out.

Dear Curious Cat,

I've grieved that Leonard Miller's bullet only hit your fiancé. Too bad you weren't with him that day. You deserve what he got. But look at you, turning your tragedy into dollar signs.

Guilt or innocence is not something to be judged by a two-bit blogger with a drama-loving readership. Maybe it's time you saw firsthand how speculation ruins lives. Judgment that has nothing to do with truth. See how it feels.

Enjoy the ride, if you
survive it.
Your New Friend

Cathy dropped the note. Was this a threat of some kind, or just an angry reader trying to mess with her? The mention of Leonard Miller, who'd murdered her fiancé and walked away scot-free, dredged up the rippling anger that had plagued her in those first months after his death.

She swept her hair out of her eyes and looked around. There were a few others walking to their cars, a couple of cars pulling out of parking spaces. No one looking her way. Anyone could have left it anytime today. Her silver sports car wasn't hard to spot, and all her readers knew she'd been attending this trial every day.

It occurred to her that she should call the police, but she had to get home and write her blog before the rest of the press beat her to the punch. Before pulling out of her space, she typed a text to her closest circle—her three siblings and Michael Hogan, one of her closest friends and the brother of her murdered fiancé.

> Just found a note stuck on my windshield by some unsatisfied reader. Sort of a threat. Never dull.

Dropping the phone onto her seat and sticking the note and envelope under her purse so it wouldn't blow away, she pulled out of the garage and into traffic, her long black hair flapping in the wind.

If the person who left the note was watching, she hoped she looked carefree and unflappable, even if it wasn't true. Inside, she seethed. Her sense of justice cut like a razor, reminding her of the victims in the cases she was covering. She knew what it was like to have a killer walk away without a conviction, thumbing his nose at those who would never be the same.

For those victims, she wrote on, doing her part to make sure the killers paid. She hadn't been able to help society by working as a prosecutor—that seemed more about making plea deals than putting criminals behind bars. Court cases weren't about justice. They were about finding loopholes. One cleverly conceived scheme by either side could influence the jury, if a case ever made it to court in the first place. Her skills were better used doing her own investigations and alerting readers to evidence that judges suppressed.

She'd given up her job in the district attorney's office and set to work writing about the cases that captured her attention . . . exposing the killers who spun their stories and manipulated the jurors. She was no longer constrained by suppressed evidence or gag orders.

Over the two years that she'd been doing this, she'd gotten several death threats. None of them had resulted in any attempts on her life. This one was probably just another scare tactic. When two million people followed your blog, a few of them were bound to be crazies.

But she wouldn't let some cryptic note ruin her day. She had a blog to write. She'd worry about it later.

CHAPTER 3

Michael Hogan felt sorry for the woman whose husband had cheated on her, so he let her keep talking, even though he had places to be.

"This girl used to work as his secretary," Laura Hancock said in a slow drawl, dabbing at her tears with the handkerchief he'd handed her. "She worked for my husband for three months, and I didn't care one bit for her, so I made him fire her. Something about the way she dressed . . . all sexy and provocative-like . . . and the haughty way she acted with me. Like she had the upper hand in some game I didn't even know we were playing."

"Yes ma'am." Michael wanted to cut her off—this was dragging on way too long.

"I didn't know he kept seeing her. I mean . . . I knew there was something going on with him, or obviously I wouldn't have hired you to follow him. But I didn't have a clue it was her."

Michael wished he hadn't given her the picture of the two kissing in a parking lot in broad daylight. Maybe he should have just told her what he'd found. Images had a way of implanting themselves on a person's mind. But she'd paid him to take pictures.

"What should I do?" she asked, looking up at him with wet eyes.

Oh, no. He wasn't going there. "Ma'am, I don't do counseling. I just get the facts, the timeline, the photos. I would encourage you not to make any immediate decisions. Talk to someone who can help you with this. Maybe a pastor?"

"I don't go to church," she said.

"Well, sometimes when you're going through a tough time, a minister can help. Sometimes churches have counseling ministries and support groups."

He could tell she wasn't listening. "What do your other clients do when they find out their spouse has been stepping out on them? Do they file for divorce?"

"Honestly, I don't know. I don't do follow-up."

She gave him a dull look, like he was the least helpful person she'd ever met. That was okay. He wasn't going to cross the line from private investigator to marriage counselor, no matter what she needed.

She finally stacked up the pictures, shoved them back into their envelope, and headed out, armed with the ammunition she needed to force an ultimatum or slaughter her husband in court. But he didn't feel good about it.

There was nothing rewarding in this work. Nothing at all.

The picture on his wall drew his gaze for the hundredth time today. His grandfather, his father, his two brothers and him in Panama City PD dress blues.

That was before he'd disgraced them all.

Right now, he had to go follow some dude who was

supposed to be wheelchair-bound but shot hoops every afternoon with his buds. A few pictures of him doing jump shots, and the worker's comp attorney who'd hired Michael would be happy.

Through the window, he watched the scorned woman go out to her car, parked beside the old, out-of-order gas pumps that reminded him every day that his office used to be a convenience store. It was the best he could get for the rent he could afford. The place was practically falling down. The roof leaked every time it rained, and he'd pulled the sheetrock off the ceiling in the back rooms, trying to fix the problem. But it would take a lot more than he'd been able to do on his own. Money was too tight, so he had to make do with buckets when storms hit.

His thoughts went back to the woman getting into her car, and he said a quiet prayer for her marriage. But there were times when it seemed that God had his hands over his ears. He hoped this wasn't one of those times.

His phone chimed. He picked it up from his cluttered desk and saw the text from Cathy.

> Just found a note stuck on my windshield by some unsatisfied reader. Sort of a threat. Never dull.

Sort of a threat? What did that mean? Quickly, he pressed speed dial to call her. He heard the wind as the call went live. She must be in her car with the top down.

"Hey, Michael. I shoulda known you'd call."

"What are you talking about . . . a threat?"

"Somebody left a note saying they were gonna show me what it feels like to be judged . . . or something to that effect."

That wasn't so bad, Michael thought. "So . . . they didn't say what they were going to do?"

"No. But it ended with, 'Enjoy the ride, if you survive it.' Oh, and the person mentioned Leonard Miller."

Michael's lower lip stiffened. "What did he say?"

"Seemed miffed that I wasn't killed with Joe."

Some unseen vice clamped across Michael's rib cage. "Okay, you've got to call the police."

"No, I don't have time. I just got out of court and I have to get my blog written. Then I have to go to the TV station, because FOX News wants to interview me about the trial."

"Cathy, call the police. If you don't, I will."

"But it's just some whacko trying to scare me."

"Fine. Maybe it is. But the police need to be aware."

He heard a long, exaggerated groan. "All right. I'll call them as soon as I get a minute."

Sometimes she made him crazy. "No, now. I'm coming over, Cathy. I'll meet you at your house."

Again, that long, protracted groan. "All right, Michael. I'll call them." She paused. "Juliet's calling. Why did I ever tell you guys? I gotta go."

"See you in a few."

"Right."

She cut off the call, and he sat holding his phone, staring at it as if he could see the person who'd put that threat on Cathy's car. He didn't like it, and even if it was just another blowhard trying to incite fear, he would get to the bottom of it.

His subject would shoot hoops again tomorrow. This was more important right now.

CHAPTER 4

Cathy's older sister sounded overly concerned, as usual. Cathy rolled her eyes and went back over the note.

"Do you want me to come over?" Juliet asked.

"No! Michael is coming. If you want to talk to him after the police leave to make sure I'm toeing the line and not flinging myself into the gunfire of a killer, call him. But honestly, if the police take too long, I don't know what I'll do. I have to get my blog out. People are waiting."

"It's not like their lives depend on reading your blog."

"Thanks. I appreciate your support."

"I'm just saying. That blog might get you killed. You're talking about killers. They don't like it."

Juliet was only two years older—just thirty-four—but she acted like Cathy's mother rather than her sister.

"Cathy, give the police a list of all the cases you've talked about lately. All the people you've tried and convicted in your blog."

"I haven't tried and convicted anybody, Juliet. I've just exposed things I've learned about their cases. We still have freedom of speech in this country."

"Tell that to the guy who's promised you a bumpy

ride." Cathy heard her nephew talking to her sister, Juliet answering. Then her sister was back. "Hey, have you talked to Jay?"

"No, I've been in court all day. I'm sure I'll hear from him and Holly when they get my text."

"I'm worried about him. He's been so depressed."

"Yeah, custody battles are brutal."

"What if he doesn't win?"

"It'll kill him." Cathy changed lanes and headed onto the exit ramp to her small house across the street from the beach.

"We just have to keep praying. You do still pray, don't you, Cathy?"

She hated when her sister got on this subject. "Yes, Juliet, I pray."

"I'm just asking. It's not like you talk about it a lot."

"And I don't want to talk about it now. I have to go. I'm almost home, and I promised I'd call the police."

"Call me the minute they leave."

Cathy sighed. "I'll call you when I'm finished with FOX."

"No, Cathy. I need to know!"

"'Bye, Juliet." Cathy hung up and dialed the police station, which she had on her speed dial, since she constantly had to call them to verify facts. This wasn't 911-worthy.

She knew the sergeant who answered, and she told him she needed to file a complaint. He would send someone right over.

Maybe she'd have time to get some of her blog written before they showed up.

But as she pulled into her driveway, Michael drove up in his Trailblazer. Great. The guy was never late.

She pulled her car into the garage, then got out and watched Michael striding up her driveway. As always when she saw him, she thought of Joe. He looked so much like his brother. His charcoal eyes, his dark hair, the laugh lines, the way his mouth was shaped . . .

"You call 'em?" he asked as he approached her.

She turned away from him and tried to banish Joe's image from her mind. "Yes, I called. They're on their way."

"Let me see the note."

She leaned into her car and got the note, holding it by one corner, and handed it to him. He pulled some latex gloves out of his pocket and pulled them on, then took it carefully.

"Come on in," she said. "It's hot out here."

He stood still, reading the note. She saw the color spreading across his tightening jaw, his cheeks, his ears. His eyes narrowed. "I don't like this, Cathy."

"Me either, but what can you do?"

She pushed the door open that led into her mud room, set down her things. He followed her into the kitchen. "How long ago did you call?"

"Like thirty seconds. It wasn't a big hurry."

He checked his watch, then met her eyes. "Go write. I'll watch for them and let them in. I'm sure you have juicy stuff you want to get out."

She grinned. "I do. When the jury went out today, Sara Chesney looked at her attorney and winked. I'm pretty sure no one else saw it. My readers are gonna love that."

"So much for the grieving aunt."

"Got that right. I'll be in my office. If anybody tries to kill me, stop them, will ya?"

"Not funny."

She laughed as she headed back to her office.

. . .

Michael paced in Cathy's living room as he waited for the police to arrive. Something about her house always made him feel comfort. Maybe it was because he'd seen Joe sitting on that couch so many times, his feet propped on her coffee table ottoman, watching a game on her 46-inch screen. Cathy and Joe had bought this house together to live in after they were married. She had moved in first, and Joe was going to join her after the knot was tied. But that day had never come.

Sometimes when Michael was in here, he could almost imagine Joe walking into the room from the kitchen, a Mountain Dew in his hand.

That old sense of failure tightened his chest again. Leonard Miller, his brother's killer, was out on the streets somewhere, hiding out because of the public sentiment against him, probably continuing his life of crime.

How many more people would die before they finally got him off the streets? How many more cops?

Michael's mouth went dry, and he went to the kitchen and reached into Cathy's fridge, got out a bottled water. He heard a car in the driveway, and he looked out, saw the police car. Two men got out. Michael knew them both. They'd all entered the police academy together, but he had been promoted faster.

When his career ended, he'd been a detective in the Major Crimes Unit, while they were still patrolling the city.

He went to the door and opened it before they rang the bell. "Hey, guys," he said. "Thanks for coming."

"No problem." Cryder shook his hand and came inside. "When I heard this call was from Cathy, I said I'd take it."

"Is she here?" Dillard asked.

"Yeah, she's here." Michael stepped into the hallway and called, "Cathy, they're here!"

He heard her theatrical grunt.

"Cathy, did you hear me?"

"Yeah, I heard," she said. "Show them the note, will you? I'm almost finished."

He sighed and turned back. "She's writing her blog." He got the note, which he'd placed in a Ziploc bag, and set it down for them to read. "She's not taking this too seriously, but it's a pretty pointed threat."

The cops read the note. "She have any idea who wrote it?" Dillard asked.

"No, none."

Suddenly she floated into the room. "Hey, guys. Glad it's you two they sent. You can hurry this along, can't you?"

"Where was the note, Cathy?" Cryder asked.

She told them about finding the note on her windshield and Michael's insistence that she call them. "It's not that big of a deal. I get death threats sometimes. Occupational hazard."

"Michael was right to make you report it," Dillard said. "Just for the record."

"Dust it, see if there are fingerprints," Michael said. "See if there's any security video in the parking garage that would show the person coming to her car."

Cryder puffed up. "This is low priority, Hogan."

"It shouldn't be. It's a death threat."

Cryder turned back to Cathy. "Cathy, who have you made mad lately?"

She sighed. "How long do you have? This guy needs to get in line."

"Might not even be a guy," Michael said. "If the tape caught the person putting the note on her car, we'll know that. Cathy, I want you to make a copy of the note before they take it. Leave it in the bag."

She shrugged. "Okay."

When she disappeared into her office, Michael turned back to his friends. "Guys, don't blow this off. I'm thinking she needs a bodyguard. If you know anybody who's interested in making some extra cash, let me know."

Cryder laughed. "Why now? Did you get her one for every threat she's had before this?"

"No, but I didn't know about the others until weeks after they happened. I do know about this one."

"She's not gonna go for that," Cryder said.

Michael knew that was true. "I'll talk her into it."

"Who's paying for it?" Dillard asked. "You?"

Michael wanted to say yes, but he'd barely been able to pay his rent last month. "I said I'd talk her into it. Think about who might want the job."

Cathy came back with the original note and handed it to Cryder. "Guys, what else do you need from me? I'm slammed for time here."

They had her sign the complaint, then they left the house. Michael stood at the front window, watching as they drove away.

"I heard what you said about a bodyguard," she said from behind him. "That's excessive, Michael. I don't want somebody hanging around me all the time. It slows me down."

"Just for a couple of weeks, until we see what this person's gonna do."

"I said no. I have a gun and a concealed weapon permit. That's all I need."

He turned to face her. "I could do it."

She crossed her arms. "Michael, what good would that do? You're not even allowed to carry a gun."

The reminder made him feel useless, but he swallowed his bitterness back.

"I'm sorry," she said quickly, stepping toward him. "I didn't mean that as a stab. I just meant that there's no use in babysitting me. I'm a big girl. I can handle this."

"What time do you have to be at the station?" he asked.

"Six thirty. I have to find something to wear and do my makeup and try to tame this hair. I shouldn't have put the top down."

"I'll wait."

Again, a grunt. "Michael, that's ridiculous."

"I read your blog this morning. You told your fans that you were going to be on FOX tonight. It's a no-brainer for someone who wants to do you harm. If I'm with you, it might be a deterrent."

"But it's a satellite feed. My readers don't know where I'll be shooting it."

"Seriously? You think it's hard to figure out that it's one of the stations in Panama City?"

She seemed to consider that for a moment, then the resistance on her face drained away. "All right, I guess, if you insist, but you don't have to hang around until I leave. Don't you have someone to spy on?"

Michael knew he should try to get his pictures of the worker's comp fraud so he could get paid.

"Do you have your security alarm set?"

"I'll set it."

"All right, I guess I can leave and come back. Don't answer the door for anyone you don't know."

"I won't be a prisoner in my own home, Michael."

Why was she so stubborn? "Cathy, just cooperate for a little while, will you? I'm trying to keep you safe."

Her face softened into a smile, and she stepped toward him and gave him a hug. His heart slammed against his chest. Instant guilt rushed through his veins.

"I appreciate it," she said. "I don't mean to sound ungrateful."

His mouth suddenly went dry. He looked down at her, taking in the almond shape of her eyes, the delicate shape of her nose, her wet lips. It was no wonder his brother had fallen for her.

She gave him a little shove. "Now go, so I can work."

He drew in a deep breath. "All right. But call me if anything happens."

"You know I will."

"I'll be real busy spying on an NBA wannabe who's supposed to be confined to a wheelchair."

"Sounds like fun."

"Oh yeah, big fun. I love my job." He hated the sarcasm in his own voice.

"It's still important, what you do," she said softly.

The last thing he wanted from her was sympathy. "Go, write. Your readers are waiting to hear about Sara Chesney's wink."

Her phone rang, breaking her gaze. She pulled it out of her pocket. "What now?" Her younger sister's picture filled the screen. "It's Holly," she said. "Michael, will you talk to her while I write my blog? Tell her I'm fine, that I've had the police here . . ."

"Sure." He took the iPhone and swiped to answer. "Holly," he said, "it's me, Michael. Cathy told me to fill you in while she—"

"I have to talk to Cathy!" Holly shouted, cutting him off. "It's Annalee . . . she's dead!"

Cathy, who'd clearly heard Holly's panicked voice, turned back. "What is it?"

Michael put it on speakerphone. "What did you say?"

"Annalee was murdered. Jay found her."

Cathy's startled eyes locked with Michael's. "What? How?"

"I don't know. Jay was over at her house . . . he called

just now and said the police are there . . . that they're questioning him."

The color drained from Cathy's face. "We have to get over there. Where is Jackson?"

"He's at day care. That's why Jay called. He wanted me to pick Jackson up."

Michael moved closer to Cathy as she swayed, put his arm around her to steady her. "Are they sure she's dead?" he asked. "What happened to her? Where was she when he found her?"

"He didn't say. I don't know anything. I want to go over there."

"Have you called Juliet?"

"He tried her first, but she didn't answer. I'll try her again now."

"Okay. We're on our way." Cathy clicked the phone off. "Michael, we have to hurry."

He grabbed her purse and thrust it at her.

CHAPTER 5

A throng of police cars glutted the street in front of Annalee's house. "This is unreal," Cathy whispered as Michael stopped his Trailblazer.

"There's Holly and Juliet," Michael said, pointing. Cathy saw them getting out of Juliet's BMW on the other side of the cruisers. Holly's two-tone hair—platinum blonde and hot pink—strung into her eyes as though it hadn't been washed in days. Cathy's twenty-eight-year-old sister wept openly like an abandoned child as she followed Juliet between the cars. Juliet, thirty-four, wasn't crying. Instead, she wore a stoic look of maternal determination as she scanned faces, her short-cropped red hair ruffling in the warm breeze.

The police had roped off the yard and an area in front of the property. Jay's car sat in the driveway. As Cathy got out of Michael's truck, her sisters came between the cars toward her. "Can we go under the tape?" Juliet asked.

"No, it's a crime scene," Michael said.

"I don't care. I'm going." Cathy ducked under the tape and started up the driveway. Her sisters followed, but Michael waited, hands in his pockets, as if he knew they wouldn't get far.

The log officer stopped them, addressing Cathy. "Ma'am, please go back."

"We're family," Cathy said. "Where is Jay, the husband?"

"He's in the house, but you can't go in there."

"Please . . . he needs us," Juliet said. "We're his sisters. Can you tell him we're here?"

"He's being questioned. You'll have to wait. You need to get back behind the tape."

As the uniform lifted the tape for them to pass back under, Michael reached out to shake the cop's hand. "Michael Hogan," he said.

The cop's eyebrows shot up. "Yeah, I know who you are."

"Is my brother here, by any chance? Max Hogan?"

"Yeah, matter of fact, he is."

"We'll wait behind the tape, but could you let him know I'm out here and need to talk to him?"

The cop waited for the sisters to duck back under the tape. When they were in compliance, he headed inside. Cathy studied her sisters. Juliet stood with her chin up, stoically waiting for the next blow. She was strong; she could take it. But Holly . . .

Her younger sister wasn't strong. She was a wilting willow, blown and tossed around by the wind, covered with emotional bruises from her own choices and the choices of those around her. Holly was shaking. She brought her hands to her face and gave in to her grief.

Cathy held back her own tears.

Michael's brother Max stepped out the front door. Though Max was the middle brother and only a year's difference separated him and Michael, he couldn't be more different. His expression was grim as he came up the driveway, dressed in jeans and an untucked button-down. "Hey, man. I thought you might show up." He came toward Cathy, gave her a quick hug. "You okay?"

"No," she said. "We want to talk to my brother. He's traumatized, and he needs us."

"He's busy. My partner and I have been questioning him."

Cathy opened her mouth to protest, but Michael said, "Talk to you alone?" Max looked from one sister to the other, then motioned for Michael to step to the side. Cathy put her arm around Holly and waited, hoping Michael would get the story.

. . .

Michael followed his brother to the edge of the yard. "What's going on, man? What can you tell me?"

Max turned his back to the sisters and kept his voice low. "It's not looking good for Jay."

Michael stared at him, letting that soak in. "What do you mean? He just showed up and found her, right?" He realized from the look on his brother's face that there was more to it than that. "What? You don't think he did it!"

Max drew in a long breath. "Michael, I know you're close to this family. You're not gonna like this."

"Tell me."

"He's looking guilty. He shouldn't have been here. They've been battling out their custody case, haven't spoken to each other except through their lawyers in a year. Suddenly today he shows up here? And his gun was found in the bathroom . . . where we found the bullet. She was shot."

"*His* gun?"

"Yes. And his story is insane. Something about a clown coming out of her house when he drove up."

Michael's heart plunged. "He said that?"

"Yeah, can you believe it? A clown in a curly wig with his face all painted up. Big shoes flopping across the lawn."

"Well, did you check the yard for those prints?"

Max slapped his forehead. "Wow, you really think I should? What would I do without my ex-super-cop brother?"

Michael ignored his brother's sarcasm. "I'm just saying, even if you don't believe his story . . . Just check it out. Why would he make up a story about a clown?"

"Why? Are you serious? Why does anybody lie?"

"Jay is not a killer. Why would he blow smoke about something that didn't even sound credible?"

"Maybe he didn't think it through. He wanted his kid, man. Couldn't handle being an every-other-weekend dad. You told me about that yourself."

"He wouldn't murder Jackson's mother. He would never do that to him."

"People do strange things when they're angry."

Michael saw that Cathy was watching him, so he turned his back to her and slid his hands into the pockets of his jeans.

"I hate it for Cathy," Max said. "She's been through a lot. We all have. But this isn't gonna be good."

"So are you on the case?" Michael asked him.

"Yep. Lucky me. Gotta get back."

"Yeah. Call me when you get finished here, will you?"

"If I have time."

Michael watched as his brother went back into the house. He fought the longing to go in there, get one look at the body, the crime scene. What clues could he find that his brother might miss? Max was new in Major Crimes. His partner, Al Forbes, had been good once, but he was close to retirement and seemed to be marking time until he could collect his pension.

Cathy crossed the driveway toward him. "What did he say?"

He didn't know what to tell her. "He just said that . . ." His voice trailed off. "That she was shot. That they found the murder weapon and the bullet in the bathroom where Jay found her."

"Good. Maybe the gun is registered to the killer. Maybe there are prints."

"Right." The word came out flat, without energy.

Cathy caught his inflection and studied his face. "Michael, what are you not telling me?"

He swallowed as her sisters came toward them. Juliet's eyes were probing.

"Michael, my brother's wife is dead," Cathy said. "Tell me what you know!"

He pulled in a deep breath. "The gun was Jay's. They're thinking that maybe . . ."

She sucked in a breath and turned back to the door. "No," she said through her teeth. "My brother didn't do this." Before he could stop her, she ducked back under the tape and flew up the driveway.

"Cathy, wait!" Michael said. "You can't go in there!"

The logging cop blocked her. "Ma'am, I told you—"

"I'm Jay Cramer's attorney," she said, throwing her chin up. "I need to see my client."

The cop looked irritated that she'd thrown him a curve ball. "Just a minute. Don't come any further." He went to the door and stepped inside.

"Cathy!" Juliet said. "You're not practicing law!"

"I've kept my license current," she said. "Jay needs a lawyer."

Michael couldn't help smiling. Leave it to Cathy to think on her feet. The cop came back out and motioned for her to come in. Without another look back, she went into her sister-in-law's house.

. . .

Cathy stepped into the house she hadn't entered since Christmas sixteen months ago, before Jay realized his marriage was in trouble. It looked like something out of *Southern Living*, with furniture Jay was still paying for and extravagant, well-placed accessories on every surface. Annalee had a knack for decorating and spending money. A cop stood at the bottom of the stairs. "Where is he?" she demanded.

"In the living room."

Cathy cut through the kitchen and into the living area, where Al Forbes had Jay in a wingback chair in the corner, questioning him like a criminal. Jay's eyes were wet, his nose red from weeping. She had seen him like this a couple of times since his wife asked for a divorce, but now he seemed traumatized, jerky and shaking. "Not another word, Jay," she called out. "Detective, I need a moment alone with my client."

That clearly didn't make Al happy, but he had no choice but to comply. "Cathy, I'm just trying to solve your sister-in-law's murder. Please don't keep him from cooperating with us." He pulled his doughy body up. "I'll be upstairs," he said. "Call us when you're ready to resume questioning."

Cathy watched him leave, then turned back to her brother. Jay got up and hugged her fiercely. "I'm so glad you're here."

She blinked back her tears and pulled him down with her on the love seat she'd given him and Annalee for an anniversary gift years ago. "Jay, I want you to tell me everything that happened, from the beginning. Don't leave anything out. And keep your voice down so they don't hear."

"I've already told them everything," he said. "I don't have anything to hide."

She closed her eyes. "Oh no. You should have asked for an attorney right out of the gate."

"I didn't know they would try to pin this on me. I

just found her, that's all. It was the clown, but I don't know if they're even looking for him."

"The clown? What clown?"

He shook his head as if to clear his thoughts. "I got this email from Annalee at work, saying she wanted me to come over and talk to her away from the attorneys, that she wanted us to come to an agreement—just me and her about what was best for Jackson. So I dropped everything and came."

That didn't sound like Annalee. She had been vicious in her attacks on her husband. The marriage had fallen apart because of her own infidelity, and she'd been trying to rip Jackson from his life and take everything Jay owned. She'd gone as far as making allegations about child abuse, all of which his attorney would debunk in court. She wasn't the conciliatory put-my-kid-first type. She never had been.

"When I drove up, there was a white truck outside on the curb. I pulled into the driveway, and out comes this clown through the front door. Dressed in a bald head with curly red hair on the sides, face all made up, red outfit, big shoes. He waved, then flopped out to his truck and drove away."

She tried to visualize it. "Did he say anything? Did you talk to him?"

"No. By the time I got out of the car, he was gone. I didn't know she was dead or I would have stopped him."

Perspiration beaded on her upper lip. "When you went into the house, was there anything out of place? Did you notice anything unusual?"

"Just that she didn't answer the door. And water was

running under the bathroom door . . . It was locked. I kicked it in."

No wonder they were suspicious. The clown story, the splintered door . . .

He wiped his jaw with a trembling hand. "She was dead in the bathtub, fully dressed, with a gunshot wound in her chest."

Cathy looked toward the staircase. "Did you see the gun?"

"No. I was just focused on her. I called 911 and did CPR. But it was too late." His body shook as a sob rose up inside him, and she hugged him. "Now they think I did it because I bought that gun. But it was here, in the house. The clown must have used it."

The clown. Even as he said the words, Cathy knew they sounded ridiculous. How would this sound to the police . . . the press? She knew they'd be showing up any minute now. Some self-important rookie would leak the story, and they'd write about the clown, and people would laugh, and Jay would become a laughingstock and be convicted in the court of public opinion.

He'd be just the kind of defendant she wrote about. But of course it wasn't true. Jay wasn't violent, and even if he were, he'd never be stupid enough to make up such a ridiculous-sounding story.

"I can't think who would have killed her. I don't know very much about what was going on with her lately, other than what she was doing to me. I saw her every time I came to pick up Jackson or bring him home, but she never spoke to me. She couldn't look me in the eye after she claimed I'd hurt him."

It was no wonder, Cathy thought. Annalee had changed her mind about her lifelong commitment because of her own forays into infidelity and had sent Jay packing when he had the gall to confront her. In grief and anger, he'd complied and stormed out. He'd lost his home and his child in one cruel night, and he hadn't even seen it coming. Then, to bolster her custody case, she'd accused him of child abuse.

Cathy tried to rein her thoughts in and think like an attorney rather than a sister. "Okay, the first thing we need to do is show the police the email. Did you talk to anybody before you left work? Anybody who might remember what time you left?"

"Yes, I told Janet."

Cathy made a mental note to talk to his secretary. "And did you stop anywhere along the way?"

"I got gas. I was almost on empty."

"Where?"

"The Exxon on 21st Street. I still have the receipt in my car."

"Okay, I'll need that."

"Why? That doesn't prove I'm innocent."

"If they can figure out the time of death, and you can prove you weren't here then . . ."

"That's a long shot, isn't it, since I may have come minutes after it happened?"

Cathy rubbed her face. The story sounded ludicrous, but she knew her brother. He wasn't a liar or a murderer. He cared about people . . . even Annalee. "Okay, let's just think this through. The clown is the killer. He comes over with the sole purpose of murdering

Annalee and pinning it on you. The clown getup keeps him from being identified. The costume is red, so you don't notice the blood. Now, how did he get in?"

"I don't know. I didn't see any sign of a break in."

She set her purse on the floor and dug into it for her notepad. She still had all her notes from the Chesney trial. She flipped to a blank page. "So he gets in somehow, and goes for your gun."

"He'd have to know where she kept it. I think she kept it in the bed table, but I don't know that for sure. We didn't even keep it loaded when I was living here."

"Maybe she heard him breaking in and got the gun."

"If she was scared, wouldn't she have called the police before she'd run to the bedroom to get the gun? And what about the email?"

"Maybe he forced her to write it," Cathy said.

"But why? If he had her email me, then killed her, he wouldn't wait around until I got here. He would have gone out the back door, slipped away without my seeing."

She tried to think like this clown. "Maybe he *wanted* you to see him."

Jay considered that for a moment, then brought his hands to his head. "No wonder they think I did it!" He sucked in a ragged breath. "Jackson. Would you get Juliet to go get him? He needs somebody he loves. I don't want him left at the babysitter's. And I want to be the one to tell him."

"Of course. But look at me."

He slid his hands down his face and met her eyes.

"Jay, you need to be strong for him. You can't panic

and fall apart. You have to stay clear. I'll make sure the police do their job and don't just blow off what you said."

"A clown," he said. "Who's ever gonna believe me?"

"That's why the guy wore a clown suit—to make your story sound ludicrous. But you know what? If he drove home like that, people saw him. Sitting at a stop sign or at a red light, it's hard not to notice a guy in a clown suit. Someone will come forward."

Jay leaned back and looked at the ceiling. "Why is God letting this happen to me? The divorce and custody battle was unbelievable enough . . . losing my home . . . losing my son . . . losing my wife. The accusations. But now to have her murdered, and me be the main suspect?"

"You don't know that."

"Oh no? They were questioning me like a suspect. I found her. It's my gun. I have a ridiculous story about what happened."

"The truth is the truth, no matter how it looks."

"Tell that to them," he said. "Some guy is laughing his head off because he got away with it, and I'm gonna take the fall."

Cathy hoped that wasn't true.

CHAPTER 6

He had to get rid of the clown suit, as soon as he parked the white pickup truck back where he'd gotten it. He hoped the parking space was still free. But if it wasn't, the co-worker who owned the truck would just think his memory had lapsed. He'd never realize that his keys had been lifted off his desk and his vehicle had been involved in a crime.

He pulled into the parking lot, slowed as he went past the other cars lined up. The space was still empty. Perfect. He pulled the truck in, grabbed the garbage bag. The clown suit and shoes and the mask with the bald head and wig attached were balled up inside it.

If they found it, they would see the blood spatters among the polka dots. He couldn't just throw it away. He had to make sure it was never found.

He went into the building, walking purposefully down the hallway with the bag in his hand. He stopped by the office where the guy with the truck worked. As usual, he wasn't at his desk.

He went in and dropped the keys on the desk where he'd found them, then slipped back out.

The incinerator room, where they disposed of

bio-hazardous material, would be the best place to dispose of the suit. He headed to the back door and out to the separate building where the fire continuously burned. He stepped in, felt the heat in the air warm several degrees. Sweat broke out on his skin. He opened the door to the flames that licked up from a basement compartment and tossed the bag in.

Instantly, the fire swallowed it. He stood there for a moment, watching as the orange and yellow tongues did their dance below. If there was a hell, was that what it looked like?

He closed the door and stepped back, wiping the sweat from his brow. How ridiculous, thinking about hell. He didn't even believe in such a thing.

He stepped out of the building, letting the humid wind cool him somewhat. He looked from left to right. A few employees had clustered around the back of the building to smoke. None of them noticed him. They never did.

But soon he would be somebody.

He straightened and took a deep breath, headed back in to finish his work. They would never be able to connect him to Annalee's death now. The smoking gun had Jay's name on it. The only other evidence was nothing but ashes floating around in the flames.

So many problems solved in one day. He hadn't felt this good about himself in years.

CHAPTER 7

While Cathy was inside, Michael got his binoculars and his evidence kit out of his car and did a visual sweep of Annalee's front lawn. He looked for footprints along the street edge of the grass, but the yard was too dry. The property wasn't roped off on the sides of the house, so he walked around it slowly, looking for a sign of a break in. The screens were still on the windows, but one window appeared to be unlocked. The killer could have gone in through there, but would he have stopped to put the screen back on?

He reached the backyard, saw that they had roped off an area around the back door. He zoomed his binoculars in on the door. Again, no sign of break in.

When he'd finished scanning the windows all around the house, he went back to the street. There were woods on both sides of the property. It was possible that the killer had disposed of some of the evidence before getting off the street. The wig, maybe? The costume?

He went into the trees near the street, looking for anything the killer could have tossed out his window. There were a couple of drink cans. He pulled a Ziploc out of his evidence kit and bagged them. He doubted they were from the killer. An empty Coke can wouldn't have been at the top of his list of things to dispose of.

He walked along, picking up stray pieces of trash—an empty water bottle, an old trash bag, more cans here and there. He bagged everything to give to Max, just in case. But it looked like the killer hadn't dumped anything here.

He doubled back, checking again. When he reached the house, he saw Juliet and Holly sitting in Juliet's car, the doors open. Holly was still a wreck. Juliet just stared toward the house.

If only he could get in there and take one look at the crime scene . . . but Max would never allow it. Max's pride was too great to consult with Michael on anything—especially a homicide case. Even if Max did care about his younger brother's opinion, he'd say that Michael was too close to the family and couldn't be objective.

He supposed that was true.

But there were so many things he wanted to know. If she was shot in the bathtub, had there been water in it before or after? Were there signs of a struggle? Was there blood anywhere else in the house? If he could just see where she was found, he might be able to piece together how she'd gotten there, when she'd realized she was in danger, where and when the killer had made his presence known.

But it was out of his hands, and that was his own fault. He had to trust his brother and the police department that had booted him.

CHAPTER 8

When the police insisted on continuing Jay's questioning at the station downtown, Cathy told them she would take him in. Outside, as her sisters met Jay with hugs and tears, Cathy took Michael aside and filled him in on Jay's story.

"I need your help," she said. "Will you go to Jay's house and look on his computer for that email Annalee sent him? Print it out and bring it to me at the police station."

"Sure," he said. "You got a key?"

"Yes." She dug in her purse for her keychain, found the one with Jay's name on the label, and pulled it off the ring. "Michael, if his story gets out to the press, no one's going to believe it. I wouldn't."

"Do you?"

"Yes, of course. He's my brother. He wouldn't do that to his child's mother."

She glanced toward Jay, locked in Juliet's embrace. "Whoever did this, they deliberately set it up so that his story would be outrageous."

Michael had that look on his face that told her his instincts were fully engaged. "We need a detailed description of that clown suit. I could go around to some costume shops, see if anyone rented or bought one lately." He glanced around the expansive lawn. "Jay said the clown walked across the grass. I looked at the yard and didn't see any prints. It's been dry lately, but there might be some prints in the bathroom or footsteps on the carpet since his feet may have been wet when he left."

"Do they know what they're doing, Michael? Can Max and Al handle this?"

"We have to trust them. We have no choice." She could tell from his popping jaw that he doubted their competence. "It'll be okay. Max is well trained. And Al is experienced."

"Al Forbes was coasting two years ago when you and Joe were in the department," she said. "He's hanging on while the clock runs out, and you know it. The easiest way to get a quick conclusion to this case is to charge Jay and stop investigating."

"I hope you're wrong," Michael said. "I don't think my brother will do that."

But Cathy knew there was a big difference between Michael's ethics and Max's.

"You're not really representing him, are you, Cathy?" Michael asked.

"I have to."

"No you don't. You can hire somebody else."

"He's my brother! Nothing is more important."

"But you're rusty, Cathy. You haven't practiced law in two years, and you've never worked as a defense attorney."

"All I know is that he needs me right now. Maybe if this goes further we'll pull in somebody else. But this is where I belong." She looked at her watch. "Oh, no. I'm supposed to be on TV tonight. I have to make a call."

Quickly, she called the producer at FOX, told him that she'd had a family emergency and couldn't be there tonight, but pointed him to the blog she'd already written for the latest information on Sara Chesney's case. As she hung up, she realized they probably wouldn't invite her on again . . . unless it was to talk about her brother's case.

"You okay?" Michael asked her as she clicked the phone off.

"Yes. I have to be."

"You'll call me if you think of anything else I can check on?"

"You know I will. I trust you a lot more than I trust them. Follow any lead you get. We can help Max out on this case whether he likes it or not."

She went to Jay and pulled him from Juliet and Holly. Her brother looked wrung out, as if he were the one who'd bled out on the bathroom floor. "We have to go," she said. "Michael will take us to my house to get my car. Max and Al are meeting us at the police station."

Jay gave another round of tearful hugs, then he slipped into the passenger seat of Michael's Trailblazer. Cathy climbed into the back. As Michael pulled away from the police cars, he patted Jay's shoulder. "You okay, man?"

Jay just shook his head. "We have to find that clown. Are they even looking? He's probably taken off the wig by now, changed clothes . . . Every minute that passes, he gets farther away."

"I checked the woods along the road. I didn't find anything like that, but I turned the little bit of trash I picked up over to Max." Michael reached into his glove compartment, got out a small notebook. "Here, draw what the clown suit looked like."

"I can't draw."

"Do the best you can. Write the colors out beside it."

Jay's hands were shaking, but he started to draw.

"While you're drawing, tell me about the email you got from Annalee," Michael said.

Jay let out a long, despairing sigh. "It just came out of the blue. When it came, I felt this huge sense of relief, that maybe we could finally sit down like two people who used to love each other, and agree on something that was best for Jackson."

"So maybe it didn't really come from her."

Jay frowned and looked up. "No, it came from her address. I checked."

"Did it sound like her?" Cathy asked.

Jay looked out his window for a moment, as if trying to remember. "It looked rushed. Misspelled and abbreviated words."

"That's not like her," Cathy said. "Annalee's a grammar freak."

"Well, yeah, but I just thought she was rushing to type it. You think the clown sent it from her computer?"

"I don't know," Michael said. "I need to look at it. Cathy gave me a key to your place. You mind me going in and having a look at your email?"

"No, that's fine. I got her email at the office, but I read it online on my Gmail account. It should show up in my Inbox at home, because I didn't delete it." Jay leaned his head back, swallowed hard. "So it wasn't from her. She never had a change of heart. There was never going to be a conversation without the lawyers."

Cathy noted the wistfulness in his tone. She tried to imagine what had happened. How had the clown gotten in? An extra key . . . a garage door opener . . . an unlocked door? Had he found Annalee in her office and taken her upstairs at gunpoint? Cathy didn't know whether Annalee had been shot in the tub or standing in the bathroom. The clown was clearly staging things to implicate Jay. Using Jay's gun, leading him to find her body . . .

But no matter where he'd shot her, she was just as dead. And Jay looked just as guilty.

"Would he have needed to know her password to send something from her email account?"

Jay rubbed his forehead. "She uses Google mail. Last I knew, she was always signed in. She checked her mail multiple times a day and didn't have to type her address and password every time. If he used her laptop, he could get instant access." He closed his eyes. "I should have seen that it wasn't her writing style. I'm so stupid."

Michael patted Jay's shoulder again. "Don't worry, buddy. I'm on this. And I think we can count on Max. He knows I'm gonna ride him about this. He'll want to stay a couple of steps ahead of me."

Jay didn't say anything, just shook his head as if that was little comfort.

CHAPTER 9

After Michael dropped Cathy and Jay off at Cathy's car, he headed to Jay's apartment. The two-bedroom rental looked as if he'd just moved in. No pictures on the walls. Garage-sale furniture in the living room—nothing but a recliner, a worn couch, and a small TV. Michael glanced in Jay's bedroom. A mattress lay on the floor, and next to it stood a card table with a computer on it. Boxes were stacked against the wall. He opened some and glanced inside—books, tools, shoes. Jay hadn't even unpacked from his move.

Michael had been to Jay and Annalee's home once for an engagement party for Cathy and Joe. It was elegantly decorated with heirloom pieces and exquisite details that only a professional designer could have pulled off. Now Jay was here, living like a college freshman.

He turned on the light and sat down on the folding chair in front of the computer. He rolled the mouse, and the screen came to life.

Jay's Google email sprang up, already loaded. Since Jay had gotten the email at the office, it wasn't already open on this computer, but it should still show up in his

Inbox. Michael scrolled through Jay's email from today and found the one from Annalee.

Frowning, he read through it, looking for any clue that she had written it under duress, or hadn't written it at all. As Jay had mentioned, words had been misspelled. He did a search for any other letters from Annalee. A list came up; all except today's were dated over a year ago. They were all flawless, even the ones written on her phone. No misspellings, accurate punctuation, full sentences.

He printed out a few of them for comparison, along with today's email.

He went back to Jay's Inbox, then clicked on Sent to see if Jay had replied to her. There was a short email.

I'll be right over. Leaving now.

If the police decided Jay was a suspect, they would seize his computer and study that day's correspondence to help establish a timeline of his actions and whereabouts. Michael decided to print it all out himself, just to make sure Cathy had what the cops would have.

He opened one letter after another. Most were business emails and correspondence to co-workers. But then he saw one that made him freeze.

Jay had sent a note to his sisters, fifteen minutes before Annalee sent him her invitation to come over.

Just wanted you to know that I'm taking care of things so that I'll have Jackson back with me soon.

Annalee will soon be out of the picture. A guy's gotta
do what a guy's gotta do. My son needs me.

Michael's stomach dropped. Why would Jay write
something like that?

He stared at it a moment, his heart pounding. The
police would see this and think it was ironclad evidence that he'd premeditated her murder.

What could Jay have meant? And why hadn't Cathy
mentioned it?

He set his elbows on the desk and rubbed his eyes,
trying to think. She probably hadn't had time to check
her email today, and Juliet and Holly weren't big email
users. Probably none of them had seen the letter yet.

He couldn't delete it—that would be tampering with
evidence. Besides, even if he did, they'd find it on Jay's
hard drive or his server. It was too late. He printed it
off, then grabbed the stack of emails. He had to call
Cathy and let her know what he'd found.

CHAPTER 10

Cathy's phone chimed as she was sitting down with Jay in the interview room at the police department, but she ignored it.

Her brother was falling apart. That dazed look in his eyes had turned into deep grief, and he'd dropped his head into his arms and was sobbing. She lowered her head against his and rubbed his back, wishing she could take this weight off of him.

The phone stopped ringing, then chimed to let her know she had a text. She didn't want to turn away from Jay even for a minute, but she glanced at her phone and saw that it was from Michael. Must be important. She quickly read his text.

Call me. Found something.

Her pulse quickened. "Jay, I have to call Michael. He says he found something."

He lifted his head, wiped his face and his nose. "Yeah, go ahead. Maybe he has a lead on the clown."

She clicked on Michael's number, waited for it to ring. When he answered, she said, "Hey, Michael. Whatcha got?"

"Cathy, I'm at Jay's." His voice sounded strained. "I've been printing out his emails from today. The one Annalee sent him . . . and the one he sent to you." There was a pause. "Did you get that, by any chance?"

She tried to think. Had she even checked her email today? "No, I didn't get it. I haven't checked email since lunchtime."

Jay pulled a tissue out of a box and blew his nose.

"Cathy, it's incriminating," Jay said in a low voice. "I don't understand why he didn't mention it."

Her mouth went dry, and she swallowed hard. "Well, okay. Hold on and I'll read it."

As he waited, she looked on her phone and clicked on the envelope icon, opened her mail.

"What are you doing?" Jay asked.

"Checking the email you sent me."

Jay frowned. "What email?"

"The one you sent earlier today."

Jay sat up straighter. "I didn't send you an email today."

She found it, clicked on it. "Yes, you did. Here it is."

"Cathy, I didn't. What does it say?"

She read aloud: "Just wanted you to know that I'm taking care of things so that I'll have Jackson back with me soon . . ." Her voice trailed off as the implications hit her.

"What? I didn't write that!" Jay snatched the phone and read the next sentence. "Annalee will soon be out of the picture."

Cathy felt the blood draining from her face. "You have got to be kidding me."

Jay kept reading through his teeth. "A guy's gotta do what a guy's gotta do. My son needs me."

He slammed his hand on the table. "Unbelievable!" he yelled. "I did not write that email!"

Cathy heard Michael's voice from the phone. "Cathy!"

She took the phone back. "Yeah?"

"He's saying he didn't send it?"

She closed her eyes. "Yes."

Jay grabbed the phone out of her hand again. "Michael, the guy has hacked into my account too. I would never write something like that. It has to be the same guy. My password was my birthday. It probably wouldn't be hard to guess. The killer must have signed onto my Google account." He looked at Cathy, his eyes desperate. "Cathy, this clown . . . this killer . . . is setting me up. Why?"

Cathy's heart plunged, and she looked out the small rectangular window in the door, to the police milling around beyond it. They were going to go crazy with this. They wouldn't even look for anyone else. A clown . . . Jay's gun . . . the custody battle . . . the email . . .

She felt sick. She took the phone back from her brother. "Michael, we have to stop him."

"I'll do what I can."

"He believes me, doesn't he?" Jay asked.

She knew Michael heard, but he didn't answer right away. "Michael, my brother is not a killer."

"I know that, Cathy."

"He loves his son. He wouldn't take his mother from him."

Again, "I know."

"He did *not* kill her!"

"Cathy, what matters right now is how this looks to the police. I'm going to start looking for the clown. Preempt their finding the email by showing it to them now. If you don't and they confiscate his computer—and they will—it won't look good."

She looked at her brother. He had backed into a corner of the room and was shaking his head, staring at nothing, as if trying to imagine how much worse this could get. How was she going to get him out of this?

CHAPTER 11

Michael left Jay's house with the printed emails, dropped them on his passenger seat, and drove to a costume shop on the south side of town, close to the beach. The store was a combination bridal shop and costume store, with the rentable wedding gowns filling the front half of the shop, and racks and racks of dingy, over-worn costumes in the back.

He went in, hoping he could convey a sense of authority so they'd give him information.

The man behind the counter smiled a friendly smile. "Help you, sir?"

"Yes," he said. "I'm an investigator working on a case, and I was wondering if you could tell me if anyone has rented a clown costume in the last week or so."

The man's eyes narrowed. "An investigator? You mean a cop? You got any identification?"

"No, not a cop." The words still twisted in his gut. "I'm a private investigator."

"Well, I don't know if I should give out information about my customers. Did one of them do something illegal?"

"One of them may have committed a serious crime

today wearing a clown suit. Unless you want **to be** implicated yourself, I suggest you look through **your** records to see if it was your suit."

"Implicated *myself*?"

Michael had known that would get his attention.

"Look, I'm not responsible for anything anybody does wearing my costumes. I'll look."

The guy moved his computer mouse until his display came to life, then typed in a few things. As he waited for his search results, he glanced at Michael again. "Wait a minute. I know who you are. You're that cop who lied on the stand." He snapped his fingers. "Michael Hogan, right?"

Michael's voice went flat. "Yes, that's who I am."

"Yeah . . . ," the man said, staring at him as if fascinated. "Shame about your brother. I'm really sorry."

Biting his molars hard, Michael nodded.

"They said you were a real good cop. It was all just a crying shame."

Michael cleared his throat. "About the clown suit . . ."

"Yeah, sure." He put on his glasses and looked at the screen. "This week, you say?"

"Right. Or better yet, tell me the last time any of your clown suits were rented out, and if any are still out."

The man studied the screen. "We have several clown suits, different styles, different sizes. We rented one last month. Two this month so far . . . Any idea how big the person is you're looking for?"

"Five-ten, average build, unless the shoes gave him height . . . or the wig added inches. Here's a picture." He showed him Jay's crude drawing.

The man shook his head. "That wouldn't be either of these. Rented these to some regular customers, two girls who go to the children's hospital to entertain the kids. Petite little things."

"Did you rent *any* to a man?"

He clicked around a little more. "No, I'm sorry. I just don't show that any of our larger-sized ones were rented. Besides, I don't have a costume that looks like this. Mine are yellow, not red."

Michael couldn't give up so easily. "Do you sell any of your costumes? Can people order them here?"

"Yeah, sometimes."

"See if anybody has ordered one."

The man did another search, then shook his head. "No, I didn't think so. We get lots of orders around Halloween, but not that many this time of year. No clowns."

Michael hesitated. "Are there other shops in town?"

The man looked pained to have to speak of his competition. "Yeah, there are a couple. You could try the Party Hearty. They have a few clown costumes—mostly cheap stuff that I wouldn't be caught dead selling. And there's a store called Dance, Etc. over at Pier Park. It has dance costumes mostly, but they sell other costumes too."

"All right," Michael said, jotting the names down. "Could you do me a favor and print out pictures of the clown costumes you carry?"

"Sure," the guy said. "No harm in doing that."

As he waited for the prints, the owner turned back

to Michael. "Whatever happened to that guy that killed your brother?"

Michael's jaw locked. "He was acquitted."

"Oh yeah, I remember that. Crazy. But I mean, where is he now?"

"He's disappeared," Michael said. "We don't know where he is."

"That's too bad. It was so clear he was guilty. To get off on a thing like that . . ."

Michael took the pictures, thanked the man, and went back to his car. Before pulling out of the parking space, he sat staring at his steering wheel, trying to compose himself.

Too bad.

The man had no idea how bad it was. To the general population, his brother's case had been entertainment. To his family, and to Cathy, it had been a gutting that had left them hollow and raw.

Besides his brother, who'd been his best friend, it had cost Michael his career and reputation.

He closed his eyes and prayed that the day would come when he would find the bottom feeder who had murdered Joe, and make sure he finally got justice.

For now, he had to keep going, without that satisfaction. Time had eased the anger and anxiety, but it hadn't done much for his bitterness. Michael had not only been a disgrace to the police force, but he was a disgrace to Christianity. That he had gotten on the witness stand and publicly lied . . .

And now, the bitterness that churned inside him was

a terrible witness to people like Cathy, who needed to see strength in his faith, rather than turmoil.

He constantly let her down in that regard. But worse, he constantly let God down.

He started the car, backed out of the space, and headed to one of the other shops in search of Jay's clown.

• • •

A couple of hours later, Michael had only three names of people who had rented or bought clown suits that would fit a man of five-ten, and they were all women. He supposed Jay could be wrong about the clown being a man. But none of the suits matched the description Jay had given anyway.

He had hit a dead end.

He decided to drive the route the killer might have taken leaving Annalee's house and see if there were any video security cameras along the way that might have caught his white truck on tape.

He found a few on traffic lights at some of the major intersections the guy might have taken. But he didn't have access to those. He'd have to ask his brother to check them out. Max would bristle at the suggestion, but Michael didn't care as long as Max got the tapes. Max had flunked the detective exam twice before passing, and Michael had reached that goal first. Max had a huge chip on his shoulder and frequently misinterpreted what Michael said about his older brother's investigations. But there was a lot riding on this. Max would have to get over it.

When Michael had exhausted the possible routes and made note of all the cameras he found, he went back to Annalee's. Police were still searching her house, and by now, neighbors had walked up the street to watch the activity. Two local television news vans had set up shop on the street.

Michael got out of his car and scanned the property. From what Jay had said, the clown had driven in the direction away from the other houses down the street. He wouldn't want anyone to be able to confirm Jay's story.

The clown would have removed his wig as he drove home, but the makeup would still have been on his face. Someone would have noticed at a red light, wouldn't they? Unless it wasn't makeup. If it were a mask, he could have just pulled it off. Still . . . someone might have seen the ruffled polka-dot collar.

He walked over to the neighbors, listened quietly for a moment to a couple of women talking.

"Custody battle," he heard one of them saying in a low voice. "They've been fighting for over a year."

"In a knock-down-drag-out over their son," the younger woman said. "If they don't go after her husband, they're crazy."

Michael seized the opportunity. "Excuse me."

The two women turned around. One looked about sixty, the other in her forties.

"Do you ladies live around here?" he asked.

"About half a mile up the road," one of them said. "We're cross-the-street neighbors from each other."

"Did you know Annalee?"

The older woman squinted at him in the end-of-day sunlight. "Who are you?"

"I'm an investigator," he said, deliberately leaving off the word "private."

Probably assuming he was one of the police detectives, the younger woman said, "Oh yeah, we knew her. She came to neighborhood association meetings. Is it true she was shot?"

Michael evaded the question. "Did either of you happen to see anyone in a white pickup truck on the street today?"

The younger one shook her head. "I just got home a little while ago. I've been working all day."

He turned to the older one. "And you, ma'am?"

"No, I've been inside all day. I didn't see or hear anybody. Is that who did it? Somebody in a white pickup?"

"We don't know yet. I'm just checking out everything. Do you know of anyone in the area who might have had a birthday party today? For children, I mean?"

They looked at each other like they couldn't figure out the question. "I don't know anybody," the younger one said.

"No, it's Monday. People usually have parties on weekends."

He considered how to phrase the question. "So . . . have you seen anyone around in a costume?"

The older woman's eyebrows popped up. "You mean a clown costume?"

Hope bloomed. "Yes."

"No, but one of the other police officers asked us that a little while ago." She brought her hand to her throat

"Is somebody in a clown costume breaking into houses out here?"

Disappointment deflated him. "We're not sure, but you should be diligent to lock your doors. Arm your alarm systems. Stay alert when you come and go."

"They need to be looking at that husband of hers," the younger one said again. "She said he was abusive, and he would do anything to get that boy. She said he was fighting her tooth and nail. If you're looking for a clown suit, I'd start by looking in his closet."

He didn't bother to tell them he'd just been in Jay's closet and there was nothing of the kind.

Suddenly feeling weary, he decided to head back to the police station and give Cathy the emails, pictures, and names of the women who'd rented clown suits. Maybe Jay had made a mistake about the color. But if the suit was yellow, he probably would have noticed blood splatters. Or would he miss that among all the polka dots?

Whatever the case, Cathy should at least show Jay these pictures. Michael wished he could help her more.

CHAPTER 12

Juliet saw Jackson's excitement when she picked him up from day care. He loved coming to her house because she had a swimming pool and kept popsicles in her freezer. Juliet tried hard to evade questions about when Mommy would come to pick him up, and chattered instead about the dog Jackson loved who couldn't wait to play with him.

Holly sat in Juliet's passenger seat, blotting tears from her eyes. Though Juliet was used to her depressed sister falling apart at the drop of a hat, she didn't have much patience for it today. She turned the rear speakers up so Jackson could sing along with Cookie Monster, then poked her sister.

"Stop that right now," she said in a low voice. "You're going to get him upset."

Holly didn't answer, just compressed her lips and tried to hold back her tears. "Sorry."

"I know it's hard, but pull yourself together. For him, if not for me."

She knew what Holly was thinking. Her sister, who was especially sensitive, was imagining some violent clown breaking into Annalee's house, walking her to the bathtub, and shooting her through the heart.

She was taking inventory of all the horrible things that had happened to their brother in the last year. She was thinking how unfair life was. How unfair God was.

But those thoughts wouldn't help them get through the night.

"If you need to go home when we get to my house, I can handle him," she said.

"No, I want to help. And I want to be there when Jay comes back."

"Then dry up. I'm not kidding."

Juliet didn't mean to be cruel. But they would all have time for tears later. Right now there was work to be done. The children had to be fed, her own boys had homework, and there would be swimming and reading to keep Jackson distracted from asking inevitable questions.

Weariness overwhelmed Juliet, but she banished it too. She needed strength tonight. Too bad Bob was out of town and couldn't help. Her husband had a lot of his own stress, and she tried not to be needy.

They got back to her house, a mid-century, sprawling home like something out of the *Brady Bunch*, and her boys, Zach and Abe, met her at the door to tell on each other.

"Mom, Zach was on my computer and he changed all the settings," the nine-year-old said.

"I didn't touch his stupid computer. It has a virus! I could fix it if he'd let me."

Juliet got out of the car. "Guys, I have Jackson with me. He's staying with us tonight."

Abe's eyebrows shot up and he ran to the car's back door, threw it open. Jackson laughed, and squirmed to unhook his seatbelt. "Hey, dude. Mom, can we swim tonight?"

"You bet we can," Juliet said, waiting for Abe to move. He was already unhooking Jackson's belt.

"I'm going off the diving board," Jackson said. "Aunt Juliet, will you catch me?"

As she answered and got him out of the car, Zach, her brooding twelve-year-old, stepped toward them. "Aunt Holly, I saw your cab when I got off the bus. Why are you crying?"

Juliet shot daggers at her sister. "She's not crying, are you, Holly?"

"No. It's my allergies. Pollen's really kicking up today."

"Pollen?" Zach asked, turning to his mother. "I'm allergic to pollen, and I'm fine."

Mr. Smarty-Pants knew too much for his own good. "Holly, go see if I have any frozen pizzas for the boys. I'm going to get Jackson settled."

Jackson had a delighted smile on his face as he came into the house and greeted the excited Yorkie. He picked up the dog and let him lick his face. "Mommy says if I get good grades in kindergarten that I can get a puppy. I told her I want one like Brody."

Juliet's heart burst. Tears closed up her throat, burned her eyes. She quickly shoved them back. "Bet you're hungry, Jackson. Want a snack?" she asked, as if everything in the world was just as it was when her nephew had last seen her.

Until his father got home to tell him how drastically his life had been altered today, that was exactly how it was going to be.

. . .

As Juliet went to the guest bedroom with Jackson and Abe, Holly found two frozen pizzas and shoved them into the oven, then microwaved a few hot dogs so Jackson would have something to satisfy his appetite until the pizzas were ready.

Zach, who wasn't buying the whole allergy thing, came into the kitchen. "What's going on, Aunt Holly? Is it about my dad?"

Holly turned to him. "Your dad? No. What would make you think that?"

"Because he's out of town. Something's wrong. You've been crying."

Holly hated herself. Why couldn't she control her emotions? She was a basket case. "No, Zach," she said quickly. "It's nothing to do with him. I'm sure he's fine."

"Then what? You admit you've been crying, right?"

"I cry all the time," Holly said. "You know I'm Debbie Downer. What else is new?"

He sighed, clearly frustrated, then headed for the TV in the keeping room adjoining the kitchen.

Holly lunged at him. "No, don't turn the TV on!"

He swung around. "Why not?"

"Because . . . it's too much noise."

"Mom always lets us watch TV. We were watching before she turned it off."

"Let's just talk, okay?"

Zach stared at her. "You don't want to talk, remember? Nothing's wrong. Everything's just fine. You've been bawling your eyes out, and Mom's eyes look red, and she comes home with Jackson . . ." His voice trailed off. "Is it something to do with them? The custody thing?"

The microwave chimed, so she turned away and got the hot dogs out. "Zach, just quit asking questions, okay? We'll tell you everything later, but right now we just want to keep Jackson happy."

"Where's Uncle Jay?"

"He's tied up right now."

"But he never gets Jackson on Mondays."

Holly wanted to scream. Instead, she put her hand on her nephew's shoulder and looked into his eyes. "Zach, you're way too smart for your own good. But you need to be mature right now and understand that we can't talk about this yet. I'd appreciate it very much if you'd just play with the kids, keep the TV off, and help your mother and me keep Jackson distracted."

Zach wouldn't give up. "Uncle Jay got custody, right? That's why Jackson's here. But that wouldn't make you cry. Unless they're happy tears."

"Yes," she lied. "That's it. They're happy tears." She grabbed the plate of hot dogs and thrust it at him. "Take these outside for Abe and Jackson. We'll eat by the pool. It'll be a little while before the pizzas are ready, though."

Satisfied that he'd "guessed" the right answer, Zach took the plate. "I won't tell them." He walked to the sliding glass patio doors and turned back. "Will he be happy or sad?"

Despair tore at her face again. She turned away from him. Sad, she wanted to say, but her own sorrow prevented her from getting the word out. Jackson was never going to see his mother again.

Instead, she checked the pizza. Why hadn't she preheated the oven? Now she didn't know when to start counting the time. She was going to burn the thing, or the middle would still be frozen. She would ruin it.

She should have waited for Juliet. She was no help at all.

"Aunt Holly?"

Why wouldn't he let this go? She closed the oven, unable to face her nephew again. "Zach, I think we can assume that the news is going to upset him. So keep what you think you know to yourself. Can you do that?"

"Sure. I can keep a secret from little kids."

"Good," she said.

When he stepped outside with the hot dogs, she sank onto a bar stool and melted into tears again.

Her poor brother. How did these things keep happening to him? Unlike her, he didn't deserve any of his bad luck. He was a good father, and he'd been a loving husband, an awesome provider. His choices should reap blessings, not tragedy.

She heard bare feet slapping the tile floor. "Can we swim now?" Jackson asked.

"Yes," Juliet said, following him into the kitchen.

"The pool is probably a great place for Aunt Holly." Then she mumbled, "Her face will be wet anyway."

Holly forced a happy smile. The little boy was distracted by his cousins.

"Aunt Holly, you have mascara smudges," Juliet whispered. "Why don't you go wash your face?"

Holly nodded and started for the bathroom. Suddenly, Juliet grabbed her arm and turned her back. Holly met her older sister's eyes, dreading whatever was coming. But Juliet only pulled her into a hug. Holly clung for a second, then drew in a deep breath. Strengthened, she went to wash her face.

"Yay, Aunt Holly made hot dogs!" Juliet cried for Jackson. "Are you hungry?"

Holly appreciated the child's shout of affirmation. At least she had done one thing right.

CHAPTER 13

The bathroom floor was cold. Holly sat on it, her back against the wall, elbows on her knees. Why had Juliet chosen these cold travertine tiles? She made a mental note that Juliet would probably like a rug for Christmas to put here. Then again, there probably weren't that many people who sat here on the floor.

Holly always seemed to be crying these days. Cathy thought Holly was clinically depressed, and maybe she was right. The latest developments in her life had not brought Holly joy or peace. She found herself dysfunctional and full of dread, and that was even before Jay's wife was murdered.

Holly pulled her purse onto her lap, dug through for her phone, and as she did, she saw that wand again, rolled up in a plastic bag. Her stomach sank, and she felt a little sick. She pulled it out and unrolled the bag, held it out in front of her. That plus sign told her everything she needed to know.

In less than eight months, she would be giving birth.

Her father would have been horrified, though he certainly had skeletons in his own closet.

Her mother, who died just three years ago, would

have been filled with shame. Disgrace was a heavy burden to bear, though Holly's mom had been familiar enough with it. Juliet would probably cry and declare that all her warnings to Holly over the last few years had come to pass.

Cathy would be quietly disapproving about the whole thing, privately judging her, yet trying not to look like she was.

They would want to know who the father was. Could she tell them that it happened on a drunken binge, after a night of clubbing with her friends? She had awakened the next day, trying to remember the name of the man she had gone home with. Hating herself.

It looked so glamorous on TV when the *Jersey Shore* gang slept around. It looked like freedom, not bondage. But here she was, trapped.

And now her family would be grieving over Annalee's death. Cathy would probably help defend Jay. How dare Holly take any of the family energy from her brother by telling them of her predicament?

Holly forced herself to her feet and went to the sink, stood in front of the mirror. She suddenly hated the hot pink streaks in her hair. They screamed "party girl." What had she been thinking? A child would be embarrassed to have a Katy Perry wannabe for a mom. Her child . . . what a joke.

Maybe she could just not tell her family, make it go away . . .

They would never know that she had disgraced them again. Disgraced herself.

She thought back on all those sermons her father

had preached when they were young, all four children lined up on the front pew, threatened within an inch of their lives into sitting still and quiet. Those long sermons about sex outside of marriage, abortion, sin in general . . . Her father hadn't meant many of them, since years later he had an affair with a church secretary.

Talk about disgracing the family. She didn't want to think about that now. The fact was that this was her dilemma, and it was nothing like the dilemma her brother faced. She had to get over it.

She could deal with it quickly . . . put it all behind her . . .

She rolled the wand up in the plastic, stuck it back in the zipped pocket in her purse. She could hear her sister and the kids out by the pool, splashing and laughing. Juliet was holding it all together somehow, the poster child for Strength. Holly, on the other hand, was the model for Stupidity.

She splashed water on her face, dried it off, and drew in a deep breath. Then she clicked on her phone, checked her voice mail. The taxi company she contracted with had probably tried to call with some fares. But there were none. Quickly, she checked her email.

She saw one from Jay. She frowned. When had he sent it? She clicked on it, thinking it had come from the police station. Then she saw it was sent earlier today. He'd sent it to all his sisters.

Just wanted you to know that I'm taking care of things so that I'll have Jackson back with me soon.

Annalee will soon be out of the picture. A guy's gotta
do what a guy's gotta do. My son needs me.

Holly gasped and almost dropped the phone. Had
he sent this before he went to Annalee's house? Surely
he hadn't meant to do anything drastic.

The nausea that had been plaguing her each morning rose up to constrict her throat. She lunged for the
toilet, heaved into the bowl.

A guy's gotta do what a guy's gotta do.

Had Jay been that desperate? He still might have won
the custody battle. Holly rinsed her mouth, grabbed
her purse, and stumbled out of the bathroom to show
the email to Juliet. The doorbell stopped her.

No one else was in the house, so she went to the
front door, looked out the peephole. Annalee's brother
and mother stood there, both of them looking distraught. Tears sprang to Holly's eyes again as she
opened the door.

"Warren," she said. "Mrs. Haughton, come in."

Annalee's mother leaned on her walker as if she
could barely stand. Cancer had weakened her body,
so that she was almost an invalid. Holly could only
imagine what she was dealing with since she'd found
out about her daughter's death. She hugged her, but the
woman was stiff, unresponsive. "Mrs. Haughton, I'm
so sorry about Annalee. We're all so upset."

"I just want to see my grandson," she muttered, her
voice phlegmy. "Where is he?"

"He's outside swimming. Juliet hasn't told him. Jay
wanted to tell Jackson himself."

As they stepped into the foyer, Holly looked up at Warren, Annalee's brother. He looked shaken, distracted as always. He had asked Holly out a dozen times, but she'd never been attracted to him. He wasn't bad looking, but he had as much trouble as she had holding a job.

Her friends would label him the man of her dreams, since she was usually drawn to losers. Thankfully, she wasn't drawn to him.

Now, the hollow look in his eyes told her he was hurting, so she gave him a hug. "Warren, are you okay?"

He ignored the question. "What are they saying about Jay? Do they think he's the one who did this?"

"No, no, they're just questioning him," she said. "He's the one who found her."

"What . . . what did he say?" Annalee's mother asked. "About her . . . being in the bathroom?"

"I haven't been able to talk to him privately," Holly said. "Cathy's with him at the police station. He's coming straight here when they let him go. Please, come sit down."

Mrs. Haughton made her way to the couch in the den, dropped down, and looked out the large picture window toward her grandson, splashing in the pool without a care in the world. Her eyes were red-rimmed, her skin lax and drooping. She breathed hard, her shoulders rising and falling with the effort. Pain—probably emotional as well as physical—etched deep, craggy lines into her face.

"We'll take him now," Warren said, peering out the window.

Holly gasped. "Jackson? No, you can't! He's fine. We've fed him, and Jay wanted us to put him to bed. When he gets home, he can decide when Jackson needs to be told."

"We don't want him with Jay," Warren bit out.

Holly realized where this was going, and she stood straighter, lifted her chin. "My brother did not hurt his wife, and he's never hurt his son, despite what Annalee claimed."

"He found her," Warren said. "He hasn't been over there in a year except to pick up Jackson. You think it's a coincidence that he just happened to walk in right after somebody murdered her?"

Holly thought of the email she'd just read. She still had the phone in her hand. She slipped it into her pocket. "I don't know what happened. I don't know why it happened. All I know is that Jackson is better off staying here. Mrs. Haughton, I know you don't feel well, and you're probably in shock. It's not a good time for you to be babysitting."

Mrs. Haughton shook her head weakly, as if she had nothing to say to that.

But Warren wasn't giving up. "We can take care of him."

"It's not a good idea," Holly said more emphatically. "I think his father is the best judge of what's best for him."

"His father could be a murderer." Warren started to the back door. "I'm going to see my nephew."

Holly blocked his way. "You're not going out there, Warren."

Warren stared at her, and for a moment she thought he might press the issue. He was bigger than she, but she didn't fight fair. This could get ugly. But suddenly, his shoulders slumped. "Holly, I just want to make sure he's okay."

"You're gonna have to take my word for it. There's no sense in upsetting him." She pointed to the window. "Look at him. Nothing's gonna change by sheltering him from this tragedy until he has to find out. Let him play! He's five!"

Mrs. Haughton brought her gnarled hand to her face. As she melted into sobs, Warren went to sit beside her. Rubbing her back, he said, "Mama, are you all right?"

"She's right," Mrs. Haughton rasped. "Let's just let him be. He's okay here." She struggled to her feet again and Warren helped her up. As Mrs. Haughton grabbed her walker, she said, "Please call me when you hear what's happening to Jay. Or anything involving the investigation. I don't know if they'll keep us informed."

"Okay." Holly grabbed a notepad out of her purse and jotted down her phone number. "I'll give you all three of our numbers—mine, Juliet's, and Cathy's. You can call us anytime for an update."

"Let us know if they lock him up," Warren said.

Holly felt nauseous again. "Look, there's a lot of confusion right now. Everybody's wound up. The police are doing their jobs. They'll get to the bottom of this and realize that Jay didn't do anything."

As they reached the front door, Warren turned and looked out the back window again. Jackson jumped off the side of the pool into his Aunt Juliet's arms, sputtering and laughing. You couldn't tell she was grieving about her sister-in-law. Holly knew better, but Warren clearly didn't.

"Family celebration, huh? I guess Jay figured out how to get Jackson, didn't he? He wasn't going to win the custody battle. Annalee was too good a mother. So he took matters into his own hands."

Again, Holly thought of that email. If only she could delete it so no one would ever see it. "What happened to Annalee today was a tragedy. But it has nothing to do with what they were going through. She's the one who emailed him, asking him to come over."

"Absolutely not," Warren said. "She would never do that."

"They were in love and married for years. They have a child together. You don't think it's even possible that she would want to bypass the lawyers and just have a conversation about what was best for Jackson?"

"No, Warren's right," the old woman wheezed. "She was bent on keeping Jackson . . . no compromise. She wouldn't have done anything . . . to jeopardize the custody battle."

Holly was getting weary of the conversation. "I know you're upset. I understand everything you're going through, and I know it's doubly worse for you, Mrs. Haughton, because of your cancer and everything. But please, I'm just asking you to give us a little time. Please, just go and let us take care of him tonight."

She opened the front door and stepped out onto the front porch, allowing Mrs. Haughton the room to shuffle out. "I'm so sorry for your loss," she said again. "Mrs. Haughton, are you gonna be okay?"

Annalee's mother didn't answer. She just focused on getting down the porch steps.

"Warren, call me if you need anything. I can bring food."

"We don't need anything from you or anybody else in your family," Warren clipped.

She waited until they got in their car, and then she went back in. She pulled her phone out of her pocket and read Jay's email again. A thin layer of perspiration formed on her lip. She slid the glass door open and stepped out on the back patio. "Juliet, can I talk to you for a minute?"

Juliet was getting out of the pool. She put a towel around her shoulders and came toward Holly. "What is it?"

"Mrs. Haughton and Warren were just here," Holly whispered.

Juliet brought her hand to her mouth. "Why didn't you tell me?"

"They wanted to take Jackson. But I talked them into waiting."

"Good," Juliet whispered. "I appreciate that."

"Come sit down with me a minute," Holly said. "I need to show you something."

They pulled chairs together next to the pool so they could keep an eye on the kids. Jackson had floaties on his arms and played near the steps at the shallow end. Abe splashed around him.

"What is it?" Juliet said.

Holly handed her her cell phone with the email pulled up. "I just noticed this email. Jay sent it, minutes before the murder."

Juliet stiffened and took the phone, read it. Holly watched the color in her face change.

"Oh no," she whispered. She stared at the phone. "He didn't mean he was going to kill her. He probably had some new strategy for working things out with her."

"I'm just worried how it looks," Holly said.

"Who did he send it to?"

"All three of us."

"No! This is bad."

"Aunt Juliet! Look at me!" Jackson called from the pool. "I can do a somersault in the water."

Juliet forced a smile, then nodded as Jackson did a somersault. "That's good, Jackson! Do another one!"

She waited as he did, then cheered again. After a second, her expression crashed again. "What should we do? Should we call Cathy?"

"Probably," Holly said. "I'm thinking I could go to Jay's house, get on his computer, and delete it."

"No, that's not right. We can't tamper with evidence."

"But we can't let them find it . . ."

"They'd find it anyway. Besides, it's wrong. We can't do that."

Holly's face twisted. "Why did he write it?"

"I don't know," Juliet said. "But I think our brother is in a lot of trouble."

CHAPTER 14

Cathy took Michael's advice and showed the police the email that came from Jay's account.

"So let me get this straight," Al said, studying Jay. "You want us to believe you didn't send this email?"

"I *didn't* send it," Jay said. "The killer sent this email. This is evidence you can't ignore."

"Sure is," Max muttered, his chin in his palm.

"Not evidence indicting Jay," Cathy said. "Max, you have to connect the dots here. The email that came to Jay from Annalee's computer. The email that supposedly came from Jay. It all leads somewhere. You can track down servers. You can use this to find the real killer."

"And so what if the server they were all sent from was Annalee's?" Max asked. "That doesn't prove anything. Jay still could have sent them from the house before he called 911."

Jay slammed his hand on the table. "Aren't you listening? Are you deaf?"

Cathy put her hand over Jay's. "Max, the killer's jerking you around too. You can check the timing of Jay's story. What time he sent his reply to Annalee from his office server, what time this email came from wherever it came from. You can talk to his secretary about when he left. You can check his gas station receipt. This clown is playing an intricately planned game. If you don't follow these leads, he's going to make *you* look like a clown. He's probably getting a real laugh out of all this right now."

"Maybe you're the one laughing at us, Jay," Al said.

"Al, you have to listen," Cathy said. "If you care that there's a murderer out there getting away with it on your watch, then you'll check out Jay's story."

Max looked at Jay. "We're gonna need your computer and all your login information."

"No problem," Jay said.

"We'll go get it and bring it back to you," Cathy said.

"Or we could go get it," Max said. "You don't mind us going into your apartment, do you?"

Jay started to answer, but Cathy touched his hand, stopping him. "You don't have a warrant, gentlemen. We'll bring you the computer."

"I don't have anything to hide," Jay said. "I'll give them my key."

"Absolutely not," Cathy said.

Max looked at Jay again. "It's your call, Jay. We can get a warrant."

Cathy shot Jay an adamant look. "I guess I'll take my attorney's advice," he said. "But I can get the computer to you tonight. I can get Michael to bring it in."

Cathy wanted to kick herself for offering it at all. It was sloppy attorney work. In an ordinary case, she would have searched through every email Jay had sent in the last year before she handed over the computer, so she'd know what the police would find. On the other hand, they would have seized it tonight anyway. They had enough to establish probable cause. Any judge would issue a search warrant, if not an arrest warrant, based on the incriminating email alone.

"I'm giving it to you in good faith," she said. "I know there's nothing on it that will implicate Jay, because he isn't guilty. I'm assuming you're also looking at Annalee's computer. You'll be able to tell if the killer signed onto Jay's account from it, and compare it to Jay's documented whereabouts at the time. Maybe there are prints on her keyboard. There are tangled threads in all this, and it's your job to untangle them."

Her words clearly didn't smooth out Max's ruffled feathers. "We're going to untangle them, Cathy."

"Did we do a stupid thing by showing the letter to you?" Jay asked. "Are you going to make me regret it?"

Max shoved his chair back from the table and got up. "Go home, Jay. You haven't been charged with anything."

"So you'll follow through on these leads?" Jay pressed.

Max took a deep breath. "Take him home, Cathy. He's about to make me mad."

Relieved that they hadn't arrested him, she walked Jay back out to her car. The midnight air was cool. Cathy crossed her arms and groped for some positive thoughts. But she couldn't seem to find any.

"They're going to arrest me tomorrow, aren't they?" Jay asked in a dull voice.

"Maybe not," she said. It was the best she could offer him.

CHAPTER 15

Cathy glanced over at her brother in the dark car. His head was leaned back on the seat, his eyes closed. Grief and misery pulled at his face, and in the occasional headlights, he looked much older than thirty.

"Jay, are you sure you didn't send that email?"

He opened his eyes. "You don't believe me?"

"I do, but it's been a traumatic day, and you might have forgotten."

"Cathy, I would never write those words. What could I possibly have meant? No, the same person who sent the email to me from Annalee's computer also hacked into my email account. And he's getting away with this."

It was beginning to rain. She turned her wipers on and tried to see through the blur on her windshield.

"So the killer was with her when he got on your account and wrote the email that went out to us. Then he got on her account and sent the email inviting you over."

"Or he made her send it." A haunted expression came over his face. "He must have tortured her before he killed her. How long was he there with her?"

She didn't want to imagine it. "I don't think she

wrote it. It wasn't her style at all. When he sent the email inviting you over, she might have already been dead. He turned on the water and waited for you to come. Then bopped out and passed you, so you'd get a good look at him."

"So I'd sound like an idiot when I told the truth."

Yes, that was exactly what he'd planned. She drove quietly for a moment, trying to think through the resources the police department would have. They could trace the emails back to the servers from which they were sent. That could prove that they hadn't been sent from Jay's home or office. The timeline would surely prove he couldn't have committed the murder, wouldn't it? Or would they simply think he'd killed her, then rushed back to his office to create his alibi? Who knew how Max and Al would think or how they would present it to the DA?

"What has he done to me?"

"Let's just go in and talk to Juliet and Holly."

She cut the car off. Jay grabbed her arm before she could get out. "Sis, I hope you believe me. Somebody's setting me up. I'm being framed. They're going to arrest me."

"Don't panic. Just take care of Jackson and yourself. Get some sleep. I'm working on this."

"What am I gonna tell him? How do I tell my child that he's never going to see his mother again? I didn't want to win custody this way. It'll break his heart and traumatize him for life."

"He's probably asleep by now. You don't have to do it tonight."

The grief on his face ripped open Cathy's old wounds. "I just need to say good night to him," he said. "I need to hold him and talk to him." His voice broke, and he covered his face again. "What if he wakes up? What if he asks me where his mother is?"

"You just tell him that you're having a sleepover at Juliet's. Tomorrow, when you're fresh, when you've had time to think, you can tell him. He has the rest of his life to deal with it." Her voice broke as she said those words.

"The rest of his life."

The rain pounded harder, hitting the windshield in dime-sized dots.

"I loved my wife, Cathy. I didn't want to lose her. I wasn't the one who started all this. If I could've had my deepest wishes, I would've saved my marriage. I still love her."

"I know that, Jay. I believe you."

"The public's gonna try me and convict me. They'll start speculating, and everything is gonna add up to me being a killer. The same kind of person that you talk about on your blog."

Suddenly, it hit Cathy. The note she had gotten on her windshield that day. The one that threatened her, told her to enjoy the ride, if she survived it. What had it said? She tried to think of the exact words. Did she have a copy in her purse? In all the chaos with Jay, she'd completely forgotten about it. She grabbed her purse and looked through it, but didn't find the note. She'd left the copy at home. She had gotten the call about Jay and run out.

"Cathy, are you listening to me?"

Her heart raced. "I have to call Michael."

"About the email?"

"No. Yes . . . that and some other stuff. I need to think. Let's go in and I'll call from inside."

She followed Jay into the house. He accepted hugs and tears as Juliet and Holly fawned over him, got him something to eat and drink, sat him down and massaged his shoulders. They weren't pelting him with questions, which was good. They were just letting him talk and unwind.

She took her phone and went into an empty room to call Michael.

He answered quickly. "Cathy, did they let him go?"

"Yeah," she said. "We're at Juliet's. But listen, I've been thinking of something. The note on my windshield this afternoon . . . It said that I was about to see what it felt like to have people speculate and judge. That I'm about to have a bumpy ride. You don't think it's about this, do you?"

Michael was silent for a moment. "I hadn't connected it. With all the stuff with Jay . . ."

She went to the window, looked out into the night. The families on Juliet's street seemed to be sleeping. Few lights shone in the windows. No cars drove by. If there were stalkers, she couldn't see them. "It has to be connected," she said. "Whoever wrote that note set Jay up. We have to let Max know it might be connected. The prints on that note might be the prints of the killer."

"I'll call him right now."

She hoped his brother would pay attention.

CHAPTER 16

Jay hadn't slept a wink, and when Jackson bounced awake that morning, Juliet distracted him with pancakes.

Now, as Jay sat outside by Juliet's pool with his child, he knew he couldn't wait any longer.

"I like skipping school today," Jackson said. "How come you don't have to work on Tuesday?"

"I took the day off so I could hang out with you."

Jackson beamed and sipped from his juice box. "Would Mommy let us do it again?"

Jay's heart seemed to have swollen too big for his chest cavity, each beat painful. Yes, now was the time. He couldn't keep putting Jackson off. "Come here, buddy."

Jackson abandoned his juice box on a wrought-iron table and came to sit on Jay's lap. "What?"

"I need to talk to you."

"Okay."

As his son looked up at him, waiting, Jay blinked back tears and glanced toward the glass patio doors. Juliet stood there watching him. She turned away when their eyes met.

Jay looked down at Jackson. "Buddy, something bad has happened to Mommy."

Jackson's round gaze narrowed. "What happened?"

"Mommy . . . well, she . . . Somebody hurt her. We don't know who it was yet."

"How did they hurt her?"

Jay hesitated. Should he tell his kindergartner that his mother was shot in cold blood? Was it necessary for him to know that she'd bled out in the bathtub? He cleared his throat and hoped Jackson couldn't feel him shaking.

"The person . . . well . . . he had a gun . . . and he shot Mommy."

Jackson's face twisted. "Is she in the hospital?"

"No, son." He tightened his arms around him, not wanting Jackson to see his face. "Mommy's not in the hospital. She was hurting so bad that Jesus decided to take her on to heaven."

Jackson's mouth fell open. "Uh-uh. She's not dead!"

"Son, I know it's hard . . ."

Jackson jerked away and slid off his lap, glaring at him, red-faced. "She did not go to heaven! She's not dead! I want to call her!" He grabbed for Jay's phone in the holster on his belt. "Gimme your phone!"

"Honey, she's not there."

"Yes, she is!" Jackson screamed. "I wanna talk to Mommy!"

Jay reached for him, but Jackson wouldn't come. He backed away, getting too close to the pool. Jay got up and grabbed him, wrestled him, and held him close as he squirmed. "Son, I'm so sorry. I love you. And I loved her."

"No, you didn't! You hated her! You never came over. You didn't even talk to her or call her!"

How could Jackson ever understand that those hadn't been Jay's choices?

Unable to hold back his own tears any longer, Jay began to weep. After a moment, Jackson stopped fighting. Jay felt his little boy's shoulders shaking as a low, sobbing moan erupted from his throat.

"You're always mad at each other," Jackson choked out.

Jay couldn't deny that. Jackson had seen and heard them fighting before the attorneys told them not to talk to each other. Memories flew back of Jay's reaction to learning Annalee was cheating on him. The rage had overwhelmed him.

Jackson had heard that screaming fight and all the accusations. When Jay packed his things to move out, Jackson locked his arms around Jay's leg and begged him not to go. Annalee had wrestled him off and ordered Jay out of the house. He'd closed the door to the sound of his son's anguish. But that was well over a year ago.

"I didn't want her to die," Jay rasped.

Jackson wiped his face and pulled back, looking up at him. "Are they gonna put the shooter in jail?"

"They will when they find him."

Jackson rubbed his eyes too hard. "She didn't even tell me 'bye.'"

"She wanted to, buddy. She wanted that more than anything."

They clung together for a long moment, weeping against each other's shirts. Finally, Jackson said, "Are you gonna come live with me now?"

"Yes," Jay whispered. "It's you and me, buddy."

CHAPTER 17

As expected, the police got the search warrant for Jay's apartment. There was nothing Cathy could do to stop it.

Exhausted after only a couple of fitful hours of sleep, she poured herself a tall cup of black coffee and decided to head to Michael's for a strategy session.

She went out to her car but didn't put the key in the ignition. For a moment she just sat there in the darkness of her garage, staring at her windshield.

"God, what are you doing to our family?"

She'd had an on-again off-again relationship with God since she was a child. Sometimes she'd been on speaking terms with him, and other times she'd had the crushing sense that he had something against her. What had she and her siblings done to deserve the way their lives had unfolded?

She closed her eyes and thought of all those sermons her father had preached, week after week, as she and Juliet tried to keep Holly and Jay quiet on the front pew. The family image was crucial. They were to appear like the perfect children, taught to respect the sanctuary and the man who was speaking. Taught to fear God.

And fear him they did. Questions weren't accepted about their burgeoning faith, until everything fell apart.

She didn't want to think about that now. Her father's unfaithfulness to her mother, his abrupt fall from pastor to outcast, and her family's sudden homelessness when the church evicted them from the parsonage . . . had all resulted in a 180-degree turn in her thinking about faith, love, and the body of Christ.

There were times when she blamed God completely. Despite her father's hypocrisy, hadn't her mother served God faithfully? Hadn't the children been behaved and obedient? Why did they deserve to live in the only place they could afford—a garage apartment offered by strangers who heard of their dilemma?

Where were the loving shoulders for her mother to cry on? Why had she been a pariah too?

Cathy shook herself out of her reverie and told herself to snap out of it. She had work to do. Her brother needed her. Her nephew needed her.

Everyone needed her.

She started the car and backed out of the garage, trying to bury her bitterness. She'd buried it when her fiancé was murdered, when his killer walked free, when Michael was the one punished. But this time, it was burying her.

It was as if God had allowed her to be crushed in the avalanche of bitterness, trapped under its weight. Yet he warned against it. How could she escape?

Under it all, she did still have a remnant of faith. "There's a purpose for all this," she whispered. "There must be. I know you're not mean. I know you love us."

That knowledge kept her going to God, even when her fists were clenched. Even when there was no human understanding for the things humans did.

Her cell phone rang as she pulled into a parking space in front of Michael's office. She didn't recognize the number, but she answered anyway. "Hello?"

"Cathy, this is Max. I know it's early. Did I wake you up?"

She sighed. "No, I'm just pulling up at Michael's. What's up?"

"I wanted you to know there were no other prints on that note that was put on your car. Just yours."

She sighed. "Great. Is there anything else you can learn from it?"

"Not really."

"Well, you'll keep it as evidence, won't you?"

"We will, but I'm not sure it's relevant. Gotta go. Just wanted you to know."

Feeling defeated, she went into the small building that had once been a gas station and convenience store. The front room, which was supposed to look like a small waiting room, had a pea-green sofa Michael had picked up at the Goodwill store. His living area was the old storeroom at the back of the building. At least he had a bathroom and shower there.

"In here, Cathy!"

She stepped toward his office door, a walled-off half of the front area. Michael sat at his desk, still wearing what he'd had on the last time she'd seen him.

"Hey," she said, dropping her bag on an easy chair in the corner. "Didn't you go to bed last night?"

"No," he said. "I've been up, trying to figure this out."

She glanced at the dry erase board, where he'd made copious notes about the case, as he would have if he'd been the detective assigned to it.

She sank into the easy chair, pulled her feet beneath her. "Something you can add to the list. No prints on the note left on my car."

"Didn't think there would be." He got up and wrote "Note on car—no fingerprints" in the evidence column. "But it was handwritten, so that could help us later. When we figure out who it is, we can compare handwriting samples."

Cathy stared at the list of all the evidence he had so far. The emails, the gun, the clown, the truck, the timeline . . . She was tired and her head hurt, but she couldn't let it slow her down.

"Let's make a column for the cases you've been writing about," he said.

She got her laptop out of her bag, opened it. She pulled up her site and scanned through it. "There are so many."

"We can rule out the ones who are in prison now. And since Jay seems sure the clown was a man, we can rule out the women."

She scanned through the list of male defendants. "Okay, Brooks Lewis is free. He was acquitted, but I always thought he was innocent and said so on my blog. Clive Taylor only got a year in prison, and he's out by now. I did say some pretty stinging things about him, because I thought he was as guilty as sin."

Michael scribbled "Clive Taylor" on the board. "Who else?"

As she went through the list of possible men who might have a grudge against her, Michael sat down next to her. She scrolled through her blogs she'd written in the last year, re-reading some of what she'd said about the men suspected of horrendous things—murder, rape, child abuse. She'd told it the way she saw it, and that didn't always make her friends.

"I don't usually think about how I'm making the suspect feel," she said. "But looking at this now, I'm surprised I wasn't the one who was murdered."

"Good point," Michael said. "Why doesn't this guy want *you* dead? Why would he be satisfied to kill your sister-in-law? If Annalee's killer is the same guy who threatened you, it doesn't make sense."

She shook her head. "It's got to be more than that. I mean, I could see him setting me up for a crime. Making me look like a person of interest. Showing me how it feels to have people speculating and judging. But to kill Annalee, who has so little to do with me, only so he could set up my brother in hopes of hurting me . . . I agree with you. It's a stretch to connect those dots."

"He did mention Leonard Miller." That name was already written at the top of the board, in a different color ink. Cathy figured it had been there for the last two years.

She winced at the reminder of the man who'd murdered Joe. "Would Miller do this, knowing we'd love nothing more than to nail him for another crime?"

"I know it's unlikely," he said. "But sociopaths can't be accused of logic."

"But what would he have against me? And how

would he even know about Jay's divorce problems? Besides, there's no evidence that he's in town. His face was all over the news here, and the town hates him. I don't think he'd come back."

"I wish he would," Michael muttered. "I'd just love to find him."

"Well, let's not let him get us off track," Cathy said. "The note warned me something would happen. I can't help but think the two situations are connected."

"But it could just be a coincidence."

She breathed a laugh. "Thought you didn't believe in coincidences."

He rubbed his tired eyes. "Well, I don't think things happen out of the blue. Everything has a purpose. But as a detective, I think when there's this much reach to connect two things, maybe we're on the wrong track. Maybe this person had it in for Annalee and just set up Jay to keep the heat off himself. Maybe it has nothing at all to do with you."

Cathy didn't know whether to be relieved at that prospect, or disappointed that one of their leads led nowhere. "It was another clue. And we don't have all that many."

Michael got up and went back to the board. "I'm still waiting to hear if security video caught the person putting the note on your car, if any of the security cameras on the main roads from Annalee's house might have caught a white truck, and where this clown suit might have come from. But I can't guarantee Max and Al have pulled those tapes."

He went to his desk and pulled out Jay's crude

drawing of the clown. "I've been googling clown suits, looking for one that looks like this."

"You'll probably find dozens of stores that carry that style."

"Maybe. Maybe not. It's not just the costume. It's the wig, the makeup, the shoes. If I can find the store that sold any of that to our zip code in the last few weeks . . ."

She sighed. "Michael, how do you have time to do all this? You have to make a living."

He shrugged. "It's what I do best. It's better than spying on Medicare frauds and cheating husbands."

"We could pay you."

He looked insulted. "I don't want money. I just want to help you out and get your brother off. And I have to admit . . . if Leonard Miller's involved, then I'm all over this."

She swallowed and met his eyes. Sorrow connected them for a moment too long. He looked away. "So where do we go from here?" she asked.

"Keep looking through the blogs and figuring out who may have had the potential to do this. It feels like a rabbit trail, but there might be something there. I'll keep pressuring Max to find any videos, even if he won't let us see them. And I'll keep working on finding the costume."

She closed her laptop and got up. "I'll let you know when I get the list of what they confiscated from their search of Jay's apartment." She started out, hesitating at the door. "Jay told Jackson about Annalee this morning. Juliet said it was really heartbreaking." Her voice broke, and she blinked back tears. "Jackson needs to be back in his own home, but with the investigation, it's impossible for them to get back in there. The divorce wasn't final, so the house is still Jay's. But with him as a person of interest and the house sealed . . ."

"We'll have to help them rule him out as soon as possible."

Tears seeped through her lashes. "Yeah."

"And in the meantime, I want you to hire a body-guard for yourself."

"I'm not doing that, Michael."

"Cathy, if this is connected to you, this guy's danger-ous. He could hurt you."

"I'll be careful. I'm carrying my gun in the car. I'll be all right."

He rubbed his forehead. "Will you at least promise me that before you go anywhere predictable, you'll call me so I can go with you?"

"Michael . . ."

"Cathy, promise me."

She sighed. "All right. I will. This whole thing is just . . . surreal. Like I'm living through a foggy night-mare." She got her bag, slid the strap on her shoulder, and dropped her laptop in.

"Cathy?"

She looked up at him and pulled the bag to her chest, holding it like a shield.

"Are you all right?"

She forced a smile. "Yes, I'm fine."

As more tears pushed to her eyes, she turned and

left his office. She got into her car, grabbed one of the wadded tissues on the passenger seat, and dabbed at her eyes.

This was almost as bad as she'd felt two years ago, when she learned Joe had been killed on a drug bust. Almost as bad.

Michael was one of the few who understood, because it was his grief too.

As she drove out of the parking space, she glanced back at his office. Michael stood at the window, watching her drive away.

CHAPTER 18

The police came to Juliet's at noon that day, pushing through the local media that had set up shop on the sidewalk. Juliet saw them coming and ordered Zach to take Jackson upstairs to watch a movie.

As the police knocked hard on her beveled glass door, Juliet pulled Jay into a desperate hug. "It's going to be okay, Jay. If they arrest you, it's just temporary. I'll get everybody praying, and we'll work day and night to solve this crime and get you out."

Jay seemed to brace himself. "Just take care of Jackson. I want him to stay with you. Keep him busy and away from the news."

The knock came again, louder, more urgently, followed by the doorbell ringing.

They couldn't wait any longer. She put her hand on the doorknob and looked back at him. "Ready?"

He nodded and she opened the door. Two uniformed officers stood there, and behind them, out by the street, cameras rolled. "Mr. Jay Cramer?" one of the officers asked.

"Yes." His voice was flat, resigned. "Come in."

They stepped in, and Juliet closed the door, blocking out the onlookers.

"Mr. Cramer, we have a warrant for your arrest for the murder of Annalee Cramer."

He nodded. "Okay. If we could just talk quietly so my son won't hear . . ."

"Daddy!"

Juliet's stomach flipped as Jackson ran up the hall.

"Daddy, come watch *How to Train Your Dragon* with me."

Jay looked as though he might pass out. He turned from the police and squatted down, getting eye level with Jackson. "Son, I can't come right now. I have to go help these policemen."

Jackson stared up at them. "Is it about Mommy?"

Jay worked his mouth to keep the emotion from showing. "Yes, it's about Mommy," he said. "I need for you to stay with Aunt Juliet and be a good boy, okay?"

Jackson looked uncomfortably up at the cops, then turned back to his dad. "When will you be back?"

Jay frowned. "I'm not sure right now. But you're gonna have some more sleepovers with Aunt Juliet. And I'll call you and let you know, okay?"

Jackson didn't answer. How much more could he take? Jay got back to his feet and turned to the police. He lowered his voice. "For him . . . could we just not do the cuffs?"

The younger cop looked down at Jackson and gave him that small mercy. "Yeah, okay."

Jay forced a smile. "'Bye, buddy. Maybe Aunt Juliet will watch that movie with you."

"Of course I will," Juliet said, tears welling. "You go help them. We'll be just fine, won't we, Jackson?"

Jackson nodded as Jay gave him a kiss and hurried out the front door with the cops.

The reporters' cameras were flashing and rolling, and they yelled questions at Jay as soon as they saw him.

Juliet quickly closed the door.

"Who are those people out there?" Jackson asked.

"They're people who want to talk to Daddy about your mommy."

"Oh." Jackson seemed to consider that. Juliet hoped he wouldn't consider it too long.

"Come on, sweetie," she said, forcing enthusiasm into her tone. "Let's go watch *Dragon*."

CHAPTER 19

Cathy stopped her car at her mailbox before pulling into her driveway and pulled out the mail. She hadn't checked it at all yesterday, so a stack of it awaited her.

She quickly flipped through it. Bills, bills, junk mail, and some handwritten envelopes that looked like fan mail. She glanced at the return address of each one.

Seattle . . . Tulsa . . . and one that said only, "Your New Friend."

Her throat closed and her heart began racing. Fingerprints, she thought. She shouldn't touch it. She set the stack of mail on the passenger seat and drove up the driveway. She ran into the house and got some latex gloves from under her kitchen sink. Then she went back to the car and carefully opened the envelope.

Suddenly her phone rang. She jumped as if she'd been caught at something. The caller ID said *Juliet*.

She clicked the phone on and held it between her shoulder and ear. "Hey,"

"Cathy, they arrested him!" Juliet's voice was muffled, low, as if she didn't want to be overheard.

Cathy grabbed the phone. "Oh no. When?"

"Just now. I can't talk. I have to distract Jackson."

"Did Jackson see it?"

"Yes, but Jay told him he was going to help the police. They didn't use handcuffs."

Cathy closed her eyes. "All right. I'm headed to the police station."

Before she started the car, she pulled the note out of the envelope.

It was handwritten.

Dear Curious Cat,

So sorry about your brother. I hope the country doesn't try and convict him before he's had the chance to defend himself. That would be a tragedy.

Are you going to blog about him? Are you going to tell them his side of the story? Oh, I hope you do.

Isn't this fun?

Your New Friend

Cathy's heart jolted. Her hands trembled as she checked the postmark. It had been mailed yesterday from Panama City's zip code.

So he was local.

She racked her brain for what to do. Yes, she'd give the note to the police, but she needed to keep a copy of it. She took a picture with her iPhone, checked it to make sure it could be clearly seen.

Then she emailed it to Michael with the subject line, "Another Message."

Her head was throbbing, and her mind raced with courses of action.

This person had murdered her sister-in-law. He had left her nephew motherless. He was trying to ruin her brother. He was toying with her as if this were a game.

Rage blasted through her. She got her .38 out of the console in her car, held it as she went into her house. The place seemed clear, but she didn't let her guard down.

Biting her lip, she went to her computer and pulled up her blog. She clicked on NEW POST and started typing.

> To the bottom-dwelling psychopath who
> murdered my sister-in-law:
> I will find you. You think you're clever, but you'll make mistakes. You already have. We know things about you that you didn't know you revealed. It's just a matter of time.
> Get ready. The ride's about to get bumpier.
> Curious Cat

She hit Send and waited as the letter showed up as a new blog post. Then slamming her chair back against her credenza, she checked the chambers of her revolver to make sure it was loaded. Grabbing her keys, she went back to her car.

Now she could go to the police station and take care of her brother.

. . .

He laughed as he read her blog. His plan was working. He was smarter than anyone gave him credit for, and soon they would give him the respect he deserved.

But it did bug him that she claimed to know things he hadn't anticipated. What could she know? He'd disposed of the clown suit. It was a pile of ashes in the incinerator. There was nothing to connect the murder to him.

And there would be nothing to connect him to the next one. He'd thought it all the way through. It was the perfect plan, with a perfect result.

He wasn't a psychopath. He was just a deep thinker, one who did what was necessary to take care of himself. Others waited for life to happen to them, and they took the cards they were dealt. They deserved to be victims, but not him.

He was too smart for that. He could shuffle the deck the way he wanted, and choose his own hand. And when it was all over, he would not be remembered as a bottom-dwelling psychopath, or even as a killer.

Not even Curious Cat could trace these deaths to him.

CHAPTER 20

N o, not here. Take a right after the red light. Then a quick left. Could you stop by the bank up there and let me run in so I can pay you?"

Holly sighed and made the right turn. Her passenger would probably skip out the back door of the bank without paying. But what could she do? It wasn't like she could run a credit report every time someone called.

"I have to keep the meter running while you're in there," she said, turning into the bank's parking lot.

"Of course, no problem. I'm not gonna run out on you, if that's what you think. I need you. I just got my license revoked for getting another DUI."

Holly glanced in her mirror at the woman. "Sorry about that."

The woman was quiet as she dug into her purse. "Yeah, but I'm going to meetings and trying to get my life together. Don't want to lose my job just because I can't drive. So if you'll just wait while I run in." She opened the door, started to get out. "You really will wait, won't you? I really do have to get to work."

"Yes, I'm not going anywhere."

The woman who looked too classy to have a DUI trotted in. Holly watched her.

The passenger seemed more like Cathy than like Holly. Holly couldn't imagine her sister having a DUI. Cathy didn't have time for foolishness like revoked licenses and surprise pregnancies.

And she sure would never be caught dead driving a cab.

As she watched for her passenger to come out of the bank, Holly's phone buzzed, and she saw Juliet's face on her screen. She clicked it on. "Hey, Sis. What's the bad news?"

"Jay just got arrested."

She sucked in a breath. "No! Did you call Cathy?"

"Yes, but they should have told her first, and they didn't. They took him in, and now Jackson's asking all sorts of questions."

"I'm coming over after I drop off my passenger."

"Don't tell anybody. I know you like to talk to them."

"Juliet, I'm not sharing our family's dirty laundry. But it doesn't matter, because this is going to be all over the news. Probably even nationally because of Cathy's blog following."

Juliet sighed. "I know. Poor Jay. What are we gonna do?"

The woman came back out of the bank, her skirt blowing behind her in the breeze. She slipped into the backseat. "Thank you. We can go now."

Holly nodded. "Juliet, I have to go. I'll see you in a few minutes."

"Okay. Drive careful."

Juliet couldn't resist mothering her. Holly cut off the phone and glanced in her rearview mirror. "Where now?"

"433 Westhaven Street."

Holly glanced back at her as she pulled out of the parking lot. "What do you do?"

"I'm an event planner. Parties all the time." She said it as if the concept disgusted her. "Ironic for someone who has issues with alcohol. Parties can ruin your life."

"Tell me about it," Holly said. "I used to take pride in my partying." She thought of telling the woman that she was pregnant, that she didn't know how she'd tell her family, especially when they were going through such a tough time already, that she wasn't equipped to take care of herself, much less a little baby. ·

After all, she'd probably never see the woman again.

But that was absurd. There was no one she could tell. No one at all.

She dropped the woman off and gave her her card. "If you need a taxi again, ask the agency for me. I could use the business."

"Sure will. I feel more comfortable with you than with some guy." The woman got out, then bent back in through the open window and handed Holly the fee. "What are you doing driving a cab, anyway?"

Holly shrugged. "Girl's gotta make a living."

As she drove to Juliet's house, her left hand rested on her stomach. How big was the baby at this stage? Did it have eyes? A brain? Was it already a boy or a girl?

How would this child feel, having a loser mom raising him? Or her?

What would she tell him when he was old enough to ask about why she drove a cab?

Well, see, I could have gone to college like my sisters. I could have gotten grants and loans, but I figured I'd wing it.

Or she could tell the truth.

I barely graduated high school and lost every other job I had because of hangovers and oversleeping. Cab driving suits me. I can set my own hours and no one can fire me.

No, it wasn't something she would have chosen. She hadn't grown up wanting to be a cab driver. Her mother would turn over in her grave.

Her overachieving sister had tried to talk her out of it and had made phone calls to get her other jobs. Eventually, Cathy had quit trying, because Holly managed to embarrass her every time.

Now even Juliet accepted what she had to do to pay her rent. She'd lost umpteen jobs, and when no one would hire her because of her own record of failures, she had started thinking outside the box.

She saw a want ad for taxi drivers, and applied. She'd been hired, and for a while had driven the agency's cab. Then a friend retired and offered to sell her his taxi.

In the interest of keeping her working, Juliet and Bob had loaned her the money to buy it. Ever since, she'd been her own boss, though she still took calls from the agency.

At least she couldn't fire herself.

But neither of her sisters would respond well to her pregnancy. Her family had been staunch pro-lifers as far back as she could remember. They would never consider abortion an option, but an unwed pregnancy was a fate worse than death, at least to Juliet.

Guilt raged through her as she drove to her sister's house. Here she was, thinking about herself at a time like this. What kind of person was she? Her brother was traumatized after finding his wife dead, and now he was being blamed for her murder. His child was at Juliet's, confused and asking questions. And Holly's mind was on her own plight. It was just like her.

She hated herself.

She reached Juliet's house where three TV vans were parked and pulled her taxi into the driveway. As she did, a police car pulled up, with a silver Cadillac trailing it.

Holly got out, hoping they'd thought better of Jay's arrest and brought him back. Maybe Cathy had pulled some legal strings.

Instead, Warren and his mother got out of the car. What now? Were they going to try to take Jackson again? Holly slammed her door and ran into the house, "Juliet!"

Her sister was at the door in seconds. "Shhh. Jackson's sleeping."

Holly tried to catch her breath. "Juliet, it's the police and Warren and his mother"

"The police? What do they want?"

"Jackson, I'll bet."

Juliet looked out as the group made their way through the reporters. Holly felt her sister go rigid.

As they reached the front steps, Juliet said, "My

brother isn't here, and Jackson's asleep right now. You'll have to come back later."

"Ma'am, we have a court order."

One of the police officers handed her a folded sheet of paper, and Juliet opened it, her hands shaking. "We have to take Jackson Cramer from you and place him in the custody of his grandmother."

Juliet's mouth fell open, and she couldn't seem to speak. "No," Holly said, "Jay wanted him to stay here. His father gets to determine where his child will stay."

"His father has been charged with murder," Warren said. "We talked to a judge this morning, who ordered that Jackson come home with us. My mother is his next of kin."

Juliet kept staring at the order. "It's a temporary order until we can have a hearing. But no one even gave Jay a chance to tell the judge where he wants Jackson to stay? This was decided without him?"

Holly suddenly felt sick. She couldn't throw up right here, in front of the press and the police. She tried to hold it back. Juliet took a step forward, touched Mrs. Haughton's arm. The woman looked weak, and her labored breathing suggested this was not easy for her. "Mrs. Haughton, you know Annalee would have been worried about Jackson's state of mind. I promise you he's fine here. He's taking a nap. Jay told him about his mom, so it's been a tough day for him already. Please . . . let him stay. Don't do this."

"He's my grandson," Mrs. Haughton said, breathless, as if that was all she could manage to get out.

"And he's my nephew," Juliet said. "He loves being

here with his cousins. I'm set up for kids. And you're not well."

"*I'm* well," Warren cut in, "and he's my nephew too. The judge says he's coming with us. Are you going to get him, or am I?"

And then the nausea came, roiling up in Holly's stomach, rising to her throat. She left the doorway and ran for the bathroom. Barely making it in time, she bent over the toilet and wretched.

"Aunt Holly? Do you have the flu?"

Holly finished heaving and looked up to see Jackson, standing sleepy-eyed in the bathroom doorway. "Maybe I do. Honey, I thought you were taking a nap."

"Where's Aunt Juliet? Is my daddy back yet?"

Tasting the bile in her mouth, Holly took his hand and tried to lead him back to the stairs. Surely Mrs. Haughton would think better of taking this child away right now. Surely Warren would care more for his nephew's fragile state of mind than for his own "rights" in removing him.

"Jackson!" Warren's voice startled them both, and Jackson turned around.

"Hey, Uncle Warren."

"Jackson, come here, bud."

Holly's nausea made an encore. Holly raced back to the bathroom and threw up again. When she looked up, Juliet was standing in the doorway. "Holly, are you all right?"

She nodded. "Yes . . . just upset."

Juliet left her alone to clean up and went back to the

front door. When Holly came back out, the travesty continuing, Jackson stood in front of his uncle, who had stooped to his eye level.

"Jackson, Grandma and I want you to come to our house for a while. We want to spend some time with you."

Jackson looked at him. "Did you know Mommy died?"

Warren looked at his mother, who bent more over her walker, as if her grief prevented her from holding herself upright.

"Yes, we know. We're all really sad, but we want to make sure you're okay. If you came, it would make Grandma feel so much better."

Jackson gazed at his grandmother. Holly hoped the guilt-inducing tactics weren't working. "Grandma's going to be sad no matter where Jackson is. Won't you, Mrs. Haughton?"

Mrs. Haughton couldn't seem to answer.

"I was gonna swim in a little while," Jackson said. "Aunt Juliet said—"

"We'll do something fun at Grandma's," Warren cut in. "You can sleep over and—"

"No, I want to sleep over here until Daddy comes back."

"But your daddy's going to be gone for a while. Let's get your stuff. Grandma's not feeling well. We need to get her home."

Jackson's big eyes sought his aunts. Speechless, Juliet struggled with tears. Holly knew she was censoring her words, considering Jackson's reaction. But Holly didn't care about that. Rage beat in her face. "Warren, this is making things worse. Don't be so selfish. Think, for once!"

"Holly, don't make it harder for him," Warren said through his teeth.

"But you know this isn't what his dad wants!"

"Jackson," Warren said in a sterner voice. "Show me where your stuff is."

When it was clear the police would demand compliance, Juliet tried to paste on a happy face and convince Jackson that he'd have fun at his grandmother's. But the child wasn't buying it.

Holly called Cathy while Juliet helped pack up Jackson's things, but there was no answer. She was probably with Jay. When Jackson began to cry, Warren just moved faster, stuffing Jackson's clothes into a suitcase.

"Uncle Warren, I don't wanna go!" Jackson cried. "Please, can I stay here?"

"No, bud. You have to come with us. Just for a while. It'll be okay. We'll watch a movie. I'll take you to the pet store, and we can pet some puppies."

The child clearly wanted none of it. He reached for Juliet. She picked him up and held him. "It's just for a little while. They can bring you back to swim later, can't you, Uncle Warren?"

Warren didn't answer. He just zipped up the bag.

Jackson wailed louder as Warren took her from Juliet's arms, the police standing beside him, ready to intervene if anyone tried to prevent this. As Warren carried the distraught child out to their car, his grandmother hobbling behind him on her walker, Holly wanted to scream and throw something.

"This is absurd!" she told Juliet. "Why did you just let that happen?"

Juliet burst into tears. "I had no choice. They had a judge's order."

"We could have stalled until Cathy called back!"

"I didn't want to get Jackson more upset. Look at him!"

"It's going to be all over the news. The little boy whose mother was murdered, carried, crying, out of his aunt's house. They're going to milk this for all it's worth."

"We need to pray," Juliet said. "We need a whole series of miracles."

But Holly doubted God even cared. It was the exact reason she had given up praying long ago.

CHAPTER 21

I want my son back with my sister!"

Jay had remained relatively calm since being arrested, but since Cathy told him that Jackson had been removed, he'd begun to shake and pace the floor. Al and Max watched him carefully, as if taking mental notes about his behavior. "This isn't right. I'm his father. *I* say where he stays. I haven't lost my parental rights just because you guys are barking up the wrong tree!"

Cathy tried to quiet her brother. Insulting the police wasn't going to do any good. "Detectives, I need a moment alone with my client."

Al uncrossed his legs and slowly got up. "Let us know when he's ready to resume."

As they walked out, Cathy turned to Jay. "I know this is upsetting. I'm upset too. I'm working on getting him back."

"How can you do that? You're also working on getting me out of here and solving this murder. You can't do everything, Cathy." Perspiration shone on his face. "I want to get another attorney. An experienced lawyer who can focus on getting me out of this."

She gaped at him. "You're firing me?"

"No, but I need a heavy-duty criminal defense attorney."

She crossed her arms and threw her chin up. "You don't think I'm heavy-duty?"

"Cathy, this is not about you. I want you to work on getting Jackson back with Juliet until I get out of here. And maybe you can follow some leads and figure out who killed Annalee. If you're tied up in all these interviews with me, you can't do that."

She had to admit, there was wisdom in what he was saying. She wasn't that experienced in murder cases, and she hadn't practiced law for the last two years. He did need someone top notch. She couldn't let her pride get in the way.

She sighed. "Then I'd recommend Lawrence Pratt. I can call him right now. He's gotten a lot of high-profile defendants acquitted of murder charges."

"I don't need someone who gets guilty people off. I need someone who gets *innocent* people off." He dropped back into the chair. "But right now, I don't even care. Just go take care of Jackson. He must be so confused. Being told his mother is gone, that he'll never see her again this side of heaven, and watching me being arrested. Then being forced to go to a house where his grandmother is slowly dying. Why does she want him?"

"I think she's just not thinking clearly," Cathy said. "Warren isn't helping matters."

"But Warren has never even spent time with Jackson alone as far as I know. He never pays any attention to him."

Cathy shook her head. "Maybe he's just trying to do something for his sister."

"Don't defend him!" Jay bit out.

"I'm not," Cathy said. "But grief does different things to people."

"The only person whose grief matters to me is Jackson's. Why can't they think of him? Cathy, don't I still have parental rights? They can't take my child away against my will until I've been convicted of something, can they?"

"They do have the right to make arrangements for a child's custody when his only remaining parent isn't able to care for him. And when his grandmother filed for custody . . . well, she's the closest kin. She knows the judge really well. He's a friend of the family. He probably thought he was doing the right thing, taking care of Jackson so he wouldn't go into foster care."

"Foster care?"

"I'll petition the court to put him back with Juliet until the hearing. Then we can present all the facts."

But Cathy knew her reassurances were weak. They did little to calm Jay down.

As Cathy left the police station, she knew she had to get Jackson back to her sister's. Even being charged with murder hadn't upset Jay as much as his child's plight.

She supposed that was how it should be. The best way to help him was to find this killer so Jay could have Jackson back.

She hurried home and made a phone call. Her first choice for Jay's attorney, Lawrence Pratt, agreed to take the case. He would go visit Jay in the next hour or so, freeing her up to file a motion to get Jackson placed back with Juliet. But first, she checked her blog to see if she'd heard back from the killer.

There was nothing from him in the comments, and she quickly logged on to her email. If he contacted her, it would give them another clue to his identity. The police had taken the latest letter as evidence, but she doubted they were following up.

"It's just a letter from a reader, Cathy," Max had said. "There's nothing threatening in this email. No reason to think it's even from the person who left the note on your car. The signature isn't unique. You could have dozens of emails signed 'Your Friend.'"

"But not 'Your *New* Friend!' They both had the same kind of message. It wasn't a coincidence." She sighed. How could she prove it was the same person? He was able to hide now, because the previous correspondence had come from Annalee's computer or through the mail. If she could lure him into emailing her, they could trace it back to another server, which would help them narrow their search.

But he was too smart to give them the satisfaction of an immediate answer. She had no doubt he'd read her message. Everyone had. It had even made the national news cycle. She hoped he was stewing over what she knew, watching out windows for the police.

She would just have to wait for the next message.

CHAPTER 22

Michael pulled into a coffee shop parking lot and got out of his Trailblazer, stretching the fatigue from his body. He couldn't slow down now. He needed coffee.

He went in and ordered a strong brew, black.

"How would you like it? To-go cup or a mug?" the woman asked.

"Got an IV?"

"No, sorry."

He chuckled. "Okay, a to-go cup then."

He waited as she poured the cup, then he dumped some sugar into it, paid for it, and went back to his car. What now? He should go back to his office and work on finding that clown costume. But something pulled him in another direction.

Michael had driven by Leonard Miller's mother's house a million times since the trial, hoping to find an unusual car there that might belong to his brother's killer. At some point, it only stood to reason that Miller would come back to see her. He wasn't banned from coming into town. He was free to go wherever he wanted.

But Miller knew that if he did, he would be recognized by citizens who thought of him as a cop-killer, and the entire police force would be tailing him in hopes of catching him committing another crime. If he went one mile over the speed limit or let his tag expire by one day, he would be hauled in. His chosen vocation—drug dealing—would eventually land him in prison for sure.

Michael made his way to that neighborhood, where the commerce of drug dealing fueled the street thugs. As he turned onto the street, he saw at least a dozen cars parked in front of Miller's mother's house.

Were they having a party in the middle of the afternoon?

He drove in front of the house, slowed, and tried to see what was happening. Someone who'd just pulled up got out of the car with a casserole dish covered with tin foil.

Either someone was sick, or someone had died.

Michael's heart began to race. Leonard Miller could be inside that house right now. If something had happened to his mother . . .

Hope clawed its way into his heart. Passing the house, he drove to the nearest convenience store and bought a newspaper. Before he'd even made it back to his car, he found the obituary page.

SHEILA RAE MILLER, 71 YEARS OLD . . .

Leonard Miller's mother had died. The funeral was going to be that afternoon.

So it was possible that Leonard Miller had left the notes for Cathy and killed Jay's wife. He was probably in town at the time.

Michael had to see him.

He went back to Mrs. Miller's house and parked behind one of the other cars in the long line of vehicles out front. Miller wouldn't know his car.

Michael ducked into the backseat, got his binoculars, and waited for someone to come in or out of the house. His side windows were blacked out so no one would see him, and the front seat looked as if no one was in the car.

As he waited, he got on his computer and listed phone numbers for all the places he found that had the kind of clown suit he was looking for. He made those calls while he watched to see if Leonard Miller had indeed shown up.

Finally, people began coming out of the house. It was probably time for the family to head to the funeral home. He waited, watching, but never saw Miller. Where was he?

Finally, when all of the cars had pulled away, Michael got back into the front seat and headed to the funeral home.

He pulled into the line of cars at a grave site and shoved his sunglasses on, watching as people surrounded the tent where the casket stood. He got out of his car and headed into the crowd.

As he got a glimpse of the people inside the tent, he saw the man he was looking for. Leonard Miller, with a pale face and a gold front tooth, the tattoo on the back of his once-shaved head now covered with hair. After he killed Joe, that tat marked him wherever he went. Now, with his hair grown back in, Michael saw the male-pattern baldness that Miller had been trying to hide. Clearly, that common baldness was better than the tattoo that so easily identified him.

Michael went back to his car, sat behind the wheel, and waited for the funeral to be over. When it was, he would follow Miller and see where he was staying.

The funeral lasted a half hour or so, and the crowd broke up quickly, everyone walking back to their cars. Michael couldn't find Miller and wasn't sure if he'd missed him leaving, or if Miller had remained behind, shaking hands.

Suddenly, someone knocked on his window.

Michael turned and saw the man he'd been search-ing for standing at his passenger door. Old rage clamped like a vise around his chest. Setting his chin, he got out and went around the car, standing full height, eye-to-eye with the man who had changed his life. "So you're here."

"I'm a free man," Miller said. "I came to bury my mother."

"My condolences." But Michael knew his voice lacked sincerity.

"You got a problem, dude? You watchin' me for a reason?"

"I had a feeling you were back in town. You don't own a clown suit, do you?"

Miller's face twisted. "What? A *clown* suit?"

Michael waited for the full range of Miller's reaction to the question.

"Dude, I don't know what you're trying to connect me with, but I been with my mother the last few days. I was with her when she died. You can talk to people at the hospital. I ain't done nothin' to nobody here."

"I will talk to them," he said. "Which hospital?"

"Bay Medical. Knock yourself out." Miller started to walk away.

"When did your mother die, Miller?"

He turned back. "Sunday."

"Then you were free yesterday."

Miller stared at him for a long moment. "Whatchu tryin' to pin on me? I was with relatives and at the funeral home."

Right. Michael would check that out, though he doubted relatives would be forthcoming. He could have killed Annalee. But why? The question churned through his stomach.

"You better enjoy being a free man, Miller. One of these days you'll get what you deserve."

Miller laughed. "Are you threatening me?"

Michael glared at him. "Just making a prophecy, that's all."

Miller kept chuckling as he strode to a black Pontiac at the front of the line, and Michael watched him pull away. He couldn't follow him, because too many other cars got between them, but he did get his tag number. Soon Miller had vanished.

But now Michael knew for sure that Leonard Miller

was in town the day Annalee was killed. He had no idea what the man's motive could be, but it was possible he'd done it.

If Miller was involved, Michael would make sure he didn't get away with it again.

CHAPTER 23

The burning, acidic knot in Juliet's stomach kept her from eating with her family that night. Her husband Bob, who'd just arrived home after a week away at a medical conference, made conversation with the children, going over the steps Abe would take in approaching his science project.

He avoided looking at her, as if he knew she'd fall apart if given the least prodding.

When they'd finished and the boys had scurried away to pretend to do homework, Bob caught her in the kitchen. "Are you okay?"

"No, I'm not," she admitted. "I'm worried about Jackson. I couldn't do anything for my brother except take care of his son . . . and now I can't do that."

"Cathy's on it. She's going to get him back, and the police will sort all this out and let Jay go."

She wasn't sure she could believe that.

"Juliet," Bob said, taking her chin. "Look at me."

She met his eyes.

"It's going to be all right. You have to believe that."

She sighed. "I know. And that's what I keep telling

my sisters. But it doesn't seem like it's gonna be all right. It's looking really bad." She put the last of the dishes into the dishwasher and pressed the button to start it. "Listen, now that you're home, I need to take a casserole to a friend. Can you help the boys with the rest of their homework?"

He gave her a narrow look. "You're suffering over your brother, and you're taking someone a casserole? Don't you think you deserve a day off?"

"Mercy doesn't ever take the day off. Will you watch them?"

"I have some work I need to catch up on tonight."

She quenched the urge to repeat what he'd just said . . . that she was suffering over her brother and needed to be served instead of serving. He'd spent the last few days in a cushy hotel. Couldn't he give her a break for a few hours?

As if he read the emotions on her face, he said, "No, it's fine. You do what makes you feel better. I'll take care of them."

He probably hoped she wouldn't take him up on it, that she'd insist he get his work done. But she didn't. This was too important.

"I might be late. I was thinking of going to see Juliet and Holly afterward. We have a lot to talk about."

"Sure, of course. We'll work on the science project some more. We'll be fine."

"Thanks." She took her purse and the casserole and headed out the door, knowing that if she took the time to tell the kids she was leaving, she'd burst into tears and get them all upset. A thousand questions would follow . . . about Jay and his dead wife . . . about him being in jail . . .

She got into her SUV and pulled out of the garage. She thought of calling her sisters to go with her on her mission, but that probably wouldn't be helpful. No, she'd go alone.

She drove the few miles to her dead sister-in-law's childhood home, where Mrs. Haughton and Warren, and now Jackson, lived. It was a Tudor-style house with a once-beautiful Yard-of-the-Month garden out front, which Mrs. Haughton had tended with her own hands until she got too sick to get back up from kneeling in the dirt.

Though the yard was neat, since she probably hired someone to keep it, it had lost its former glory.

Juliet hoped she'd get the chance to check on Jackson, to reassure him, to give them some tips on how to care for him. Maybe she'd even talk them into letting him come home with her. If he'd cried and grieved, maybe they'd already seen how foolish it was to move him.

She rang the doorbell and waited. No one came, so she knocked on the door. Finally, she heard the creaking of footsteps moving across the floor . . . slow, plodding . . .

Was Mrs. Haughton coming to the door herself? She felt suddenly guilty for making her do that.

The door slowly came open. Mrs. Haughton stood looking through the six-inch opening, her oxygen tube pinched under her nose. She leaned on a cane, the tank on wheels beside her.

"Mrs. Haughton, I'm sorry I got you up. I'm not here

to fight with you over Jackson. I just wanted to do what I'd do for anyone. I wanted to bring you a meal."

The woman's pale face seemed to soften, and she stepped back from the door. "Come in. I can't carry that."

Juliet nodded and stepped inside. The house was stale, stuffy, as if it hadn't been open in weeks. She'd read somewhere that carbon dioxide had a way of building up in a home that hadn't had a cracked window or open door. What was little Jackson breathing?

She looked around, saw the drawn drapes, the prescription bottles on the coffee table amid snapshots of Annalee and Warren as children. The drugs would be a hazard for Jackson. Why hadn't they put them away?

"Mrs. Haughton, where is Jackson?"

"Warren took him to get a Happy Meal."

Juliet nodded, disappointed. "Then . . . is he doing all right?"

"He's fine. I'm his grandmother, Juliet. We're not strangers."

"I know." She looked down at the casserole dish as the woman slowly lowered to the couch. "I'll put this in the refrigerator."

Mrs. Haughton nodded, and Juliet went into the kitchen. She hadn't been in there since Mr. Haughton died and they'd gathered for his wake. The dishes were put away, and everything seemed relatively clean.

She put the casserole into the refrigerator, quickly assessing the contents for things Jackson could eat. Not much there. No fruit, no fresh vegetables. Just a few Tupperware containers with unidentifiable contents.

Three two-liter bottles of soda, some jelly. She closed the refrigerator and went back to the living room.

Mrs. Haughton's eyes had settled on the wall across from her, and in that moment, Juliet saw the mother's grief. Her heart melted and she sank down next to the older woman. "Mrs. Haughton, my heart's breaking for you. I can't imagine what you're going through. Is there anything I can do to help with the funeral?"

Mrs. Haughton spoke in halting phrases, drawing breaths between them. "We can't bury her . . . until after the autopsy and the . . . Medical Examiner releases her. When that happens . . . Warren will take care of the arrangements . . . I don't know what I'd do without him."

"I'm sure he's been a comfort. But now, with the responsibility of taking care of Jackson, you might have your hands full."

Mrs. Haughton didn't answer, so Juliet changed gears. "How is he . . . emotionally? Is he upset? Crying?"

"He lost his mother. What would you expect?"

That would be a yes, Juliet thought. "At his age, it's probably best to distract him. That's why I was playing with him, letting him swim . . ."

"Swimming won't bring his mother back."

"No, of course it won't. But it's a heavy load for a little boy to bear."

The woman brought her chin up. "If you've come here to shame us . . . into letting Jackson go home with you . . . you're wasting your time. He's where he should be. He's well cared for here."

"I'm sure he is." It was useless, this visit. Juliet looked

at her hands. "His room . . . I'm sure it wasn't set up for him. Is there anything I can do to help with that? Make up a bed? Change sheets?"

The woman blinked, as though she hadn't thought of that. "No, we'll manage just fine."

"Okay. I just wanted to offer . . ."

Mrs. Haughton stared again, and silence fell heavy between them. Finally, Juliet spoke again. "I hope you're not talking to Jackson about his father having any part in this. That would only compound his grief."

She could tell by the look on Mrs. Haughton's face and the way she avoided her eyes that they had done just that. Juliet felt suddenly light-headed. She managed to get to her feet.

"I guess I'll go. Mrs. Haughton, please be sensitive with him." Tears stole out of her eyes.

Mrs. Haughton's eyes filled too. "I know how to care . . . for my grandson. I'm not dead yet."

Juliet went to the door, unable to continue this sham of a visit. As she stepped from the house, she prayed a desperate prayer for her nephew.

Back in her car, she sat for a moment, not yet wanting to go home. Bob didn't provide any comfort, really, but she couldn't blame him. He had an important job and had patients and his staff on his mind. Annalee's death didn't really affect him at all. Even Jay's arrest hadn't put a dent in Bob's life. How could he be expected to understand what she was going through?

She checked her watch. Seven thirty. Still not too late to make a visit to the nursing home, where her stressful thoughts often sent her. She started her car and drove across town, pulled into the parking lot at the building with the sign OCEANSIDE REST.

She went in, saw a family visiting with an elderly grandfather in the lobby. She reached the hallway and stepped between wheelchairs, speaking to those who looked hopefully up at her as she passed. She reached the double doors that took her to the Alzheimer's wing.

A nurse noticed her and smiled.

"Hi. Where is he?" Juliet asked.

"In the garden," the nurse said.

Juliet went out the side exit door and saw him. Her father sat on a bench facing the ocean, staring vacantly in front of him.

She went to sit beside him. "Hi, Daddy."

He turned and looked at her hard, as if trying to place her, but then he only said, "Hello." There was no recognition in his eyes.

"It's a pretty evening, isn't it?"

He opened his mouth to answer, but then he faltered. He'd already forgotten the question. He gazed back at the ocean, no doubt forgetting that she sat beside him.

She didn't know why she came. Her siblings knew he was here, but they had no desire to visit him. Cathy had such bitterness about the way he'd abandoned their family, she would never come. Holly had deep insecurities because of that abandonment. Though she'd spent much of her youth wishing for contact with their father, he seemed to have forgotten he had four children. Jay didn't like to talk about him.

So Juliet came. She'd been fifteen when her father left, so she'd spent all of her formative years being molded by his values. Her love for him had turned to a deep hurt when he'd chosen his secretary over his family. But years later, when Alzheimer's had robbed him of his faculties, that secretary had abandoned *him*.

The principle of reaping what you sowed had always saddened her. She didn't want him to reap that. But she couldn't do anything about it.

When Juliet found out where he'd been placed by the woman who'd meant more than his family to him, she began to visit him. Sometimes she sat here with him, not saying a word, just remembering the father he had once been.

"Jay's in trouble," she told him. He turned to her again, his eyes revealing his effort to hold on to that statement. "The police think he did something that he didn't do. But he's a good man. He reminds me of you, when you were still at home. He loves his child."

For a fraction of a second, there was a flash of recognition in her father's eyes, then sadness wrinkled his face. Quickly, it emptied again.

"You'd be proud of him," she whispered.

She didn't really know why she'd come here tonight. Why did she expect to absorb peace and comfort from her father?

Her phone rang, and her father jumped. He looked at her as she got it out of her purse. Cathy. She answered quickly.

"Hey, Cathy."

"Where are you?"

Juliet hesitated. She didn't want to tell Cathy she was sitting with their dad. "I just visited Mrs. Haughton.

Jackson had gone out with Warren. I thought I might come to your house now if you're home."

"No, I'm not," Cathy said. "I just left the judge. He wouldn't change the order until we have a hearing."

"Oh no!" Tears sprang to her eyes. "You're kidding!" Her father looked at her again, but he didn't seem to see her.

"He's hard-nosed and doesn't like to admit he's made a mistake. We'll just have to convince him. I'm heading back to Michael's. We need to put our heads together, figure this thing out. He's been working on it and says he's had some breakthroughs. You can come."

Juliet wiped her eyes. Her hand was trembling. "Should we get Holly too?"

"Sure. Maybe between the four of us, we can think of something. I'll call her."

Juliet clicked off the phone and dug through her purse for a Kleenex. She dabbed at her eyes. This was so unlike her. She was the one who carried on. The problem-solver, the positive one. The one who kept things in perspective and took care of everyone else.

Ever since their father had left the family, leaving her mother distraught and suddenly thrust into the workforce, Juliet had been a surrogate mom. She'd taken care of her youngest two siblings, and she'd worked hard to keep Cathy on track, though she herself was only two years older.

The faith her father had taught her echoed in her mind. "We trust in God, no matter the circumstances," she repeated. "Isn't that right, Daddy?"

Again, he seemed to ignore her.

Her father's appetites had overruled his faith. He'd given up everything as a result . . . his career, his home, his children, his wife . . .

And now he'd lost his capacity to think or to make things right. Somehow, that was okay with her. But she couldn't make it okay for her siblings.

She kissed him good-bye, knowing the intimate act disturbed him as much as a stranger taking liberties. Then she left him and hurried back to her car. As she drove to Michael's, she thought of the fallout after their father had left. The church people who had always declared their love for the family wound up abandoning them as surely as her father had, and that had hurt all of them.

Unlike her sisters, Juliet had found solace in another church, where there were people who embraced her. Where it lacked, she had filled in the voids. If they didn't serve, she served. If they didn't love, she loved. If they didn't care or take meals or give hugs, she gave them.

Funny thing. Once she started, others followed suit, and now she served among a sweet fellowship of believers.

Soon they would learn what she was going through, and she knew they would surround her with love and casseroles. But for now, she hoped they hadn't made the connection.

Already the news had reported Annalee's death and had even suggested that Jay was a suspect in her murder. Her church members knew her as Juliet Cole. It would take a little while for word to filter down that Jay was her brother. She should call them and get it over with. Ask them to pray. But she couldn't make herself do it yet.

She reached Michael's office, saw that Holly's cab was already there. She must have been in the area when Cathy called. Cathy was just pulling in herself.

Juliet blotted her eyes again and blew her nose, determined to step back into her role of the hope-giver and caretaker.

Her grief would have to wait.

CHAPTER 24

Michael hadn't expected all three sisters to show up at his place tonight, but he supposed it would be helpful. He sure couldn't follow every trail by himself. He brought in folding chairs from a closet and set them in front of the dry erase boards he'd filled with his notes, then caught them up on Leonard Miller.

"Where did Miller go after the funeral?" Cathy asked.

"I lost him. Too many cars pulled out between us. He could be staying at his mother's. I intend to find out and follow him as much as I can. If he buys drugs or sells them, I'll nail him. If he jaywalks or speeds . . ."

"Why aren't the police following him?" Juliet asked.

"Because they don't have the manpower."

"Neither do you," Cathy pointed out.

"No, but I have a personal stake. And if he's Annalee's killer, this is our second chance to get justice."

Cathy dropped her feet and studied him for a moment. "The thing is, I don't want us to settle for him as the killer yet, because there are others who may have done it. If we focus just on him, then we may be as guilty as Max and Al, of seeing only one possibility and missing the other ones. I want Jay cleared, but I can't figure out what motive Miller would have for killing Annalee and setting up Jay."

"The motive was in his first letter," Holly said. "He's trying to turn the tables on you."

"But using Annalee. That doesn't make sense. And why would he risk that? He's free. There are people who have a lot more reason to get even with me. He just has too much to lose."

Michael pushed off from his desk, stood up, tapping his dry erase marker in his palm. "You're right, Cathy. So I've been looking back through your blogs and researching everybody who lives within a three-hundred-mile radius of Panama City, everybody who is currently not incarcerated, everybody who might still hold a grudge serious enough to do something so radical. I came up with three men we haven't thought of—Lex Andrews, Paul Winthrop, and William Moore."

Juliet shook her head. "I don't remember the details of those cases. What were they?"

Cathy drew in a long breath. "Moore was the guy who claimed his wife and children were murdered by intruders, and he was only shot in the arm. He refused to talk with or cooperate with police at all. And as I investigated him, I found that there were other mysterious deaths in his past. A former girlfriend who allegedly committed suicide, for one."

Michael went behind his desk and opened the PowerPoint he'd made of the suspects. Moore's face came up. "Cathy's investigating prompted police to look further into that death. They arrested Moore and charged him with the murders, but the jury acquitted him. He remarried three weeks later and now is living in south Georgia. Things came out pretty good for him, so he'd have nothing to gain by doing this."

He showed them the next picture. "This guy—Lex Andrews—is five-ten, so he could fit the description. Worked as a contractor. He was suspected of killing his wife and embezzling from her father's contracting business. When they didn't have enough evidence to charge him with murder, they slammed him with the embezzlement charge. He served a year and is out now."

"Good job, Michael," Holly said. "I didn't know he was out."

He clicked to the next slide. "Paul Winthrop is the guy who lost his child when they were camping, and after a long search, the boy was found dead. The child was autistic."

Cathy looked at her sisters. "I just thought it was odd that he only took the nine-year-old autistic child camping that night. Not any of the other children. He had two other boys, ten and twelve. Neighbors talked of their having a hard time with the autistic son. That he had raging temper tantrums, and they would hear him screaming at night. His parents had trouble controlling him and had tried to get help from all kinds of experts. My feeling was that the dad might have been at the end of his rope and decided on an easy way out."

"Wow, that's sad," Juliet said.

"What happened to him?" Holly asked.

"He was acquitted too. The jury admitted in interviews that they thought he'd killed the child, but they couldn't prove it beyond a reasonable doubt."

"Winthrop lives in a small town near Mobile," Michael added. "Close enough for a quick trip to Panama City."

Cathy sighed. "I did think he was guilty, but I don't think he's mentally unstable or aggressively violent."

"But because of your blogs," Michael said, "lots of people still consider him a child killer. He could hold a grudge for that. It could eat at him . . . especially if he didn't do it."

"But it's unlikely that he'd go after Annalee. If he wanted to kill somebody, wouldn't it be me?"

Juliet dropped her face in her hands. "Cathy, what you do is so dangerous. You're messing with murderers."

"I'm helping victims get justice," Cathy said. "I wasn't afraid . . . until now."

Michael knew her fear had nothing to do with herself. She was as brave as they came, maybe even stupidly so. But her eyes were open now that her own family had been harmed. Her sister-in-law . . . her brother.

"Any one of these men could fit the height and weight descriptions of the clown," Holly said.

"So would Leonard Miller," Juliet said.

"Yep."

"If we're going to be honest about it," Cathy said, "the connection between my blog and Annalee is non-existent in all of these cases. Even if one of these wanted revenge, it's such a stretch that they'd go after Annalee and Jay."

"But anyone who knows you knows you're close to

your family," Michael said. "Pinning a crime on one of your siblings so you can watch the judgment and speculation is not a reach."

As they all took that in, Michael clicked to a catalogue picture of the clown suit. "Switching gears, I have good news. I've tracked down the clown suit."

Cathy sucked in a breath. "You know where it is?"

"No, but I know where it was bought," he said. "I found every store online that sold that suit, and got them to check to see if they'd had any orders sent to this area in the last few weeks. And I found one. Somebody named Doug Streep placed the order. Same approximate size, same exact suit. It was sent to a post office box at the Jenks Avenue post office."

Cathy deflated. "A post office box? Did you look Streep up?" she asked.

"Yes. I found a few Doug Streeps, but none from this area. And nothing that connected them to any of you."

"That box is right here, just a couple of miles away," Holly said. "We need to watch it and see who comes to pick up the mail."

"Well, that's easier said than done," Michael said. "I can't be there 24/7. And if I'm tied up doing that, I can't track down other leads and follow Leonard Miller. Plus, there's the little matter of sleep and my arcane need to make a living."

Cathy sighed. "I know, Michael. What you've done is way beyond the call of friendship."

He bit back the urge to tell Cathy that he thought of

her as family. "I'm fine. I'm not complaining. I was just thinking I need a whole staff of PIs to help me follow all these leads. But I can barely pay myself."

"We could do it!" Holly said. "We could all moonlight as detectives. We work cheap!"

"What do you mean *we*?" Juliet asked.

"Don't you want to help Jay?" Holly demanded.

Juliet grunted. "Yes, of course I do. But we aren't trained private investigators. I wouldn't know what to do."

Michael lifted his eyebrows as he considered the idea. "Of course I would give you an orientation and a little training in what you can and can't do. But mostly you'd help by staking out the post office, making phone calls about these other guys, tracking down information on the Internet . . ."

"So nothing dangerous," Cathy told Juliet.

Juliet seemed to consider that for a long moment. "But we're dealing with a cold-blooded killer. He may even be after Cathy . . . or us."

"All the more reason to help find him." Cathy set down her laptop and got up, facing her older sister. "Look, Juliet, finding him means getting Jay out of jail, getting Jackson back with his dad, maybe even in his own home . . . The police haven't found where that suit was ordered. They don't even believe there *was* a clown. All of these leads came from Michael. The police stopped at their first lead—and they don't seem to be considering anything else."

"I gave Max the info I have," Michael said. "But you

know my brother. Who knows if he'll follow up? He thinks I'm just prejudiced because Jay's my friend."

Michael watched the emotions morphing across Juliet's face. Fear, doubt, anger . . . maybe this was too much to ask of her.

"So all we'd be doing right now is watching the post office? Making phone calls? Doing benign things like that?" Juliet asked.

"Yes," Michael said. "I'm not going to send you into harm's way. But we are trying to find the killer, so I can't promise you total safety. But I couldn't promise that, even if you don't help. If you want to help, do what you can when you can. If you don't feel comfortable, that's fine."

"Count me in," Holly said. "It's a step up from taxi driver. Part-time Private Eye. I'm stoked! I can do some of it while I'm on the clock, between calls. You've been wishing I'd make something of myself, Juliet. Maybe this is my chance."

Juliet sighed, then threw up her hands. "Okay, I'll do it while the boys are at school, if it'll help Jay."

Holly sprang out of her chair. "Woo-hoo! I'm a PI! A detective! I need some disguises. A moustache. A hat. A wig!"

Michael grinned. "You won't need any of those, Holly."

"Just know that I'm willing if the need comes up."

"She's joking about the wig," Juliet said, "but with those pink streaks in her hair, she'll stand out like a sore thumb."

"I'll put it up and wear a hat. I was thinking of bleaching out the pink anyway."

Juliet shook her head, "Holly, what are you gonna do if you catch this guy? You're five-five and 120 pounds."

"I wouldn't try to tackle him," Holly said. "I'd just be able to identify him if he was one of these guys."

"And then what?"

Michael sat on his desk. "Then she could let me know, and I'd take it from there."

"And that brings us to another thing," Juliet said. "What are you going to do, taking it from there? You're not allowed to even carry a gun."

Michael bristled. "Why do people keep reminding me of that? You think it slipped my mind?"

Juliet shrugged. "No, I know you didn't. But I'm just pointing out—"

"I'll get the police involved if it comes to that. Don't worry, Juliet. I know what I'm doing."

"I can carry a gun," Cathy said. "I have a concealed weapon permit."

"I can carry one too," Holly said. "So can you, Juliet."

"What are we, Charlie's Angels?"

"No," Holly said with a proud grin. "Michael's Angels. Jay's Angels. Annalee's Angels. *Jackson's* Angels."

Michael could see that Juliet was still conflicted, but Holly's words clearly pushed through the fear in her heart.

Cathy had opened her laptop and seemed lost in what she was reading. Michael turned to her. "Cathy, I understand if you'd rather use your time and

resources in another way," he said. "Juliet and Holly
will help me a ton."

"No," Cathy said, shutting her laptop. "I'm in. I
told Jay I would help solve this murder, and I will. The
sooner we get him out, the sooner he'll have Jackson
back. The sooner this family can start healing."

"Yes!" Holly said. "Finally I don't have to wince
when I tell people what I do."

"You're still a cab driver," Juliet muttered.

"Yeah, but that's not all I am."

Michael couldn't help smiling. The part-time,
unpaid job would give Holly purpose. Something she
desperately needed. Since he'd known her, she'd had a
series of jobs she hated. He was glad to see the rare life
in her eyes. Good for her.

"We can start orientation right now," he said.

CHAPTER 25

Juliet didn't sleep that night, and the next morning she felt like a robot getting the kids off to school. Her thoughts continually went back to Jackson. Had he slept last night? Had anyone said his prayers and tucked him in? Had they gotten him up on time and fed him a decent breakfast before school? Dressed him in clothes that he liked?

As she was cleaning the kitchen after breakfast, it occurred to her that there was a way to find out. While her visit to the Haughton house hadn't given her any information about Jackson's state of mind, she could go see him at school. She'd been active in the PTA since her children were in kindergarten, so she had a logical reason to be on the campus. She was also listed as one of the emergency contacts in case Jackson ever got sick at school, so no one could keep her from talking to him.

She forced herself into the shower and got dressed as she would on any other day. She didn't have business at the school today; there was no homeroom party, no teacher appreciation day. But if she went up there anyway, no one would know she wasn't invited.

She pulled into the school parking lot, parked where

she usually did when she did volunteer work there. Carrying an empty manila envelope, she went in, smiled at the principal who was walking to his office.

"Hi, Mr. Sanders," she said.

"Juliet," he said, hesitating in the hall. "I heard about your sister-in-law's death. I'm so sorry."

So word was getting out. Abe had probably told them. "Yeah, it's tragic."

"I hope they're not putting you to work today."

She sighed. "I just came to talk to somebody."

"Let me know if there's anything I can do for your family."

Did he know that it was her brother in jail for the murder? Had her son blurted that out too?

She dropped her head as she walked past him. She didn't want her children to have to suffer for the biases against their family.

She walked down the kindergarten hallway and went to Jackson's class, knocked lightly. Jackson's teacher, Mrs. Bernard, turned to her and smiled. She knew Juliet well, because she'd been the homeroom mother the year Abe was in kindergarten.

"Hi, Juliet. How are you?" Her soft tone indicated she was aware of Annalee's death.

"I'm okay. Just wanted to check on Jackson." She scanned the room and her gaze landed on his empty desk. "He's not here today?"

Mrs. Bernard crossed the room and stepped out into the hallway. "No, he's not here," she said in a low voice. "I heard about his mom. I'm so sorry. His dad's probably keeping him home today."

Juliet didn't want to correct her. Disappointed, she went back out to her car and sat behind the wheel. She melted into tears as she said a prayer for her little nephew, that he was being well cared for and that he wasn't upset, that someone was seeing to his needs.

Meanwhile, Juliet would talk to people who worked with Annalee's latest boyfriend. Max had told Michael he had an ironclad alibi, but she wanted to see for herself. They couldn't leave any loose threads in this investigation. Her brother's future depended on them.

CHAPTER 26

Holly pulled into the post office parking lot and drove to the far end so she wouldn't be noticed. She backed the car into a space, facing the building. She didn't want to go in there and stand around the post office boxes all day long. That would call attention to herself. The postal employees would wonder what she was doing.

Right now the parking lot was mostly empty. There were two doors to the post office. One led to the counter where customers could buy stamps or mail packages. The other led to the post office boxes lined up on the walls. She would watch the people coming and going from that door and go in if one of the men they were looking for arrived. Michael had put their pictures on her smartphone, so she flipped through them now, reviewing the details of their features, what they might look like in different clothes, different haircuts, maybe even different color hair.

She hoped she could stay awake. She hadn't slept well last night and had awakened early with morning sickness.

Her gaze drifted to her rearview mirror. The

abortion clinic was just next door to the post office—right behind her. She had been there several times before to drop off women who didn't want their cars identified by the protesters across the street. They always got nervously into her cab, hoodies up, and were tragically quiet on the drive to the clinic. When she returned to pick them up, it was always the same. Tearful silence . . . blank expressions.

Could she handle being one of them? A few protesters stood the legal distance away with signs that had unborn babies on them, babies who were only weeks old in their mothers' wombs. She laid her hand flat on her stomach. She wasn't even sure how far along she was exactly—four weeks? Five? But the thought that the little life forming inside her already had a soul and spirit and mind filled her with shame.

No, she couldn't think like that. It would be so much easier if she didn't believe that. It was no big deal. She was just delaying her motherhood a few years until she was ready.

But those ideas rattled like rocks in her head.

If there was ever an unfit mother, she was it. Self-hatred cleated through her.

A car pulled into the clinic's parking lot, and she watched in the mirror as protesters called out. A girl got out, a scarf over her head, hiding her face as she hurried up the sidewalk to the clinic.

If Holly wore a coat and a hood, maybe she could be disguised when she went for her appointment. She had tried numerous times to make the phone call to schedule an appointment, but had hung up each time they answered. She was a coward. Too cowardly to carry her child; too cowardly to get rid of it.

Unable to stand the sight any longer, she got out of the car and walked into the post office. As she stepped into the dimly lit building, the sound of the protesters' voices faded away.

Relief washed over her.

She tried to refocus and found the post office box in question. She went to lean against the postage machine. She would have to alternate between standing inside, sitting in her car, and taking calls so she could make a living. Despite the heat, she'd have to do it with her windows up so she couldn't hear the protesters, with her eyes away from the rearview mirror.

It was going to be a long day.

. . .

Holly took three calls during the time that she was watching the post office, and each time called Juliet to take over for her. In each case, there was a window of opportunity in which the box owner may have come to pick up his mail. But they could only do their best.

When she was free again, she went back to the parking lot, switching off with Juliet, who had to go pick up her kids from school. She angled her taxi a little differently this time so her rear view wasn't of the abortion clinic. She locked in on the face of everyone who drove up. No one fitting the descriptions of any of Cathy's enemies came.

Her gaze drifted back to her rearview mirror. Unable

to stop herself, she adjusted it so she could see the clinic again. If she chose to abort, she would be just one in a steady stream of patients, and it would be the end of this problem. She'd never have to tell her sisters, her brother. She'd never have to bring them further down with this news. She'd never have to shame her family as she had done already so many times before. It would all be behind her.

But could she really go through with it?

Someone knocked on her window and she jumped. Warren Haughton stood at her door, frowning down at her. Surprised, she lowered the window. "Warren!"

"Thought that was you," he said. "What are you doing here?"

She groped for an explanation. "I'm just waiting here for my next call."

"I thought you usually hung out at the airport."

Was he giving her the third degree? "Yeah, well. I'm working in town today. How's Jackson?" She looked for his car. "Is he with you?"

"No, he's home. He's hanging in there."

Holly's mind dredged up her nephew's screams as they'd taken him away. Was that Warren's version of "hanging in there"? She thought of accusing him of insensitivity and cruelty, but that wouldn't help Jackson. There had been a time when Warren had a crush on her. He'd even asked her out a couple of times. Maybe if she played to his attraction he'd at least let her check on Jackson.

"Listen, about yesterday," she said in a gentler voice. "I'm sorry I was so rude. We were all grieving and upset."

He stood straighter. "No problem."

She forced herself to meet his eyes. "How are you doing?"

His face changed, hard edges softening. "I'm okay. We were trying to arrange the funeral, but the Medical Examiner hasn't released her body yet."

Holly swallowed, sick at the thought of her sister-in-law lying on an autopsy table. "So the funeral plans are on hold? Maybe that's good. I know Jay will want to be there with Jackson."

His jaw tightened again, so she tried to connect again. "But waiting must be agony."

"It's been really hard," he said, looking toward the post office. "I didn't sleep at all last night."

"I didn't either," she said. "Did Jackson?"

"Not much. We decided to let him sleep in this morning. But he's gonna be all right."

A car with a man pulled into the lot. Holly watched him until he got out of the car. No, not one of Cathy's enemies. She turned back to Warren. "I know you love him and that you're taking good care of him," she said, "but would you mind if I stopped by this afternoon and just said hello? I could bring food so you don't have to cook tonight."

He met her eyes, stared at her for a moment as if trying to decide whether that was a good idea. "No more food. Our fridge is full. Mom's friends have been cooking like crazy. But I guess you could come by if you don't get him upset."

"I won't. Maybe I could bring him a toy or something."

"Yeah, we can't get into his house yet."

"Okay," she said. "Then I'll be there, maybe around four."

"I should be home," he said. She watched as he sauntered up to the post office, holding some letters in his hand. That was good, she thought. She could get in and see Jackson. At least maybe their fears would be put to rest. Maybe things weren't as bad as they thought. Warren and his mother did love him, after all.

Her phone buzzed—the taxi agency. She clicked it on. "Hey, Jambo. Whatcha got?"

"Pickup on Grand Avenue, 314," her dispatcher said.

Holly started her engine. "Okay, I'm there."

As she drove away, she glanced at the faces in the cars pulling in. So far she hadn't seen Andrews, Winthrop, or Moore. Maybe they just didn't pick up their mail every day, or they weren't expecting anything. Or maybe they'd only opened the box for that one order.

Discouragement rolled over her. How were they ever going to figure this out? The idea of sitting still . . . waiting for them . . . seemed futile. Detective work wasn't as exciting as she'd hoped.

Tears filled her eyes as she made her way to the address. Her brother was probably miserable in jail, sitting there where he never thought he would be, racking his brain trying to figure out the identity of the murderer who had set him up. Worrying about his child.

She wasn't sure that she was any better at being a PI than she was at anything else. But this time, her brother's future might depend on her competence.

CHAPTER 27

Cathy spent the morning on the phone and computer, tracking all the information she could find about the activities of the men on Michael's dry erase board.

Though her windows were open and the ocean breeze whispered through from the beach across the street, it was already starting to feel muggy and hotter than normal for April.

She got up from her desk and stretched, then went to the window. From her home office, she could see the ocean between the small houses across from her. A man walked his dog on the sidewalk in front of her house.

His proximity made her feel vulnerable. Quickly, she closed the drapes.

Finally she went back to her computer and checked her blog again to see if her new pen pal had written her back. There were three hundred seventy-five comments to her post addressed to the "bottom-dwelling psychopath," all supportive of her. None of the comments indicated veiled bitterness or vengeance. He hadn't replied.

Turning back to the phone, she decided to work on Lex Andrews, the man who'd been accused of killing his wife, though he'd only served time for embezzlement. After a few phone calls to contacts she had in his town, she got his place of employment. He'd gone from helping run his father-in-law's contracting firm to working at a telemarketing business. She managed to get someone from Human Resources at Andrews's job to talk to her.

"I'm just checking on Alexander Andrews, goes by the name of Lex," she said. "Is there any way you can tell me if he was at work Monday, the day before yesterday?"

"Why?" the woman asked. "Is he involved in another crime?"

Cathy paused. Of course the woman knew about his case. Everyone in that area did. "I don't know if he was," Cathy said. "I'm just checking on some things. If you could tell me that, it would really be helpful."

"Sure," the woman said. "I don't guess that's confidential information. Hold on a sec."

Cathy waited as the woman checked her records. Finally, she came back. "Yeah, he was here all day Monday. He checked out at noon for lunch, then punched the time clock when he came back about forty-five minutes later."

"Okay, that's what I need to know," Cathy said. "Any way he could have punched in and not actually been there?"

"No, someone in his department would have called

People are really stingy here. They don't like for anybody to get one minute of pay they don't deserve. He seems like a good worker. Hasn't missed a day since he started working here."

Cathy blew out a sigh. "Okay. I really appreciate it."

"Should we be concerned?" the woman asked. "My boss knew him before all that happened. He insisted on giving him a break and hiring him. But if he's involved in something else . . ."

Cathy felt a little guilty. Andrews would have had trouble finding a job after his short prison sentence and all the PR surrounding his wife's murder. He had to make a living. And what if she'd been wrong about him? If he was really innocent, and all of her blogs about him had just made his life worse? What if he'd been set up like Jay had?

As sure as she'd been about his guilt . . . maybe she'd just played into someone else's hands.

She tried to refocus her thoughts. "No, I don't know of any crime he's committed lately. I'm just ruling people out. If he was at work, then he's probably okay. Thanks for the info."

She quickly hung up and rubbed her temples. So maybe it wasn't Lex Andrews.

Next, she called Winthrop's place of employment. Of the three, the father of the autistic boy was probably the least likely to have done something violent, but if he saw Cathy as someone who had truly altered his life by making him look guilty, he might have snapped and decided to come after her. Bitterness did strange things to a person. She knew that better than anyone.

One of her father's sermons from the book of Romans ran through her mind, along with one of the many scriptures he had made her commit to memory.

See to it that no one falls short of the grace of God and that no bitter root grows up to cause trouble and defile many.

How ironic, when the first bitterness she'd struggled with in her life was caused by the man who taught her that. But her father's flaws didn't make the principle less true.

And if Winthrop, Andrews, Moore, or Miller had cultivated bitterness toward her, madness may have followed. Her own bitterness had certainly caused trouble for them.

Winthrop worked for a carpet company doing installations, the same place he'd worked during his case. She called the store, waited until a young-sounding woman answered.

"TJ Carpet," the girl said.

"Hi," Cathy said. "My name's Cathy Cramer. I'm investigating a case here in Panama City, and I wondered if you could answer some questions for me."

There was a long pause. "You're the one who kept harassing Paul throughout the trial," she said. "Why should I talk to you?"

Cathy sighed. Clearly this girl wasn't going to be an ally. "I wasn't harassing him," she said. "I was just writing about his son's murder."

"It wasn't a murder," the girl said. "The boy got lost and drowned."

Cathy closed her eyes. "This is not about that case. I just want you to tell me one thing. Was Paul at work Monday?"

The girl hesitated. "Why? What has that got to do with you?"

"It isn't classified information. Either he was, or he wasn't."

"Are you trying to start something up on him again? Because the guy is still grieving over his son. His whole family is. Can't you leave him alone?"

Cathy set her chin in her palm. "So he wasn't at work?"

"He was at work. He did three installations that day."

"Were they all in your area?"

"Absolutely. Where do you want him to have been?"

Cathy breathed a mirthless laugh. "I don't want him to have been anywhere. Someone left an anonymous note on my car a couple of days ago, and I wondered if it was from him."

The girl's voice grew more brittle. "Paul Winthrop is a good and decent man. Leave him alone."

Cathy hung up. She leaned her elbows on her desk and closed her eyes. Well, there was certainly bitterness there. If the girl who answered the phone was that angry, Winthrop was probably livid. Did he blame Cathy for putting him under the microscope? She wasn't the only one who'd harped on his possible involvement in his son's death. Lots of others had jumped on the band-wagon after her.

But she had been the first.

Yes, Winthrop definitely had reason to hate her. She couldn't be sure if the girl was telling her the truth or not about Winthrop being at work.

Rallying, she turned her attention to William Moore, who had relocated and adopted a new vocation since his trial. It was no wonder. It was unlikely anyone in his hometown would ever trust the guy again, even though he had been acquitted of the murders of his wife and children.

Now he worked for a landscaping company, doing hard, sweaty labor. She dialed the number she had found for his place of employment.

"Pine Lake Landscaping," a man's voice said.

"Hi. Who am I speaking to?"

"Jack," the man said. "The owner."

Cathy tried to sound light and upbeat. "Hi, Jack. I'm calling to verify someone's employment. Can you help me?"

"Sure. I only have five guys."

"Great. His name is William Moore."

The man paused. "Why do you ask?"

"I'm just checking to see if he was at work Monday. Could you tell me if he was?"

Again, silence. "Does this have to do with his police record?"

Cathy hesitated. "Sort of. I'm investigating a case. I just need to know if he was at work Monday. That's all. Yes or no."

"Yes, he was," he said. "He was working on a job on location, building a deck."

"And you're sure he was there all day?"

"I think he was," he said. "I sent him and two other guys to work on it. Nobody told me he didn't show up. I think I would've heard it from the client."

Another dead end. "Okay, that's what I needed to know. I appreciate it."

"But if he's up to something no good I need for you to tell me. I gave him the benefit of the doubt, but I don't want some guy working for me who can't be trusted."

"I'm not saying he can't," she said.

"So is he a suspect in another crime?"

Again, guilt stirred through her. What if she suggested he was, and he wound up losing this job? What if he, too, was innocent all along, and her blogs had ruined his life?

She rubbed her temples. No, that was crazy. She'd thoroughly investigated. All signs pointed to him. The police and district attorney had believed he was guilty. She *wasn't* wrong.

Still, she tried to backpedal.

"I don't know that he is. He probably isn't. I'm just checking a few leads in a case I'm working on, trying to rule people out, and thought I would ask."

"Will you let me know if something comes up about him? I'm trying to do a good thing by letting him work here, but if he doesn't deserve it . . ."

"He's probably not involved in the situation at all. I'm just trying to see who might have been in the Panama City area this last Monday."

"Panama City?" the man repeated. "Actually, that's where he's building the deck."

Her heart jolted. She sat straighter. "Okay, so he could have come and gone from that job?"

"Yes," he said. "He may have taken off early. I can check with his co-workers and call you back."

"Yes, if you learn that he did take off early, would you let me know?" she asked.

He agreed that he would. Cathy hung up and stared at her notepad. Moore could possibly be the perpetrator since he was in Panama City at the time the murder was committed. So he was still on their list.

Her computer beeped, indicating that she had email. She ran her finger across the track pad, brought her email program up. Then she saw it. Another message. The From line said *New Friend*. Catching her breath, she opened it quickly.

> Dear Curious Cat:
>
> Funny that you haven't been blogging about your brother like you would any other random suspect. But I didn't think you would. Doesn't matter. It's all over the news.
>
> I love how it's bringing up all those old memories. Joe Hogan . . . Leonard Miller . . .
>
> Such fun.
>
> Your New Friend

Cathy stared at the email. Was this just an angry reader, or the same person who'd sent the other messages? There was nothing overtly threatening or even incriminating in this. But in her gut, she knew it was the same guy. He'd referred to himself as "Your New

Friend" in all three notes, and now they could trace it back to a server. It was a clue, if she could keep the police from dismissing it.

She forwarded the email to Michael, then printed it out. Sliding her chair back, she grabbed her purse. She would call Max, see if he could meet her at Michael's. If he balked, she would just have to play to his ego by shaming him for blowing off evidence. But that wouldn't guarantee he'd follow the lead.

CHAPTER 28

Max was at Michael's office when Cathy pulled up. When she went in, he was already reading a copy of the email that Michael had printed out. "I don't like the reference to Joe and Leonard Miller," he said without greeting her, "but really, anybody could have written this."

Cathy dropped her purse and keys on Michael's desk. "But Miller's back in town. This is too coincidental. Have you been able to find him today, Michael?"

Michael sat low in his chair, his feet propped on the desk. He looked weary. "Yes. He's staying at his mother's, along with his two brothers. They went out around lunchtime and got burgers. He didn't drive. Doesn't look like he has a car here."

"He could have borrowed or rented a white pickup truck," she said.

"But if he ordered the clown suit, why would he have it sent here? Why wouldn't he ship it to the town he lives in now?"

"Maybe he never really left," she said. "Granted, you haven't been able to locate him, but maybe he's just been keeping his head down and using another name."

Max's silence irritated her. She watched as he got up and went to Michael's dry erase board. The disapproval on his face made it clear that he resented Michael's work on this. Max's insecurity would be inflamed if his brother had gotten ahead of him on the investigation.

"I've been making phone calls," she said. "Of the three men, we narrowed it down to—"

"What three men?" Max demanded.

Michael pointed to the names on the board. "These three that Cathy's written about."

"Of the three," Cathy repeated, "I think Moore is the most likely. He was in Panama City Monday building a deck. His boss thinks he was there all day, but he's not sure. But Max, whether it's Miller or Moore or one of the others, if this is the killer who wrote me, it proves that Jay didn't do it."

"There's no evidence it is the killer. And the fact that this person mentioned Leonard Miller doesn't mean that Miller's involved or that he *is* Miller."

Cathy paced the floor. "But don't you see? It's an opportunity, a simple opportunity to wreak havoc and play games with us. You'd think it was enough that Michael lost his career. You gotta figure Miller's been celebrating over that. Maybe it gave him enough of a rush that he wants more."

Michael's feet came off the desk. "I didn't lose my career because of him. I lost it because of me."

Cathy hated it when Michael took the blame. "You didn't bury evidence. You were trying to do the right thing."

Michael saw Max's jaw muscle constrict in and out, but he remained silent. He clearly felt the way his parents did—that Michael's perjury charge had disgraced his family name and allowed Joe's killer to walk free. "Max, you have to see that this isn't just some random reader."

"But this guy doesn't even refer to Annalee's murder or say he did it. He could just be a crackpot who heard about it."

"That's not true," Cathy said. "He signed each letter the same way. No one else would know to do that. He warned me something was going to happen, *before* she was killed."

"Same guy wrote all three notes," Michael said in a flat voice. "Open your eyes, man."

Max bristled. "I'm not the cop who makes fatal mistakes."

Cathy saw the anger in Michael's face . . . his ears . . . climbing in a red tint across his skin.

She tried to intervene. "Sniping at Michael isn't helping, Max. You know Michael didn't suppress evidence."

Michael glared at his brother. So much water under the bridge. So much grief, pain, resentment . . .

"Of course we're all sensitive," Cathy said in a softer voice. "The name Leonard Miller is like sandpaper to all three of us. But now it's my brother's life we're talking about, and my fiancé's killer. Your brother's. It should draw us all together, not push us apart."

. . .

Michael had longed for closeness with Max and his parents since Joe's death, but their silence on the subject was worse than his grand jury indictment. The fact was, he didn't blame them.

He thought back to that awful day when his brother was shot dead in the line of duty. Joe was part of a drug bust that had been planned for months, to take down a major source of the drug flow in the Florida panhandle. As the police went in, Joe had seen the perp attempting to flee. When he tried to stop him, the man shot him at close range. Michael was notified minutes later, and he met the ambulance at the crime scene. The perp got away, but several witnesses agreed that he was a white man with a shaved head and a tattoo of a bat on the back of his head. Michael rode with Joe in the ambulance, yelling at him to keep fighting as the life bled out of him. He was dead on arrival.

Later, still in a state of shock, Michael went back to the scene to see if they'd apprehended the killer. A crowd of neighbors stood watching the police activity, and an old woman came over to Michael and claimed she had seen a black man shooting the cop. Her description was completely opposite from the one that most of the eyewitnesses had given—including the other cops on the scene—but he went back to her house with her, took down her statement, and had her sign an affidavit. He realized immediately that the woman had some form of dementia. She said the same things over and over and got confused when he questioned her.

He gave her middle-aged daughter a copy of the affidavit, then promptly forgot about it. Thinking it a waste of time, he didn't bother to turn it in to the detectives on the case. Later, they caught Leonard Miller, the guy with the bat tattoo, and several witnesses gave a positive identification. Since he was one of the men they'd been investigating, it was easy to make a solid case.

But who could have anticipated that when they came to trial that woman would return to haunt him? The defense attorney called Michael to the stand and asked if he'd ever buried evidence in a police case. Michael said no, he hadn't. Had he covered up evidence concerning his brother's case? the defense attorney asked again. Thinking he was answering with complete honesty, Michael repeated that he had never done that.

Then the old woman's daughter was called to the stand, and she told how her mother had given evidence disputing the identity of the perpetrator, but that Michael had never followed up. When the defense attorney brought Michael back to the stand and asked him about the affidavit, Michael had to admit that he hadn't given it to the detectives on the case. The lead went nowhere, and the woman had dementia.

But the damage was done.

The defense attorney exploited Michael's faulty memory, making the trial and the media circus focus on him and the "corrupt police department" rather than the accused.

The defense attorney rested his case soon after

questioning Michael, leaving his contradictory statements burning on the jurors' memories. When the jury found Leonard Miller not guilty, Michael was left with the stunned realization that his own failure had enabled his brother's killer to walk free. When the trial was over, Michael was charged with perjury. Though it was a felony charge, he didn't fight it. Even though he hadn't meant to withhold evidence, that was exactly what he had done.

And felons couldn't carry guns or serve as police officers. Everything he'd worked for was gone in one afternoon. While he'd grieved over his brother's loss, he'd had to forge out a new life.

"I've just now gotten my bearings," Cathy was saying. "Just now been able to stop dwelling on what happened, thinking about him every day, every hour . . . and now, it's all dragged back up. I know it's the same for both of you."

Max ignored her confession. He was not a touchy-feely kind of guy. "Michael, I don't want you getting in the way. Let us investigate this case."

Michael shook his head. "Seriously? You didn't find the clown suit. You wouldn't know Miller was back in town if it wasn't for me. You haven't even paid attention to the letters to Cathy. Why would I pull out and trust you to get it right?"

"Don't go off half-cocked, Michael. Oh, wait, I forgot. You can't carry a gun."

The comment hit home. Michael resented the condescension, but they weren't getting anywhere. He forced himself to lower his voice. "I never go off half-cocked. I know what I'm doing. My training didn't evaporate just because I turned in my badge."

"Max, get off his case," Cathy said. "Let him do his work. My brother is innocent. Somebody has to care about that."

With an exasperated sigh, Max got to his feet, pulled his phone out of his pocket, and took a picture of the dry erase board.

"What are you doing?" Michael asked.

"Taking your notes so I can follow your leads."

That released Michael's tension as if Max had opened a pressure valve. "Good. We help each other, we get the perp off the street sooner."

When Max left them alone, Michael looked at Cathy. Her eyes glowed with suppressed rage. "I don't get why he's still mad at you. Your family knows you didn't deliberately do anything wrong. Everybody in town knows that. How could he treat you that way? Who does he think he is?"

"Max and the rest of my family will always hold it against me."

"Well, I don't." She got up, walked to the window, crossing her arms. "If I were you, I would probably have done the same thing. The woman had dementia. There was nothing you could do. Her testimony wasn't helpful, and you had a lot on your mind. Your brother had just died. It's no wonder you forgot about it."

"Yeah, but that's the thing. Law enforcement officers don't have the privilege of forgetting about testimony," he said.

She turned back to him, met his eyes. "Everything that happened in that case was a travesty. Joe getting killed, Miller walking free, and you and your career . . ." Her voice trailed off and she turned back to the window, looked out through the blinds. "I don't understand how these things happen," she muttered in a barely audible voice. "Especially to you. You're a believer. You serve God. Why would he let this—?"

"Don't go there," Michael cut in. "I trust God."

"Really?" She turned back to him. "Even after all this? Because I don't know. I've believed in God since I was a little girl, but sometimes things happen no one can explain. Horrible things. And they happen to people who love and serve God as much as they do to others. What's the point?"

It was the one thing about her that Michael wished he could change. Events in her life had shaken her faith. But how could he help her when he harbored his own bitterness? He got up and faced her, wishing he could banish the tears glistening in her eyes. "God is still there for us, Cathy. He uses everything. And I trust him no matter how this life shakes out for me."

He didn't know if her silence was contemplative or angry. Was she just biting her tongue, letting him believe what he wanted?

As their gazes locked, he took a step toward her, pushed the hair out of her eyes. The brush of his fingertips against her skin was like an electric jolt between them, and color climbed her cheeks. He put his hand back in his pocket. He should know better than to touch her. "I hope you haven't stopped believing, Cathy."

"I still have a few things to work out with God," she whispered.

"I know," he said. "It's hard to see sunshine from the bottom of the pit."

Michael hoped she would let him pull her out. But first he had to get himself on solid footing.

He held her gaze for a moment longer. Her misty eyes were a rich brown, sharp and deep. Misty. "Thank you for being such a good friend, Michael," she said. "You're always there for me."

He swallowed. "Ditto." That guilt rose up to drown him again. How could he have such strong feelings for his dead brother's fiancée? It felt like a betrayal of Joe.

She broke their gaze. "Well, I guess I better go."

He knew it. He'd made her uncomfortable. He stepped back to give her space.

"I want to try to see Jay before visiting hours are over. Now that I'm not his attorney, I have to go during visitation like everybody else."

"Okay," he said. "Let me know if anything happens."

"I will."

"And Cathy?"

She turned back to him at the door.

"Be careful. This guy is paying very close attention to you. Don't let your guard down."

"I won't. Don't worry." As she stepped out into the twilight, he watched her look both ways. Michael wondered if the perp sat nearby, chuckling at the fact that they were all putting their heads together now, talking about him. The narcissist's dream.

He couldn't let her go alone. He got his keys and waited for her to drive away, then went out to his Trailblazer and followed her. He would watch over her whether she agreed to it or not.

CHAPTER 29

Cathy drove to the jail, pulled into the parking lot, and sat in her car for a moment. Her heart was still racing from Michael's touch. What was wrong with her?

What would Joe think, knowing that she had feelings for his brother? Would it hurt him? Of course it would. She had no right. And Michael probably just saw her as a little sister, someone who needed protecting.

He had been there for her every day as she dealt with the shock of Joe's loss. When she heard that her fiancé had been murdered, she'd retreated into her bed. Juliet, Holly, and Jay surrounded her, along with many of her friends. There was no shortage of food to eat, but she couldn't swallow any of it. She wanted to be left alone in a dark room with the covers pulled over her head.

It was during those days that Michael was the only one who was comfortable to be around. He would come over and she would manage to get up for him. They spent so many hours sitting and staring at a TV screen, neither one of them registering what was on it. Silence cloaked them like a warm blanket.

Joe had been Michael's best friend. They saw and

talked to each other several times each day. The holes in his day were as gaping as those in Cathy's. When Cathy wept, Michael wept with her. When he smiled, she managed to smile too.

There were days when he would come over and say, "Let's go for a ride," and she would get in the car with him. They would park at the beach, staring out at the ocean until the sun went down and the moon rose high in the sky, neither of them saying a word. She wasn't sure when the grief had lifted, when that heaviness lightened and daily life began to overshadow the tragedy. It had happened for them around the same time, and eventually they began to laugh and joke and talk.

When she decided to quit practicing law, Michael was the only one who understood. Their passion for finding justice for murder victims was stronger than ever. As she started her blog, Michael helped her in his spare time, investigating some of the things she was writing about, encouraging her and cheering her on.

But their bond was like brother and sister, wasn't it? She wasn't supposed to fall in love with him. He would never stand for it.

She pulled down her visor, looked in the mirror, wiped her eyes. Flipping it back up, she whispered, "Please forgive me."

She shook off the thoughts and went into the jail, signed in. She'd visited this place many times as a prosecutor, but she had gone in through the back door. Now she had to sit in the waiting room like all the other family members, hoping for fifteen short minutes with her brother.

As she waited, she looked around, wondering what everyone here was thinking. Was this old hat to some of them? Did they come here week after week for years on end, trying to maintain some semblance of a relationship with an incarcerated loved one? She prayed that wouldn't be the case with Jay. If he went to prison for murder, he'd be moved to a state facility miles from here. How would he maintain his relationship with Jackson? She hoped his attorney was working hard. They had to get him out of here.

When they finally called her name, she went into the small room lined up with desks and chairs and found the one where Jay sat on the other side of the dirty glass. He looked pale and tired, and he'd already lost weight. She smiled at him, but he didn't return it. He picked up the phone and so did she.

"You okay?" she asked him.

"No, I'm not okay," he bit out. "Cathy, what is my attorney doing? Why hasn't he gotten me out of here?"

"He's working on it," she said. "Has he been by to see you today?"

"Yes, but he's moving too slow. I need to be with my son. Everything is crumbling apart!"

"Try to stay calm. We're all working on it."

"Stay calm?" he asked. "Are you kidding me? My wife is murdered, my son is taken away from me, I'm thrown in jail accused of murder . . . You think I can stay calm?"

"We just have to keep clear heads and think. The best thing we can do for Jackson is get you out of here.

I know you've racked your brain for the police, but if you could think of anyone else who might have it in for her or you . . ."

"I'm thinking. I gave so many names to them, but what do they care?"

She stared at her little brother for a moment, and sorrow overcame her. Before her mother died, she had asked to talk to Cathy and Juliet alone. "Watch over Jay and Holly," she'd whispered. "Take care of them. I don't feel like I finished raising them." She and Juliet had promised they would, but they'd done a crummy job with Holly. And Jay . . . Who could have seen *this* coming?

She burst into tears, rubbed her forehead to hide them, and looked down at the table where someone had drawn a profane picture. She felt her brother watching her. "Hey, look at me, Sis."

She looked up, met her brother's eyes.

"No crying, okay? I didn't mean to upset you. I can't stand to see you cry."

She tried to pull herself together. "It's okay. I don't know what's going on either. It's like God just has it in for our family."

Jay wiped his own eyes and drew in a long breath. Sitting straighter, he said, "Not God. Satan."

She breathed a laugh. "God isn't putting up much of a fight."

"We don't have any idea how much of a fight he's putting up. There could be angels and demons slugging it out all around us."

Were they switching roles now? Was he the older, wiser sibling? She didn't want to pop his bubble. Faith had gotten Jay through the last year. Who was she to douse it with her own doubts, when he needed it most?

She forced herself to nod. "The truth will come out."

"I just need you guys to work as hard as you can from your end. Don't leave any rock unturned."

"We won't," Cathy said, blotting her eyes. "You won't believe this, but Michael recruited all three of us to be part-time private investigators."

His eyes rounded. "What?"

"You heard me right," she said. "Michael's following up on a lot of leads, and he can't do it all himself, so he asked us to help him."

"Holly a PI?" Jay asked. "Juliet?"

"That's right," she said, chuckling. "Can you imagine?"

"I can't believe he talked Juliet into it."

"We all want to help you," she said. "We're doing everything we can."

"Thank you," he said. "I knew I could count on my sisters." Tears sprang back to his eyes again, and he rubbed his mouth.

"Stupid clown," he said. "It isn't even believable to me. How can anybody else believe me?"

"Well, we think we've got a lead on the clown suit. We found where it was ordered." She told him about the name and post office box.

"Thank God," he whispered, clutching the phone. "If you can find the clown, that's the smoking gun."

"We will find him. Holly and Juliet are watching the

post office box as we speak. I'm waiting for another call from the judge about Jackson." She switched gears. "So are you okay? Is it awful in there?"

He shrugged. "I've had better digs, but it could be worse. Just trying to keep my head down."

Their time came to an end. Cathy left and went back to her car, sat and stared for a few more minutes. She'd never in her wildest dreams imagined she'd see her brother in jail. Her mother would have been so devastated. Cathy had gotten Holly out of jail a couple of times for DUIs, but she had been so mad at her that she hadn't grieved over it. Holly deserved what she got those times. But not Jay.

She closed her eyes. Through gritted teeth, she said, "God, I still believe in you, but I'm not sure I believe you care about me." The words thrust her deeper into the pit of grief. "I need your help. You know Jay is innocent. You know who did this. We could really use a miracle."

If God only heard the prayers of the faithful, then he was certainly not going to hear hers, she thought. Her faith was as flimsy as a spider web. She expected nothing.

Juliet had said so many times that God was there, listening, even when it didn't appear that he was. Bad things happened because we live in a fallen world. Evil reigned. Satan was prowling around looking for someone to devour. He had devoured Joe and now he was devouring Jay and Jackson. Cathy couldn't get her head wrapped around that. Why hadn't God stopped these things? Why wouldn't he answer the simplest prayers of a child whose father had walked out? Why wouldn't he answer the prayers of a woman whose heart was breaking? Why did some families have tragedies over and over, while others sailed on without a blip?

Sighing, Cathy started her car and decided to go home and try to call the judge again. If she could get him to answer the phone or call her back, maybe she could get Jackson back tonight. At least one thing would be settled.

CHAPTER 30

Holly left Juliet watching the post office at four, her boys in the backseat, munching on fries and playing video games. Holly was shaky as she drove up to the Haughton house. She hoped Warren hadn't forgotten that she was coming. She went to the door, rang the bell, and remembered that she was supposed to have brought a toy for Jackson. She never thought to do the right thing. Her sister was the one known for her compassion and caring. Holly was always distracted by her own dramas.

Anxiety twisted in her chest as she heard footsteps. The door came open, and she heard Jackson crying from deep within the house. Warren peered out. "Holly, it's not a good time after all."

"Really? Because I was looking forward to seeing Jackson. Is he all right?"

"He's a little upset right now."

She looked past Warren, but couldn't see the boy in the darkness of the house. "Maybe I could calm him down." Not waiting for an invitation, she pushed past Warren into the house.

"Holly, I told you no!"

"Jackson?" she called. "Honey, are you all right?"

She heard the crying cease for a second, then footsteps as Jackson ran toward her. "Aunt Holly!"

His eyes were swollen as if he'd cried for hours, and mucus crusted under his nose. He hiccupped sobs as he came to her. She stooped down and gathered him into her arms. "I want my daddy!" he said. "Where is my daddy?"

Holly clung to him, wishing she could bring Jay to him. "Daddy's still helping the police, honey."

"Uncle Warren said he was in jail. He said they're never letting him out!"

Shocked, she stared up at Warren. "Why would you tell him that?"

"Because it's true," Warren said. "He was crying for his daddy. He needed to understand why he couldn't come."

What else had he told him? Had he said that the police thought Jay killed Jackson's mother? Was Jackson having to sort that out too? Rage burned on her face, but she tried to bite it back for Jackson's sake.

She took the child into the living room. Mrs. Haughton hobbled in from the kitchen, leaning on her cane and rolling her oxygen canister in front of her. She looked startled to see her. "Holly!"

Holly didn't care how sick the woman was; it was no excuse for cruelty. "Why have you let Warren fill Jackson's mind with things about his dad? What good can come of that?"

The old woman didn't answer. Holly sat down on the couch and pulled Jackson onto her lap, and he buried his face into her chest and wept like an orphan. "I want to go home," he cried. "I don't feel good. My stomach hurts."

She stroked his hair and kissed his forehead, rocking back and forth. "Honey, Daddy's gonna come back and get you. You just might have to wait a few days."

"He's not in jail, is he, Aunt Holly? Uncle Warren lied."

Warren dropped into a recliner, his lips compressed in anger. Holly speared him with a savage look. "He's just talking to the police, trying to help find the person who hurt Mommy." A Kleenex box sat on the coffee table, and she grabbed one and wiped his nose.

"I want to go back to Aunt Juliet's," Jackson said, hiccupping sobs. "I want to play with Abe and Zach and swim and sleep over."

As Mrs. Haughton lowered to the other end of the couch, Holly gave her a beseeching look. Mrs. Haughton turned to look at Warren, as if it were his call. "He's staying here," Warren insisted. "We'll get through this."

"But why?" Holly asked. "When he's clearly so upset, why would you make him stay?"

"We do want him to be happy," Mrs. Haughton said, stroking Jackson's back with a shaky hand. "But he's just having a rough spell. We all are. It's understandable."

Holly looked at her closely. Her face looked gray, her lips, blue. Her face was as wrinkled as a discarded grocery sack. The woman was clearly declining. The house smelled musty, medicinal, and the only light was that from the windows. What must it be like for a young child to be trapped here—grieving for his parents while his grandmother's life beat out of her?

"I think you need to leave now, Holly," Warren said.

Holly wouldn't let Jackson go. "I can't leave him like this."

Warren stood up, tried to take Jackson from her. Jackson screamed an octave higher.

Holly tried to shift gears. *Flatter him*, she thought. *Do something!* She racked her brain as Jackson clung to her. "Warren, I've always liked you," she forced herself to say. "You're a great guy, and I know you're grieving. Don't leave me with the impression that that's not true."

"I don't really care what your impression is of me," he said over the boy's cries. "My sister is dead. We're keeping Jackson here."

She wanted to put her hands over Jackson's ears. Why couldn't Warren be more sensitive to him?

"That's enough!" Warren wrestled Jackson from her. "Time to go, Holly."

Mrs. Haughton looked as troubled as Holly. "Warren, you don't have to be rude."

"Yes, I do," he said. "This is ridiculous. She came over here to stir him up."

"You said I could come! He was already stirred up," Holly said. "He was crying when I got here. I heard him."

"Of course he cries. He would cry if he was with Jay." Still holding the fighting boy, he stalked to the front door, threw it open. "'Bye, Holly."

"Warren, please."

"Leave!" he shouted.

Reluctantly, Holly stepped through the door, turned back to say something, but he slammed the door in her face.

She could hear Jackson's wails through the door, and her heart shattered. How could a person willingly let a child suffer like that? How could he plant words in his mind that he shouldn't hear, words that would keep him up all night?

She went back to her taxi, sat behind the wheel, trying to pull herself together before she pulled out onto the street. She couldn't tell Juliet what she'd found. It would break her heart, steep her in despondency. But Cathy could do something. She needed to know.

She could work harder to get him back with his aunt. Jay had to have some say in this matter. She pulled a Kleenex out of her console, wiped her face, blew her nose, and took a few deep breaths as she drove to Cathy's house.

Ironic that she had such empathy for her nephew, when she had so little for her own child. She wondered if the abortion would hurt her baby, if he or she would have silent cries, if he would kick against the needle or whatever it was they used to pull it out of her womb.

Nausea roiled up in her and she pulled over to the side of the road, vomited on the street. What kind of person was she? Was she just like Warren, putting her own needs ahead of her child's?

She closed the door, drank from her water bottle, trying to rinse the taste out of her mouth. Her hand went back to her stomach, to the little life that was growing there, the little trusting life who had no clue that its mother was considering snuffing out its future.

But she couldn't think about that now.

Her phone rang. The agency. She hoped they wouldn't realize she'd been crying. "Yeah, whatcha got?"

"Pickup at the airport. They're short on cabs today. Need you to head over there."

She drew in a deep breath. "Will do. I'm on my way." There was no time to dwell on her sorrow now. She had to make a living. Rent was due next week and she barely had enough to make it.

Pulling herself together, she headed to the airport and picked up a man who had a small carry-on bag. "Oceanside Rest Home," he said.

"Oceanside," Holly repeated. Wasn't that where Juliet said their father was living now? "Do you have an address?"

"No, I'm afraid not."

"No problem. I have a phone book. I'll look it up." She found the address, then headed that way.

"I haven't seen my mother in a few months," he said.

Holly wished he wouldn't talk. She wasn't in the mood to be chatty. "Really? I'm sure she'll be glad to see you."

"Yes, I'm sure she will." Holly turned up the radio, hoping he'd take the cue to sit in silence. But he didn't.

"You don't look like a cab driver," he said. "How long have you been driving a taxi?"

"About a year," she said, embarrassed. "But I moonlight as a private eye."

"No way," he said, amused and clearly impressed.

Pride swelled within her. How long since she'd felt any sense of self-worth? It felt good.

When they reached the nursing home, she told him

the fare and waited as he paid. She sat, watching, as he walked in.

Her father was just inside that building. She hadn't seen him more than a couple of times in over ten years. Curiosity worked at her.

What did he look like now? Would she even recognize him?

She pulled into a parking space and decided to go in. Juliet said he had Alzheimer's, that he didn't even recognize the daughter he knew best. He certainly wouldn't know Holly.

She went inside, looked around. There was a window behind which a woman sat at a desk. She leaned in. "Hi. My father is here, but I've never visited him before. Could you tell me what room he's in? Ralph Cramer?"

The woman looked him up among the hundreds of other names, then directed her to the Alzheimer's wing. Holly went through the double doors. The hallway was clear except for a nurse's aide coming toward her.

"Hi," she said. "I'm looking for Ralph Cramer."

The woman tipped her head toward the dining room. "He's in there, eating."

Holly stepped into the doorway, scanned the faces of all the elderly women, and settled on two men at a table across the room. An aide was feeding them.

"Don't you see him?" the woman asked.

Tears sprang to Holly's eyes again. "Um . . . no. I'm not sure which one he is."

"You don't know your dad?"

Holly couldn't look her in the eye. "No. I haven't seen him in years."

"Oh, let me show you." She pointed. "He's the one on the right. Nice man. Real sweet."

Holly smiled. That was good to know.

"Go on in. He may not know you, but he'll be glad to have company."

Fear stalled her. "I . . . I don't know. Maybe I'll just stand here . . . I really just wanted to see him."

The nurse's aide probably thought horrible things about her, but even that wasn't enough to make Holly approach him. She just stood there, staring across the room at the man who had left her when she was a child.

Mashed potatoes dribbled on his chin. The aide who was feeding him was rushing him. She looked bored as she shoved mixed spoonfuls into the men's mouths. They chewed too slowly, obviously irritating her.

Suddenly, Holly's fear was overshadowed by her sense of injustice. She crossed the room and took her father's spoon out of the woman's hand. "I'll take it from here with him."

The woman sat up straighter. "Who are you?"

"I'm his daughter," she said, pulling out a chair. She plopped down and looked at her dad's face with misty eyes. "Daddy, it's me. Holly."

He looked at her, and for a moment, she thought he would say, *Holly! I've been thinking about you. My little girl!*

But of course he didn't. He regarded her with the same indifference as he'd looked at the aide. Holly scooped some meatloaf onto the spoon, gently put it into his mouth. He chewed slowly.

She waited, allowing him to take his time. The aide finished feeding the other man, a little gentler now.

Holly stared at her father, trying to make him see her. "Is it good?"

He smiled and nodded, then opened his mouth for another bite. She gave him some peas. She was actually good at this. Who would have thought?

After a few more bites, he put his hand up. "I don't care for any more, thank you."

She set the spoon down. "Okay."

He sat back in his chair, his eyes glazing over. Why had she come here? What did she expect from him? He could do nothing for her. He couldn't restore any of what he'd taken from her. He couldn't help her now in her pregnancy. He wasn't going to be a jolly grandfather to her child. And he could do nothing for Jackson or Jay.

Still, it comforted her to see him.

She got to her feet, touched his shoulder. "I'll go now, but maybe I'll come see you again."

He nodded politely, then turned away.

Holly hurried out of the building to the safety of her taxi.

CHAPTER 31

Cathy fell into bed after hours on the phone with the people on Jay's list—friends and former boyfriends of Annalee. She had gotten a good bit of information about Annalee's most recent boyfriend, confirming the fact that he had a new girlfriend and was no longer interested in Annalee. His alibi had already been checked out, proving he was a dead end in the case.

At four, the phone rang, startling Cathy awake. She shook herself out of her quicksand grog and picked the phone up.

"Hello?" She heard coughing on the other end, wheezing.

"Hello?" she said again.

"Cathy." It sounded like Mrs. Haughton's voice, raspy, wheezy.

"Mrs. Haughton?" she said. "Are you okay?"

More coughing, then finally the woman found her voice. "Cathy, it's Jackson."

Cathy sat up in bed, turned on her lamp. "What is it? What's happened?"

"They're taking him to the hospital. He's sick."

Cathy jumped out of bed. "What's wrong with him?"

"He must have a stomach virus. He's been having diarrhea, vomiting, and now there's blood . . ."

Cathy's heart jolted. "Blood? You mean, in his stools?"

"He's very weak. He didn't even make it to the bathroom. Just soiled the bed. That's when I realized how bad it was." She started to cough again.

Cathy ran around the room, grabbing her clothes. "Mrs. Haughton, have you called an ambulance?"

"Yes. They're here right now. They're taking him to Bay Medical."

Cathy grabbed her purse. "We'll be at the hospital when he gets there." Not stopping to brush her teeth or her hair, she hurried out to her car. She pressed speed dial and called Juliet.

Her sister answered after three rings. Cathy filled her in, and she could hear her sister's terror as she said, "I'll be there in a few minutes. Call Holly."

Cathy woke up Holly too, then debated whether to tell Michael. Why would she call him? He wasn't in their family, and didn't even know Jackson that well. But she needed him. She clicked on his speed dial number, and waited as it rang several times. Finally, he picked up. "Hey . . . Do you know what time it is?"

"Yes," she said. "I'm sorry. I debated whether to call you, and I don't expect you to do anything except pray, but . . ."

Instantly more alert, he said, "Cathy, what is it?"

"They're taking Jackson to the hospital. Mrs. Haughton said he's really sick. Diarrhea, vomiting, blood. It sounds really bad."

"Cathy, I'm coming."

"No, don't. There's nothing you can do. I just wanted to tell you so you'd pray."

"I'll pray and come. Cathy, it's gonna be all right."

She wiped the tear rolling down her face. "Do you really think so?"

"Yes. They'll get him on a drip, get him rehydrated, figure out why there's blood . . ."

"But he's all alone. His parents . . . One dead, one in jail."

"He's not alone. He has all of you."

When he hung up, she held the phone for a moment, letting his voice linger in her head. Michael always reassured her, even when he knew things were going off the rails. He would pray as he drove.

She should do the same.

More tears flooded her eyes as she tried. "God, I know you and I haven't been on very good terms lately." But that was wrong, wasn't it? God hadn't changed. She was the one who'd changed. "Okay, *I* haven't been on good terms with *you*. My fault. I know that. Ever since the stuff with Joe being ripped out of my life . . . and Michael losing his career over something so minor . . . I've held an even bigger grudge than I already had."

She opened her console and tore a tissue out of the box there. "It just feels like you don't listen to me. That you don't hear. But I'm begging you to hear now!"

It began to rain, big drops splatting on her windshield. She turned on her windshield wipers, watched them wipe the blur away.

"He's only five. He's lost his mother, and Jay's in

jail . . . Can't you do something? Can't you heal him? Can't you do a miracle so Jay can be with him?"

Lightning flashed, and thunder quickly followed. Was that God, letting her know he'd heard? Or was it just the storm?

The truth was, she missed her faith. She missed finding meaning in her trials. She missed the sense that God had her back.

But too much had happened.

She hadn't really had that solid a faith since she was thirteen. If her father had only known the havoc he'd wrought in his children when he chose his appetites over his family. Would it have mattered?

She had held a grudge, not just against the people of God who acted so ungodly, but against the God who allowed a faithful family to be uprooted and cast out.

She never abandoned her *belief* in God. She knew he was there. But was he benevolent? Did he care about her pain?

Joe's murder during her plans for her wedding seemed like more of the same. Another slap-down. How dare she embrace joy? Didn't she know better?

Michael, sensing her failing faith, had tried to bolster it up. But he should be just as angry as she. He'd lost a brother and had his reputation and calling taken from him. He was bitter about many things, but not about God. He still prayed constantly. Still went to church. Still reminded her that God loved her and was watching.

She reached the hospital, drove around until she saw the emergency room and the ambulance entrance. She went inside and asked if Jackson had been brought in yet. When they told her it would be a little while, she went back out, pacing in front of the doors that flew open each time she passed them, waiting for the ambulance that would bring her nephew.

Within a few minutes, she saw Holly's cab, and both her sisters got out. They ran toward her and all three embraced. It was clear they'd both shed eye-swelling tears on the way over. As they let each other go, they saw flashing red lights at the edge of the parking lot. The ambulance was pulling in, but no siren screamed of its urgency.

As the ambulance driver's door opened, the light came on. Through the back window, Cathy saw Warren sitting next to Jackson on the gurney. Jackson's eyes were closed and he had an oxygen mask on. The EMT got out, and Cathy approached him. "We're Jackson's aunts. How is he?"

"He's a sick little boy." He opened the back doors.

Warren shot the sisters a look as they approached the van. "Move back," he yelled.

They stepped back as the paramedics rolled the gurney out. Cathy moved closer then, trying to see Jackson's face. It was dark, but in the dim light from the ER doors, she could see that he looked as pale as death.

The hospital's glass doors flew open and the paramedics rolled Jackson inside, Warren still beside him. The women followed.

"Cathy!"

She turned at Michael's voice. He was hurrying in behind them.

"Is he all right?"

"No." In the light, she saw Jackson's face. Gray circles under his eyes. He was asleep or unconscious. He looked so tiny lying there with an IV in his arm and an oxygen mask covering half his face. So helpless.

Michael hugged her, and she clung for a moment too long. The emergency room seemed busy, even for this time of morning, and the woman at the front desk seemed in no hurry to help the boy. "We have to wait until we can clear a room," she said, as if Jackson had come in with a sore throat. Cathy waited for the paramedics to tell the woman that this was an urgent matter, but they only went to the desk, leaving Jackson parked in the hallway, and began filling out paperwork.

"This is ridiculous!" Cathy said, her voice rising. "This is an emergency. Somebody has to help him."

Finally a nurse appeared. "You can come this way," she said, and pushed the gurney up the hall. Cathy and the others followed as the paramedics gave the nurse a rundown of Jackson's condition. They stood in the examining room while the nurses worked his clothes off, got him into a gown, took his blood, and typed things into the computer. Jackson never came awake.

All the while, Warren leaned against the wall, the only one in the situation who seemed unruffled. When the doctor came in, he asked the group to leave the room during his examination.

As they all moved toward the hallway, Juliet said, "I'm staying with him here."

"There's no need," Warren said. "I'll stay."

"No. He needs me and I'm staying!"

"Juliet, I have the custody order."

"Your mother has the custody order. Not you. She's not here."

"Well, she can't stay, so I am."

"Fine, then it'll be the two of us."

He bristled. "If you want to make a scene and wake up Jackson, then we'll get security involved."

Cathy stared at him, unable to believe how callous he was. "You don't care about him at all, do you?"

"I care so much that I'm not going to leave his side. End of story. He's my sister's son, and I'm not leaving him."

"Can you, for once, think about what's best for Jackson?"

"I think *I'm* best for Jackson," Warren said.

"Clearly, you're not!" Juliet cried. "What did you feed him? He could have food poisoning. Salmonella causes bloody stools."

"He didn't even eat supper. We couldn't get him to take a bite. He was already feeling bad. For lunch we had McDonalds, but I ate what he had. I don't think it's food poisoning. It's a virus, and he would have gotten sick no matter who he was staying with. He was probably exposed at school. He'll be fine."

The defensiveness in his tone irked Cathy.

"Could we pray?" Juliet said suddenly, the corners of her mouth trembling. "Everybody, let's just hold hands and pray."

Warren held back for a moment, then reluctantly took Juliet's and Holly's hands and bowed his head while Juliet prayed.

CHAPTER 32

As the group waited in the hall for the doctors to examine Jackson, Cathy glanced up and saw Mrs. Haughton hobbling toward them, one breathless weary step after another, leaning on her cane and rolling her oxygen tank in front of her. Cathy pushed off from the wall and went to meet her, took her oxygen tank so she wouldn't have to roll it herself.

"Mrs. Haughton, are you all right?"

The woman looked like she was near death. She wore a scarf on her head, probably to hide her chemo-thinned hair, but it was askew. She took three or four steps, then stopped and leaned against the wall to rest. "I'm sorry it took me so long to get here," she said, then stopped to cough. Cathy touched Mrs. Haughton's back as she tried to clear her lungs. Finally, she drew in a short breath. "I had to drive myself. Haven't driven in months. Warren rode in the ambulance . . ."

Cathy saw an empty wheelchair against the wall and ran to get it. "Mrs. Haughton, sit down. I'll push you."

She expected an argument from the proud woman, but Mrs. Haughton didn't protest. When Cathy brought the chair up behind her, she dropped down into it. Her chest heaved with her labored breathing, and Cathy wondered if the oxygen was doing her any good at all.

She glanced down the hall where Warren and the others stood. Warren seemed impassive as his mother was rolled toward him. "Mom," he said when they reached him, "you know you're not supposed to drive."

"I had to come," she said. "Had to check on Jackson."

"But I told you to stay home. I told you I'd let you know—"

"How is he?" she asked, cutting in. "Where is he?"

"He's in this room," Juliet said, pointing to the door. "They're examining him now."

"He's not doing well," Cathy said. "He's very sick. They're running tests."

Mrs. Haughton's hands trembled as she brought them to her face. "I would've insisted he come sooner . . . but until he had his accident on the bed . . . I didn't know there was blood . . ."

"How long has he been having diarrhea?" Juliet asked.

"For several hours," she said. "He kept saying his stomach hurt."

"But Warren," Holly said, "you didn't tell me he had diarrhea when I came to visit."

"It wasn't relevant," Warren said. "We figured he was under stress, that he was having a hard time adjusting."

"But if we had known," Juliet said, "I could have told you what to do about it. I could've told you he needed liquids, that maybe his electrolytes were off. I had medicine that he could've taken. I could have called his pediatrician."

Mrs. Haughton's shoulders were shaking. "We never should have taken him, Warren. I told you it wasn't right for him. I told you we should leave . . . well enough alone."

Cathy turned from Mrs. Haughton to Warren. So there it was. It had all been Warren's idea, not his mother's.

Suddenly an alarm blared across the hallway, startling her. The red light over Jackson's door began to flash. Nurses came running out of exam rooms, dashing toward Jackson's room.

"He's coding!" Juliet cried.

Cathy froze, staring at that light.

"Out of the way!" a man in scrubs said. "Get back! We need this area clear."

Cathy rolled Mrs. Haughton to the other side of the door. Two doctors ran toward them, a woman following them with a crash cart.

Mrs. Haughton wobbled to her feet, her glazed eyes round. "Is he dead?"

No one answered, and she dropped back into the chair as if her legs had given out.

"What's happening?" Juliet cried.

Cathy couldn't take it. Abandoning the wheelchair, she stepped inside the doorway, unnoticed by the staff. They had opened her nephew's gown and placed leads on his chest.

"Clear!" someone yelled, and they shocked him, his little body jolting up and bouncing back down.

Cathy held her breath.

"Nothing," someone shouted.

"Again. Clear!"

Again, the body jolted. Cathy winced.

"We've got a pulse."

Thank you, God! Cathy almost collapsed with relief.

Suddenly Jackson took a deep breath, coughed, and his eyes fluttered open. He began to cry.

Cathy pressed between two doctors and went to the bed. "It's okay, honey," she said, touching his face. "You're gonna be okay. You're just really sick."

His eyes focused as he looked at her. "Daddy." His voice was weak, not much more than a whisper. "Where's Daddy?"

"He's not here, honey. Aunt Holly and Aunt Juliet are here, and we're all gonna take care of you."

His face twisted and reddened, but that was a far cry better than gray and pale. Sweat broke out on his forehead and over his lip. "I don't feel good."

"I know you don't, honey. But the doctors and nurses are gonna help you. Everybody's praying for you."

If there was ever a time that God answered prayer, Cathy hoped it was now.

. . .

Out in the hallway, Michael couldn't help the niggling suspicion that had been working on him ever since he'd seen Mrs. Haughton coming up the hall, and Warren's reaction . . . or lack thereof. It wasn't normal. Warren's mother was dying of cancer, yet he looked at her with disgust and dread, as if angry that she had bucked his orders and driven to the hospital to check on her grandson.

The fact that she'd admitted that it was Warren's idea to take custody of Jackson worried him further. Why would Warren want that? It wasn't like he was close to Jackson. The few times Michael had seen Warren at birthday parties and other family events, he'd never even seen him speak to the boy. Something wasn't right.

And now as this emergency played out before their eyes, Michael watched Warren's face. Everyone else was trembling, embracing, wiping tears, terrified. Warren simply paced back and forth, back and forth, his fingers fidgeting. They'd always known Warren didn't do things like other people did. His inability to hold a job, despite his high IQ, was evidence that he didn't do life that well. Now he worked as a janitor and lived at home with his mother. At a time when she couldn't take care of herself, that was a blessing, he supposed. But he saw no tenderness in his dealings with her.

Warren checked his watch. Another alarm went off in Michael's head. He was checking the time when his nephew was in the next room coding?

No, something wasn't right.

Finally, the doctor came out of the room. Juliet and Holly almost assaulted him. "Is he okay?" Juliet asked.

"We were able to revive him. But he's in critical condition. We're going to put him in the ICU."

"Yes, okay," Juliet said.

"We need to get some papers signed. Which one of you is his parent?"

"None of us," Juliet said. "His mother died Monday. His dad can't be here."

"We're his family," Holly cut in. "We're his aunts, and this is his grandmother."

"Who has custody?"

"I do," the old woman said. "I can sign the forms. Do you know what's wrong with him?"

He shook his head. "We'll have to wait for lab results and do a few more tests. I'll let you know when they're back. We don't have any beds in the pediatric ICU, so we're taking him to the adult ICU. But he'll get excellent care there."

The doctor picked up his pace, heading down the hall. Michael left the others and followed the doctor, catching up to him. "Doc, can I ask you something?" he said, matching his stride.

"I'm in a hurry," he said. "Who are you?"

"I'm a friend of the family."

"Then I can't talk to you about this patient."

"No, I don't want you to talk about him. I just want to make a suggestion. When you're doing those blood tests, could you test for poison?"

The doctor stopped walking, turned to look at Michael fully. "Poison?"

Michael wondered how much to tell him. "I'm a former homicide detective. Michael Hogan."

The doctor's eyes narrowed. "Oh yes, I remember you."

Of course he did. "So Monday this kid's mother turns up dead, murdered. And today he's so sick he's near death. The timing just seems fishy. I want to make sure."

The doctor nodded. "I get it. Yes, we'll test him. Was he at home when his mother was killed? Was *she* poisoned?"

"No, she was shot. He was at day care. The killer is still at large. Don't you think it's a strange coincidence that he's so sick that he codes a couple of days later?"

The doctor looked back toward the room. "I guess it is. So he's staying with his grandmother?"

"Yes, and his uncle. The grandmother has stage four lung cancer. I guess we should also consider the possibility that he could have ingested some of her drugs."

"I'll test for those too. I'll call the lab now. I'm putting a rush on everything."

"Great. Thanks, Doc."

While they waited for Jackson to be moved to the ICU, the nurses allowed two people at a time to go into the room with him. Cathy stayed in the waiting room, letting Juliet go in. Warren wouldn't cede his position next to the boy, not even for his mother. Cathy didn't know what was taking them so long to transfer Jackson to ICU, but she supposed it was better that family members were able to be with him now. Once he was moved to ICU they'd probably be kept away from him.

She wondered if she should call Jay at the jail. When she first got to the hospital, she had thought she would call him when they knew something, but now that Jackson had coded, it seemed his death could be imminent. Did they let murder suspects out if their children teetered on the brink of death?

"You okay?" Michael draped his jacket over her shoulders. "You're shivering."

She grabbed the lapels and pulled it tighter around her. "Michael, I saw you talking to the doctor," she said in a low voice. "What was that about?"

"I just thought of a few more things they should test him for."

"Like what?"

"Just . . . different things."

She could tell he was evading, so she got to her feet. "Michael, is there something you're not telling me?"

"No, not at all. I don't know any more than you do."

"But do you have one of your hunches?"

He shrugged. "I don't know."

"Is it about Warren?" she asked in a whisper. "Because he's creeping me out."

Michael should have known her instincts matched his. "I never have liked the guy that much. But we'll know more when the test results come back."

"Do you think Jackson was poisoned or drugged?"

"I don't know," Michael said. "If he didn't want Jackson around he could've left him with Juliet."

"Unless this was what he planned all along."

"What do you mean?"

Cathy glanced back at the others in the room. Mrs. Haughton sat in the wheelchair, her chin on her chest. Holly seemed to be drowsing too, slumped back against the wall with her eyes closed. "I don't know," Cathy whispered. "There's just something not right about the way he's acting. His stubbornness, his hostility. And it wasn't his idea to call the ambulance; it was Mrs. Haughton's. If it weren't for Jackson having an accident in the bed, she wouldn't have known how bad off he was. But Warren knew it was bad if he was the one taking care of him. Why wouldn't he have taken Jackson to the hospital sooner, unless maybe . . . unless he planned it?"

"That's why I asked the doctor to check to see if there were any poisons in his system."

Cathy sank into her chair again, trying to work possible scenarios out in her mind. Jackson poisoned? Surely not.

Michael lowered to the chair beside her and planted his elbows on his knees, head in his hands. She knew him well enough to know he was praying. She hoped he had God's attention.

After a while, the doctor came back up the hall. Cathy and Michael got to their feet, and Holly opened her eyes.

As he stepped into Jackson's room, Cathy touched Mrs. Haughton. She lifted her head and sat straighter. "The doctor . . . he's in Jackson's room."

Mrs. Haughton nodded and tried to roll herself, but Cathy took over and rolled her to the exam room, the others following.

As they entered, Mrs. Haughton looked hopefully up at the doctor. "Do you have the results?"

He turned to her, his expression grim. "Yes, ma'am, I do."

"What is it, Doctor?" Cathy asked.

He cleared his throat, rubbed his jaw. "I'm afraid it's pretty serious. Jackson doesn't have a virus. He has *Escerichia coli*."

Cathy sucked in a breath. "E. coli?"

"How could Jackson have gotten that?" Juliet demanded.

"It's food-borne. It usually doesn't get this severe until three to four days after eating the tainted food. Is anybody else in the family sick?"

"No," Juliet said. "They're not. We would know." She turned to Warren. "What did you feed him?"

Warren grunted. "Did you hear him? He said it would take three to four days. I've only had him for two. Maybe it was what *you* fed him!"

"He ate what my kids and I ate."

"Annalee died three days ago," Cathy cut in. "Maybe it was something *she* fed him."

"We need to have everything he's eaten tested," the doctor said. "Can we get into the child's house?"

"It's a sealed crime scene," Michael said. "But I'm sure we can get the police to help us on this. But we'll need to test the food at your house too, Warren."

"Give me the key to your house," Holly said to Warren. "I'll drive over there right now and get what's in the fridge."

Warren sprang up then. "No, I'll go. What do you need, Doctor?"

"Anything he's eaten while he's been with you. Even wrappers that may have been thrown away."

"I'm the only one who knows what that is. He ate

two McDonald's Happy Meals. That was all we could get down him."

Mrs. Haughton finally spoke up. "He did have a few bites of a breakfast casserole . . . a friend brought it. We'll need to test that."

"What about his school?" Juliet asked

"Doubtful," the doctor said. "We'd be seeing other sick kids."

"What can you do for him?" Juliet asked.

"We've got to arrest the growth of the bacteria. Keep him hydrated. We're going to get him to ICU in the next few minutes. Since he's so young, we'll allow one of you to stay with him. I recommend that it's the person he's closest to."

"That would be Juliet," Cathy said.

Juliet nodded, but Warren shook his head. "You people are so arrogant. Just because you think the world revolves around you does not mean that you're the closest one to Jackson. He likes me. I'm staying with him."

"Look, we don't have time to fight about this," the doctor said. "Work it out. It'll be about an hour before any of you can see him, so you should take that time to gather the food samples."

"All right," Warren said. "Mom, I'll be back shortly. Do you want to go home?"

"No," she said. "I'll stay right here."

Warren pulled keys out of his pocket and headed down the hall.

CHAPTER 33

The ICU waiting room was full of anxious family members who looked like they had been up for days. Groups clumped together, their belongings spread out as if they were trying to make a home out of the vinyl recliners lined up in rows. Holly touched her stomach as she looked around the room, wondering what kind of parent she would be if she had the baby and something went wrong with her child. Would she be like these others, keeping vigil all night long?

Yes, she would, came the answer. She was doing that for Jackson. She would do it for her own child, wouldn't she? Maybe she did have a motherhood gene.

She snatched her thoughts back and tried to focus on her nephew. Warren was with him in the ICU, so the rest of them were exiled here. Mrs. Haughton looked as if she might not make it through the night. Her breath came out in whistling releases, and periodically she would double over coughing, trying to catch her breath. She could barely hold her head up. She kept it leaned back against the wall behind her wheelchair, but now and then it would drop forward as she dozed.

A coughing spell woke her, and Mrs. Haughton

labored to catch her breath. Holly went to sit beside her and touched her bony knee. Mrs. Haughton looked at her with yellow eyes.

"Mrs. Haughton, there's nothing you can do for Jackson right now. They won't let us see him until the next visiting time. Why don't you let me take you home?"

"I have my car," she rasped out.

"I know, but you could leave it for Warren since he came in the ambulance. I'm happy to take you home."

Mrs. Haughton looked around, as if trying to think it through. She clearly wanted to stay, but sitting here must be agonizing. Finally, she gave in. "Guess I'm of no use here."

Holly fetched Mrs. Haughton's cane, which was propped against the wall. She hooked it onto the back of the chair, then grabbed the oxygen tank, still attached to the woman by a tube. Rolling the tank beside them, she pushed Mrs. Haughton down the hall. When Holly got her into the taxi with the oxygen tank at her feet, she put the cane in the back and returned the wheelchair to the lobby. As she came back to the car, she found Mrs. Haughton doubled over again in another fit of coughing.

The woman's condition was much worse than Holly had thought. She should probably be in the hospital, herself. She got into the driver's seat, touched the woman's shoulder, and waited until she finished coughing again. "Mrs. Haughton, are you all right?"

Mrs. Haughton leaned back and took a long shallow breath. "No, I'm not all right," she said. "It's in my lungs, my liver . . ."

"I'm so sorry."

Mrs. Haughton managed to pull in a long, uninterrupted breath. "We should have let him stay at Juliet's. I knew I wasn't up to it."

Holly started the car. "Why do you think Warren wanted that?"

Mrs. Haughton shrugged. "I think he just wanted to do something for Annalee . . . since he feels so helpless. Taking care of her boy . . . was the only thing he could think of."

Something about that didn't ring true. Warren didn't seem like the kind of person who would go out of his way for his sister.

"It's so hard to believe." Mrs. Haughton paused to get a breath. "The day before she died . . . Annalee and Jackson came over for dinner. We ate in the dining room . . . like it was Thanksgiving or something."

Holly frowned. "Did Annalee cook?"

"No, Warren did. It was a feast. Roast beef and potatoes . . . everything we all like. We talked about . . . whether I should continue treatment . . . or surrender to hospice. We decided on hospice care. I was so sure . . . mine would be the next funeral."

As her voice trailed off, Holly found her thoughts drifting back to that meal Warren had cooked. Today was Thursday, so that would have been Sunday, four days ago. Enough time for the E. coli to do its number on Jackson's system.

Her mind raced as she drove. Was it possible? Could Warren have infected Jackson? If so, maybe he'd also murdered Annalee,

Holly got Mrs. Haughton home, helped her into the house, and got her settled on the couch. "Mrs. Haughton, do you think any of that food from Sunday is still in the fridge?"

"You can look, dear," she said. "He stores leftovers in those blue plastic containers. But he probably took them to the hospital . . . to be tested."

Holly went into the kitchen and threw open the refrigerator. It was almost empty. No blue containers. She'd have to find out whether he'd taken them in. She went back to the living room. "Mrs. Haughton, I would be careful with anything that's left in the fridge. In fact, if you have friends who could bring you some food, that would be great."

"I'll be fine," she said. "I have some canned soup . . . that'll be more than enough."

Holly nodded, hating to leave her alone. "Have you told your doctor yet? I mean, that you've decided to start hospice care?"

"Not yet," Mrs. Haughton said, "I was going to this week . . . but then Annalee died . . ." Her voice trailed off.

Holly had assumed the woman was on chemo, fighting the cancer in her body. "If you don't mind my asking, what's your prognosis?"

Mrs. Haughton's eyes grew dark again, and she stared at the oxygen tank. "Probably a few weeks, at best."

"Oh no. Shouldn't you be in the hospital?"

"I'm not going . . . to get better, Holly. Only worse. I hope I live . . . to see my grandson get better and see . . . justice for my daughter. But I'm at peace with dying.

And Warren has really been here for me." Tears pushed to her eyes, and she dabbed at them with dry, wrinkled fingers. "Jackson and Warren . . . are my only two left. I guess they'll split everything I leave . . . when I go."

Holly fell into silence, her mind racing. So Jackson and Warren were the heirs to her estate. Of course.

"How long has Warren been living with you?"

"Six months," Mrs. Haughton said. "Before that I hardly ever saw him . . . a blessing that he came home . . . to take care of me. Never thought I'd see that. He has problems . . . with employment and everything." She coughed again, pulled in a breath. "He's always been a special boy. But it's nice to see him have such attachments . . . to me and his nephew. I just hope he doesn't lose this job . . . because he won't leave Jackson's side."

Holly frowned, unable to match her picture of Warren with the one his mother painted. "Where is it he works now?"

"At PC Labs. He cleans up. Janitorial work . . . is so much less than he's capable of . . . but he has to work somewhere."

PC Labs? An alarm went off in Holly's brain. "What is it they do there?"

"They handle most of the . . . hospital's lab work."

Holly's throat closed. So Warren could have gotten samples of E. coli there?

She suddenly felt dizzy. She had to call her sisters . . . Michael.

Holly's heart pounded as she sprinted back out to her taxi. She got into the car, sat behind the wheel again, staring at the dashboard. Could it be that

Warren was waiting patiently for his mother to die, and just before she did, had killed his sister and tried to kill his nephew, so that he'd get the whole estate for himself? Could the man be that cruel? That selfish?

Was he a sociopath? If he didn't have a conscience, if he could kill blood relatives for money . . .

She started the car and headed back to the hospital, her mind racing ninety to nothing. If it was Warren, then he would have destroyed the tainted food. They'd been on the wrong track investigating the men who were angry at Cathy. Even Leonard Miller wasn't to blame.

Suddenly it hit her. She'd had the answer since he appeared at the post office yesterday.

When she got to the hospital, she hurried up to the ICU waiting room, found Cathy and Juliet sitting with Michael. Michael had dozed off, and Cathy had her head on Juliet's shoulder.

Juliet was wide awake. "Holly, that was sweet of you to take her home. Is she all right?"

Holly ignored the question and dragged her chair closer so she could talk quietly. "Guys, I need to talk to all of you."

Cathy nudged Michael, and he woke up, rubbed his eyes. "Hey."

"I need to tell you something I just thought of," she whispered. "Something important."

"What is it?" Michael said, leaning forward.

"Yesterday when I was staking out the post office, waiting for those men to show up, I never saw them. But guess who I did see? Warren."

Michael's eyebrows shot up, and Cathy stiffened.

"He shows up in the parking lot, knocks on my window, and says hello. Then he goes in."

"Did you follow him?" Cathy asked. "Did you see what box he went to?"

"No, I was in the parking lot, waiting in my car. I was going to go in if I saw any of those other men. It didn't occur to me to go in for Warren. He had some letters in his hand, so I assumed he was just mailing something. I mean, it makes sense that he would use that post office. He lives in the area."

"Did you see him come back out with mail?" Michael asked.

"No, I got a call and had to leave. But get this. I was just talking to Mrs. Haughton, and she told me that he served dinner to Annalee and Jackson Sunday. And here's the kicker. He's working as a janitor at PC Labs."

Cathy's mouth fell open.

"Jackson and Warren are Mrs. Haughton's only two heirs left."

Juliet slowly got to her feet, her hand over her mouth. "That's a big estate. They have a lot of money. Do you think . . . ?"

Michael nodded. "I think we've hit on something. He's taken out his sister, and now he's trying to take out Jackson before his mother dies. Think about it. If Jackson's alive when she dies, then Jay will be in charge of Jackson's part of the inheritance. Warren would never get it."

Juliet turned her panicked gaze to the door. "We've got to get him out of there! He could kill him while he's sitting with him!"

"Call Max," Cathy told Michael. "Tell him everything!"

"I'm on it. Cathy, if I were you I'd call the judge again. Go to his house if you have to. Make him understand that we have to get Warren away from him."

Cathy was already heading for the door. "I'll try to catch him at home."

CHAPTER 34

J ay didn't get the message in jail until seven o'clock that morning when the guard came to wake the inmates. As he passed out bowls of tasteless oatmeal from a rolling cart, the guard called out, "Cramer? Jay Cramer?"

Jay stepped forward, hope lifting his heart. "Yeah?"

The guard didn't even look at him. "Got a message. Your son's in the hospital."

Jay's stomach dropped. "What's wrong with him?"

"They said he had an intestinal thing. He went to the emergency room last night. That's all the message said."

Jay lunged for the door. "I need to go call . . . I've got to talk to the sheriff. They'll let me go for this, won't they? My son needs me!"

"Back up!" the guard barked out. "You don't got bail yet. You're staying right here."

"But can I at least call?"

"No phone calls till eight. That's when the phone comes back on."

"Not the pay phone. Can't I use the phone downstairs?

I can only get landlines on this one. I need to call my sister's cell phone."

"Nope," the guard said, and rolled the door shut. Jay broke out in perspiration, his heart hammering. What could be wrong with Jackson? He went to the phone to wait for eight o'clock, but two men were already there waiting to use it.

"Please . . . I need to use it first," he said. "My son is sick. He's in the hospital. I have to know—"

"I was here first," the burly man who went by the name A.Z. said. "Get in line, pal. I gotta call my wife."

"But my son could be in trouble. He's only five and he's sick!"

Anthony, the next one in line, grabbed the sleeve of Jay's jumpsuit and pulled him back. "You got a problem hearing? Wait your turn. You ain't gettin' the phone until we've made our calls."

Jay had no choice, so he waited, fidgeting. As soon as the clock said eight, A.Z. grabbed up the phone and called his wife to cuss her out for not posting bail for him. Jay couldn't imagine why the woman had accepted the collect call that was clearly from the jail. Hopefully, she would hang up on him and cut this short.

After a few minutes, the next guy called his mother and had a fight equally blood-curdling, F-bombs flying.

Jackson in the hospital. What could have happened? The guard said it was his intestines. Had he eaten something bad at his grandmother's? Was he just sick from the stress? How bad must it be for one of his sisters to call the jail and get this message to him?

When he was finally given his chance at the phone, he called Juliet, but only got voice mail. She must be at the hospital.

Now what? Jay racked his brain. He couldn't call the hospital. He didn't have a number. He tried to think of someone who still had a landline and could fill him in. Michael used his cell phone mostly too, but he did have a landline in his office. Since he lived there, maybe Jay would catch him in. He closed his eyes, tried to remember Michael's office number. Two repeating digits . . . 4545?

"You gonna make a call or what?" a guy who'd just come up behind him asked.

"Yes. Just give me a minute." He dialed the number, waited, praying. Miraculously, Michael picked up. "Michael Hogan."

Relief washed over him. Jay waited as the prison system's automated voice told Michael he had a collect call from the jail and asked if he would accept the charges. When it came time, Jay spoke his name into the phone, waited. Thankfully, Michael said yes.

Finally, the call connected them. "Jay, are you there?"

"Yes," Jay said. "I can't reach my sisters. I got a message that Jackson's in the hospital. Do you know what's going on?"

Behind Jay, the waiting man tapped his shoulder. "Hurry up, I got an emergency."

Jay shrugged the man's arm away and plugged his ear so he could hear.

"He was really sick, had bloody diarrhea last night,"

Michael was saying. "Mrs. Haughton called an ambulance. They tested him and discovered he has E. coli."

Jay had to steady himself on the concrete block wall. "E. coli? Is he gonna be all right?"

"I just left the hospital," Michael said. "He's still in ICU. I can't lie to you, man. It's bad."

The man tapped his shoulder again. Jay spun around, shooting him a death look. Sweat dripped into his eyes, even though it must be fifty degrees in the room. "How did he get E. coli? You can die of that!" he bit out. "Is he awake? Is someone with him?"

"Warren is with him."

It just kept getting worse. "Warren? No, I want Juliet to be with him. Michael, you guys have got to get me out of here. Tell Cathy to talk to a judge, get him to set bond. I'll pay anything."

The man behind him tapped him again, and rage erupted. Jay swung around. "Back off!" he shouted.

Michael hesitated. "Jay, are you all right?"

Jay felt the blood pounding in his face.

"Jay, calm down, buddy. Don't get into a fight. It'll make things worse for you."

Jay knew he was right. He drew in a deep breath, tried to calm down.

"We're working hard to get you out, or at least to get Jackson back with Juliet."

The man shoved Jay and knocked the phone out of his hand. Rage exploded in Jay's head. He started to fight back, but instead, raised his hands in the air. "Come on, man. We don't want to fight. Just let me finish my call."

The man who had come in sometime during the night looked wild-eyed and dangerous, but he was about fifty pounds smaller than Jay. When he swung, Jay caught his fist, but the guy threw a quick left hook, catching Jay on the cheekbone.

Inmates gathered around and began rooting them on, as if they'd waited days for such entertainment. In a flash, he thought he could kill the guy. But what about Jackson? They wouldn't let him out of here if he jumped the man, even in self-defense.

He forced his hands to his sides, determined not to feed the fury.

"Punch him!" someone shouted, and others bellowed agreement.

"I'm not fighting with you, man!" Jay yelled. "These guys want trouble, but you're the only one making it."

The door slid open, and two guards broke up the cluster of men egging the fighter on. Jay kept his arms at his sides, praying they'd see that he'd done nothing wrong.

One of the guards wrestled the rabid little guy out of the pod as men yelled insults and mocked him. They would turn on him next, he thought, and he'd have to make a decision how far he'd go to defend himself.

The guard still in the room backed to the door and called out, "Cramer? Get over here."

Dread stooped him. With one last look at the hanging telephone, he crossed through the loud men and faced the guard whose name tag said *Davis*. "You need to see the nurse?" the guard asked Jay.

Jay blinked and stared at him, surprised at the

question. He raised his hand to his cheek, realized it was bleeding. He could go to the nurse and get out of this madness for a while. But then he couldn't finish the call. "No. I'm okay," he said. "I just need to finish my call. That's all I want."

As he turned back from the door, he saw that someone else had already grabbed the phone.

The guard clanged the door shut. Jay brought his hands to his face and went to a bench, wiped the gash with the sleeve of his jumpsuit. How could this happen? His wife dead, his son dying? And him here in jail, powerless to help.

Why was God allowing everything in his life to be stripped away? It didn't line up. There was no sense to be made of it.

Still, he fixed his eyes on the stupid orange flip-flops they'd issued him, while he sent up desperate prayers for the life of his son.

CHAPTER 35

"Judge, you've got to listen to me," Cathy said to the man who stood in a bathrobe on his front lawn, walking his dog. "I understand why you gave the order for Jackson to be with his grandmother and why you haven't wanted to hear me out about this earlier, but I don't think you understand the situation." She explained about Mrs. Haughton's prognosis and Jackson's illness.

Judge Harper looked a little like Ed Asner, round, grumpy, and world-weary. "Was the illness caused by neglect or abuse?"

"We don't know . . . but he got sick while his uncle was caring for him." She knew better than to go down the road of accusing Warren of killing his sister and trying to kill his nephew. He would demand that she follow proper procedures for reporting a crime and expect ironclad evidence.

"My brother wants Jackson with my sister Juliet. I've got the paperwork here. He signed everything. His parental rights have not been rescinded, so he still has the right to determine who keeps his son."

The judge took the papers, stared down at them. "It hardly matters right now if the child is in the hospital,"

"You're wrong, Judge," Cathy said. "Warren is sitting with him in ICU. He's the one making decisions about Jackson's treatment. Jackson is not close to him, and he's so sick that he coded this morning. He's grieving over his mother, and he doesn't understand where his father is. He's close to my sister. She's kept him a lot, and he's comfortable with her."

"I know his grandmother. She's a good woman. I'm sure he's comfortable with her too, even if she is ill."

Cathy wanted to shake him. "He's not with his grandmother. She's at home trying to breathe. He should be with the relatives that his father chose. My brother is innocent until proven guilty, and he still has parental rights."

The judge's dog found a place to do his business. She couldn't tell by the man's face if he was considering her motion or not.

"Judge, you know me. I don't make stuff up."

"Oh, come on, Cathy. You make stuff up all the time. You write about your opinions as if they're fact. You convict people before they've even gone to trial."

"You know I'm usually right. I speculate, but I'm not pulling things out of air. I have good instincts. You've told me that yourself back when I was practicing. But all that is irrelevant. We're talking about custody and whether a father has the right to choose the caretaker for his sick child. Your friendship with Mrs. Haughton shouldn't have influenced you. In fact, it's a conflict of interest."

"Are you accusing me of impropriety?"

Cathy hesitated. "No, I'm just saying that your

friendship with that family might have subconsciously influenced you."

"It didn't. I would have placed him with the next of kin no matter who she was." Judge Harper drew in a deep breath, let it out in a huff. "The best I can do is make sure we get a quick date for a hearing. I'll need to hear both sides before I change my order."

"But it's urgent. He's in danger. Don't you think it's strange that he's stricken with a life-threatening bacteria the same week his mother is murdered?"

"Cathy, if you have an accusation to make against his grandmother—"

"Not his grandmother. His uncle. At best, he's incompetent as his caretaker. At worst, he could be culpable . . ."

The judge's face flashed. "Are you seriously suggesting attempted murder when you haven't even filed a complaint with the police?"

"The police are fixated on my brother, but it's all going to come to light soon. You'll see that you've made a terrible mistake letting the Haughtons keep custody. It'll be an embarrassment—"

The moment the words were out of her mouth, Cathy knew she'd gone too far. Judge Harper's mouth tightened with derision.

"Cathy, you've made your case and I've given you my answer. I suggest you don't press your luck. You're about to make me mad."

Cathy wanted to scream as he led his dog back into his house. They would just need to get definitive evidence to have Warren arrested. Jackson didn't have time to wait for a hearing.

CHAPTER 36

Holly had dozed off and on at the hospital, but altogether she'd probably gotten an hour of uninterrupted sleep in the ICU waiting room. According to the doctor, Jackson's kidneys had failed. He was facing dialysis. Beyond that, the family didn't know what the next step in his treatment would be.

When the morning visitation time came, Holly hurried in to see her nephew. He didn't wake up to see her. Warren sat by his side like a sentinel, refusing to move. Some good she was as a PI. Here she sat, knowing Warren was the killer but unable to prove it. He could kill Jackson under all their noses.

It would be three more hours before the next visitation. Juliet had gone home to get her kids off to school, and Michael and Cathy had left to work on the case. There must be something Holly could do. If she could just get into the Haughton house and snoop in Warren's room while he was here at the hospital, she might find evidence the police could use in his arrest.

She could take Mrs. Haughton breakfast, offer to make her coffee, and help her with her medications. That would get her in the door. She knew better than to ask Michael or her sisters. Juliet would freak if Holly even suggested it. But how else would they prove Warren's guilt?

Deciding to take matters into her own hands, she left the hospital and headed for Krispy Kreme, bought a box of doughnuts and some coffee. Throwing back the coffee, she headed to the Haughton house.

Nervous, she knocked on the door, dreading the idea that Mrs. Haughton would have to hobble to the door to answer it again. But soon she heard the woman's feet shuffling across the floor. She heard the door unlocking, then it creaked open.

Mrs. Haughton seemed out of breath and fragile as she peered out.

"Mrs. Haughton, I'm so sorry to get you up," Holly said. "I hope you weren't asleep."

She was still wearing the clothes she'd had on last night. "I was dozing on the couch," the woman wheezed out. "Is Jackson all right?"

"Yes, he's holding his own."

"Oh, thank heaven. I thought you'd come to tell me . . ."

"No, nothing like that." Holly smiled and brandished the box of donuts. "I brought you some breakfast, since Warren wasn't here to help you this morning."

Mrs. Haughton didn't answer. Hunching over her cane and wheeling her oxygen tank, she shuffled back to the couch, dropped back down.

Holly followed her in and cleared off a place on the table, set the donuts down. "Can I make you some coffee? Get you your medicine?"

The woman looked as if she couldn't think. "Yes . . . I guess so."

Holly went into the kitchen, looked around. Of course Warren wouldn't have a clown suit sitting out here. In fact, if he had one at all, it would be hidden, since he couldn't let his mother know anything about it.

Holly started a pot of coffee, poured Mrs. Haughton a cup of water for her pills, took it back to her. "I hate to ask, but may I use your bathroom?"

Mrs. Haughton waved a hand toward the hall. "It's probably a mess. We haven't cleaned since Jackson got sick here. Warren fired my maid . . . got in a quarrel with her . . ."

Of course, Holly thought. He didn't want her catching him at anything. "It'll be fine," she said.

Mrs. Haughton reached for a bottle of pills, opened it, her hands trembling. Holly headed for the bathroom. In the corner by the tub, she saw a pile of pajamas and other clothes that Jackson had soiled. The smell hung in the air, making her nauseous.

She should offer to wash those so Mrs. Haughton didn't have to deal with it, but she supposed the less she moved things around, the better. If the police had to search . . .

She came out quietly, hoping Mrs. Haughton wasn't paying attention. She stepped into the room across from the bathroom—Warren's room. The bed was made and everything was neat. She wouldn't have expected that of him. She'd figured him to be more like her, never making his bed, dirty clothes piled on his floor. Quickly she opened his closet. There were a few shirts and several pairs of jeans folded over hangers. No clown suit hung there. There was no chifforobe or armoire, but there was a chest of drawers. She crossed the room, pulled the bigger drawers open, looking for anything red with polka dots. Nothing.

Getting on her knees, she pulled the bed skirt up. Only a few pairs of shoes.

As she got back to her feet, she scanned the closet shelf. Nothing red.

Disappointed, she turned back around, looking for his trash can. Finally, she saw it under his bed table. She stooped and looked inside.

A stack of mail had been tossed away. She flipped through it without removing the letters from the can, looking at the addresses on the labels.

It was mostly junk mail addressed to Resident. She kept flipping through it . . .

Then she saw something. A sale catalog addressed to Doug Streep, at the post office box they'd been watching! Doug Streep . . . the name of the man who'd ordered the clown suit!

Should she take it with her? No, she had to leave it here. Quickly, she took a picture with her cell phone.

She slipped back across the hall into the bathroom, flushed the toilet, and ran some water in case Mrs. Haughton was listening. Hands trembling just like the sick woman's, Holly texted the picture to Michael, Cathy, and Juliet. She wrote,

Found this in Warren's room. Catalog addressed to Doug Streep!

She hit SEND. Then, trying to behave normally, she came out of the bathroom and went back to the living room. Mrs. Haughton was nibbling on a donut. Holly couldn't look her in the eye. The cancer-stricken woman had no idea what was going on in her own home. She had no idea that her own family was being ripped apart by a selfish, psychopathic son. She had no idea that she was nothing more to him than an inheritance.

"Mrs. Haughton, I have to go. Is there anything else I can get you?"

"No, I'm fine, dear. Thank you for thinking of me. Let yourself out."

Holly burst out of the house, got back into her taxi, and quickly called her sister.

"Holly?" Cathy answered, out of breath.

"Did you get my text?"

"Yes, I got it. What are you *doing* there?"

"It doesn't matter. The point is, it's there, in his trash can in his room."

"That was dangerous, Holly, not to mention illegal."

"Are you kidding me? I just proved who Annalee's killer is, and you're chastising me? Besides, I didn't break in. I took Mrs. Haughton breakfast. She invited me in."

"Where are you now?"

"Leaving their house."

"Good. I have to talk to Michael and figure out what needs to be done."

"Do a three-way call. I want to talk to him too."

"Okay, hold on."

She waited as Cathy got Michael on the phone. When he came on, he said, "Holly, good work."

Holly couldn't help smiling. "Thanks, boss."

"That gives us an unmistakable link. We can prove he's the one who bought the clown suit."

"I knew it was him!" Cathy said. "So do we call the police yet?"

"I just told Max," Michael said. "But he doesn't think it's enough for a search warrant. We haven't proven he's done anything wrong yet. It's not illegal to have a post office box or to order a clown suit. If Holly had found tainted food . . ."

Cathy grunted. "But Warren's the one who brought the food from their house. He surely disposed of the contamination. He works at the lab where they test for E. coli. He had access to it. He fed Jackson Sunday!"

"Those things will matter. Holly, again, you're doing great work."

Holly beamed. When was the last time anyone had said that to her?

"What if we went to the house and showed Mrs. Haughton what we found? Maybe she would consent to allowing the police to search her house."

"I don't think she would," Holly said. "She's protective of Warren. If she had any reason to think he could be arrested . . ."

"But if we convince her that he killed her daughter?" Cathy asked. "That he almost killed her grandson?"

Holly closed her eyes. "That poor woman. She's sitting there dying alone, and she doesn't have any idea what's going on. She can't take this."

"She has to take it, before she loses her grandson too."

"I hate to make matters worse," Michael said. "But Jay called this morning to ask about Jackson. He got cut off, and it sounded like a fight. We have to get him out of there."

"Oh no." Holly's throat closed.

Cathy managed to speak. "I'll call and get his attorney to find out what happened."

"We have to talk about this," Michael said. "Plan a strategy. Call Juliet, and all of you come to my office. We'll figure it all out."

"We have to hurry, Michael," Holly said. "Time could be running out for both Jay and Jackson."

CHAPTER 37

Juliet had gotten home at seven a.m., after spending the night in the hospital waiting room. Bob was already dressed and ready to head to his office, but he hadn't bothered to get the kids up for school.

She had thirty minutes to get them up, feed them, and drive them, since they'd missed the bus. Popping pop tarts in a toaster—something she rarely did—she dragged Abe and Zach up and hounded them into their clothes. When Abe came into the kitchen, he was wearing yesterday's outfit. The shirt still had a spaghetti stain on it.

"Abe, go change clothes. Those are dirty."

"But it's my favorite shirt," he whined. "I want to wear it."

She grabbed the pop tarts out of the toaster, wrapped them in napkins. "Change now, Abe. Your blue shirt is clean. It makes your eyes pop."

"I don't want popping eyes."

"Go!" She turned to Zach, who stood in front of her with groggy eyes. "Zach, did you brush your teeth?"

"I scraped them with my fingernail."

"That's gross, son. Go brush. Hurry."

Abe appeared back in the kitchen with the clean shirt, but the same pair of dirty jeans. She decided it was good enough.

"Get your backpack. You'll have to eat in the car."

Abe took his pop tart, bit into it. "I didn't finish my homework," he said with his mouth full.

Juliet gaped at him. "Are you kidding me? Your dad didn't help you?"

"He didn't finish helping me."

Wonderful. What had he done last night? She got the kids into the car. "Abe, you'll have to take a lower grade. It's your responsibility to do your homework."

"Even if I don't understand it? I was waiting for you to get home."

"Is Jackson gonna be all right?" Zach cut in.

"I hope so."

"What about Uncle Jay? Dad says he's in jail. What did he do?"

She winced. What had her husband been thinking to tell them that? "Nothing. It's all a big mistake. It'll get worked out today, I hope." She reached Zach's school, kissed her son before he got out of the car. "Remember who you are," she said.

She watched Zach trudge in, then glanced at Abe, who had pop tart jelly on his clean shirt. Sighing, she pulled a wet wipe out of the box on her floorboard and rubbed it off.

"I have a headache," Abe said.

"No you don't, kiddo. You're fine. Going to school."

"But I'm sad about Jackson and Aunt Annalee."

She sighed as she reached the line of cars at his school. "I know, son. I'm sad too."

"What if people ask me if my uncle killed his wife?"

"They won't know you're his nephew."

"But I already texted some of them."

She groaned. "Well then, I don't know what to tell you."

"Can't I just stay home and hang out with you today?"

"No, honey. I have a lot to do today to help Jackson and Uncle Jay."

"I could help too."

"You'll help best by going to school. The fourth grade can't possibly go on without you."

He rolled his eyes and opened the car door. "Remember who you are," he said before she could get the words out.

She smiled and grabbed his face with both hands, smacked a kiss on his mouth. He grinned and wiped it off, then scampered up the walk.

As she was pulling away, her phone rang. Cathy. She clicked it on.

"Juliet, we need a quick powwow at Michael's. Have you seen Holly's text?"

"No. I've been getting the kids to school."

"She found a catalog addressed to Doug Streep in Warren's room."

"What? How did she—?"

"We'll tell you everything at Michael's office."

Juliet turned her car around and headed to Michael's office.

CHAPTER 38

Cathy had just arrived at Michael's office when Juliet burst in with both barrels loaded. "We've got to get Warren away from him!" she cried.

Cathy felt the same way. Jackson's life was in danger.

Michael was the only one who seemed calm. "Okay, I've got a plan."

Cathy shook her head. "If it's the one about going to Mrs. Haughton, I don't think it'll work."

"Just hear me out. Mrs. Haughton is grieving over her murdered daughter and is upset about her grandson. If we tell her . . . show her . . . what Holly found, she may agree to let Max and his team search her house. They can't get a warrant yet, but if she voluntarily lets them in . . ."

"She won't," Holly said. "She'll protect her son to the death."

"Even if we show her that he's tried to kill two of the people she loves most in the world?"

Cathy stared in front of her, trying to imagine how it might go.

"But I'm not sure she's in her right mind," Juliet said. "I mean, think about it. She let Warren take Jackson home, even though she knew she couldn't care for him. She listened to him crying for hours and hours and didn't let him go back to Juliet. She sat by while he had diarrhea and vomiting, and didn't even call the doctor."

"I know," Michael said, "but my guess is that she's already thinking of things that Warren said and did. She may be in denial, but there must be things gnawing at her."

"But I wasn't supposed to be prowling around in their house," Holly said. "Wouldn't it mess up the case if it went to trial and it came out that I found the mail when I was snooping in his room?"

"You were invited in," Michael said. "You got a little nosy, but you weren't breaking and entering. And you weren't doing an illegal search, because you're not a police officer."

"So let me get this straight," Juliet said. "If Mrs. Haughton gives the police permission to search, then it's not an illegal search? And they won't need a warrant?"

"That's right. And it's probably the only way we're going to get the police to do it."

"Are you sure they will, even then?" Cathy asked.

"Yes. Max has already told me he would if he got her permission. I'll call him as soon as we hang up so he'll be ready if she gives the word."

Cathy sighed. "I guess it could work. We can be persuasive. And as sick as she is, Mrs. Haughton is a reasonable woman. She must want the truth, especially if Jackson is still in danger."

Holly closed her eyes. "We might just kill her. Hearing this is just gonna put her over the edge. I don't know how much more that woman can take."

"That's the whole point," Cathy said. "When we tell her that her son is trying to get her money, that this is all about greed, that he was taking his sister out of the equation and now is trying to take her grandson . . ."

Juliet brought her hands to her face. "I can't stand thinking about the danger Jackson's in."

"That's why we have to hurry."

CHAPTER 39

Twenty minutes later, the three sisters stood at the front door of Mrs. Haughton's house. Cathy was tense, but she bolstered herself. But Holly was breathing hard enough to hyperventilate. "Get a grip, Holly," Cathy said. "We don't have time to fall apart."

Holly bent over, hands on her knees. "I'm just feeling a little sick."

"We can do this together," Juliet said. "Just stand up and breathe."

Cathy rang the bell and followed it up with a hard knock.

"I feel horrible about this," Holly whispered. "When she answers the door, she has to get up and get her cane and roll that oxygen tank with her. And for what? So we can rip out her heart and stomp on it?"

"It's kind of important," Cathy said.

They heard a creaking, a shuffling, and finally the door opened. Mrs. Haughton's breathing sounded more asthmatic than before. Her eyes were wet and sunken. Her skin was even more gray.

Holly was the first to speak. "Mrs. Haughton, I'm so sorry to bother you again."

"Is Jackson all right?"

Cathy answered before her sisters. "Actually, he's not. We need to talk to you. Can we come in?"

"Of course." Mrs. Haughton looked stricken, and she stepped back from the door and allowed them into the house. They closed the door. The smell of stale air and disease wafted over the room. Cathy remembered those smells from her mother's illness. "Let's go sit down, if you don't mind."

A look of stark dread on her face, Mrs. Haughton shuffled back into the living room. Holly took her tank and helped her get there.

Mrs. Haughton's sunken eyes looked haunted by the time she reached her couch and sank down onto it. "Just tell me. He's dead, isn't he?"

"No ma'am," Holly said quickly. "He's alive."

The woman blew out a sigh of relief, then doubled over in a coughing fit.

"He's still in ICU," Juliet said when the coughing slowed. "His kidneys have failed."

"He's *worse*?" Her face twisted, and she brought her hand to her face. "It should be me, not him. Is Warren still with him?"

"Yes, that's why we're here." Cathy nudged Holly. "Why don't you tell her what you found?"

Holly shot Cathy a look of protest, so Cathy kept talking. "Mrs. Haughton, we need to be very honest with you about what we know about Annalee's death and about Jackson's illness."

The woman drew her brows together, her forehead pleating like an accordion. "You think the two are connected?"

"We know they are," Cathy said.

Holly looked nervously at her sisters, then patted Mrs. Haughton's cold hand. "Mrs. Haughton . . ." Her voice sounded shredded. She cleared her throat and tried again. "When I was here earlier today and I went to the bathroom, I saw Warren's room. I went in there and looked around."

"You did *what*?"

"I'm sorry," she said, her pitch rising. "It's just that things weren't adding up, and I had some suspicions."

"What do you mean?"

"The way he's been acting," Cathy said. "Warren's insistence that Jackson come home with you even though he was so upset . . . Jackson's sudden illness."

"He just wanted to . . . look after his nephew," she said with as much indignation as she could muster. "You had no right!"

Mrs. Haughton began to cough again, and for a moment, Cathy thought she wouldn't be able to catch her breath. She waited, hand on her shoulder, as the sick woman worked to clear her lungs.

Finally, Mrs. Haughton got a breath and gaped at Holly. "You searched his room?" she said, touching her chest.

"I just . . . looked around, and I saw something in his wastebasket."

"His wastebasket?" Her shoulders heaved. "You were looking . . . in his trash? What for?"

"Mrs. Haughton," Cathy interjected. "Holly was looking for a clown suit."

The woman pulled her head back as if that didn't make sense. "A clown suit?"

"Yes. Our brother told us that when he got to Annalee's house that day, he saw a man coming out in a clown costume. That's the person who killed Annalee."

Mrs. Haughton shook her head. "But that's a ridiculous made-up story. Even the police don't believe it. It didn't really happen."

"Mrs. Haughton, we've been working with Michael Hogan," Cathy said, "and he was able to find where it was purchased, and the post office box it was shipped to here in town. It was shipped to a man named Doug Streep. Does that name mean anything to you?"

"No."

Holly picked up the story. "Juliet and I sat outside the post office, taking turns watching to see if any of the men we thought might be guilty showed up to check that box."

"But it wasn't one of them who showed up," Juliet said.

Holly shook her head. "It was Warren. *He* showed up that day."

Mrs. Haughton grunted. "Just because . . . he has a post office box . . ."

"Mrs. Haughton, if you go with me to his room right now, you'll see what I saw this morning. Mail addressed to Doug Streep at the same post office box. Why would he have that mail if it's not his box?"

For a moment Cathy thought the woman might shut this talk down, but she didn't. Not yet.

"I don't know who Doug Streep is, but . . . it isn't

Warren." She dragged in a breath. "Your brother created that clown story . . . to get himself off the hook."

"He didn't make it up, Mrs. Haughton," Holly said. "It's true. Warren's getting mail addressed to Doug Streep because that's the alias he used to rent the post office box."

Mrs. Haughton hacked again. Holly shot a troubled look at Cathy. The woman got to the end of it, her words ripping out. "I want to see it. Show me."

"All right," Holly said. "Come and I'll show you."

She helped Mrs. Haughton get up, wheeled her oxygen tank, handed her her walker. Cathy and Juliet followed as she shuffled into Warren's bedroom. Holly pointed to the mail in the trash can.

"*You* could have put it there!" Mrs. Haughton said. "Prowling around in my house . . ."

"You know I didn't. You answered the door when I got here. I wasn't carrying anything but donuts. I didn't even bring my purse in."

Mrs. Haughton stared at the catalog, sweat breaking out on her temples. "Get the mail out of there. I want to see all of it."

Holly gathered it and showed it to her.

As she flipped through it, her body seemed to shake harder.

"Mrs. Haughton, do you remember if Warren ever brought a package home that might have held a clown suit?" Cathy asked.

She rubbed her eyes. "No. He wouldn't . . ."

"Are you sure? Maybe he lied about what was in it," Juliet said.

"No! I told you, there's no clown suit."

"Mrs. Haughton," Holly said, "we want you to do one simple thing, and it will prove whether Warren is guilty or innocent."

"He's innocent!" she said as forcefully as she could manage. "I don't know why he has a post office box in someone else's name . . . it's nothing to do with Annalee. Your brother did this! He was there."

Cathy wasn't going to give up. "Why do you suppose he didn't tell you earlier about Jackson's bloody stools? It's E. coli, Mrs. Haughton. He could have gotten a culture at work."

Mrs. Haughton gasped. "You think *he* hurt Jackson?"

"Worse," Juliet said. "We think he tried to kill him, and that he's going to keep trying. He's with him right now. He won't leave his side."

She gaped at them, her face reflecting her anguish.

"Mrs. Haughton, I know this is painful," Holly said. "But is protecting Warren worth losing Jackson?"

Mrs. Haughton looked from side to side, as though she didn't know what to do. "I . . . I can force him to let Juliet take over."

Now they were getting somewhere. "We need you to do more than that," Cathy said. "We want you to let the police come in the house and look around."

"You mean search this house for evidence?"

"If there was any evidence, you would want to know, wouldn't you? Don't you want your daughter's murder solved?"

Mrs. Haughton was trembling now from head to toe. Cathy kept pressing.

"Your grandson has E. coli," Cathy said. "He almost died right here in this house. Warren works at a lab where they test for E. coli. He gets your inheritance when you die, and he doesn't want to share it. He got rid of his sister, and now he's taking out his nephew."

Cathy knew her words were harsh, but gentleness wouldn't pierce Mrs. Haughton's denial.

"He's my son!" She took a step and almost dropped.

All three of them reached out to steady her. "Are you okay?" Holly asked.

"No, I'm not okay," she said. "This is absurd!"

Juliet made her look at her. "If you would just let them come in and look around, you could be sure. It could put your mind to rest. If there's nothing to find, then it's okay. But if there is something . . ."

"Then I lose my daughter *and* my son," Mrs. Haughton rasped out.

They all got quiet as she stood there, holding onto Cathy and Holly, staring into space. Finally, Cathy tried again. "Mrs. Haughton, Jackson's life is hanging by a thread."

"Then get him away from him," she said. "I'll relinquish custody."

Cathy wasn't satisfied. "If you love your grandson, you'll let the police come in here," Cathy said.

Mrs. Haughton seemed to be replaying the week's events. "I need a lawyer," she said. "I have to call." She shuffled back to the living room, dropped onto the couch, and grabbed her address book out of the end table drawer. She flipped through the pages. "I have to "

"Mrs. Haughton," Cathy said, knowing that if she called her lawyer everything would come to a halt. "Listen to me!"

The woman looked up, her eyes frantic.

"Later you can get a lawyer for Warren if he gets in any trouble. But right now, don't you want to know if he killed your daughter?"

"Of course I do!"

"Don't you want to know if your grandson was poisoned?"

"He wasn't!"

"Don't you want to know if your son is trying to manipulate things so that he'll get the whole inheritance for himself?"

Mrs. Haughton shook her head hard, her mouth hanging open in a silent cry.

"You know you have doubts," Holly said softly. "You know that Jay's story could be true. You know he loved his wife, that it wasn't his idea to get a divorce. You know he couldn't walk in there and murder her and take away Jackson's mother."

Tears escaped and rolled down Mrs. Haughton's wrinkled cheeks.

"I know this is hard," Holly said, tears assaulting her too. "I wouldn't do this to you for the world. But all you have to do is open the door and let the police come in. We can have them here in a few minutes. Mrs. Haughton, please say yes. For Annalee's sake. For Jackson's."

For a long moment the woman just trembled, wiping the tears from her face with unsteady hands. Cathy was certain that she was going to say no and call the attorney, who would make sure no one searched without a warrant. She also knew they'd probably never get one.

But finally, the old woman slid her hands down her face. "Call them," she said.

Cathy sucked in a breath. "Call the police?"

"Yes," she said. "I'll let them in."

CHAPTER 40

Max, Al, and their crime scene investigators arrived at the Haughton house within minutes of Michael's call.

They asked Mrs. Haughton to wait outside on the front porch, and Cathy and her sisters sat with her, trying to reassure her that she'd done the right thing.

Michael paced on the lawn like a caged tiger, watching everything they brought out, though most of it was concealed in evidence bags. Cathy knew he would give anything to be inside, leading the search.

After Holly had shown Max the incriminating mail, they'd logged it as evidence. Now Cathy hoped they'd find even more evidence to give them probable cause for an arrest. She checked her watch, wondering if they should have Mrs. Haughton pull rank on Warren to get him out of the ICU. But if they acted to remove him, it might tip him off. If the police would just hurry and find what they needed to get an arrest warrant . . .

The front door opened and Max stepped out. Eyebrows drawn together in a deep frown, he approached Mrs. Haughton. "Ma'am, I need to ask you some questions about some things we've found."

She looked even weaker than she had earlier, more distraught, but she nodded resolutely. In his gloved hand, he held a flat, round container. "Have you ever seen this before?"

"No, what is it?"

"It's a petri dish with the residue of a culture from the lab where Warren works."

Cathy and her sisters gasped, but Warren's mother didn't seem to understand.

"A petri dish? No, no. He's not a lab technician. He's a janitor."

"Exactly. We're going to test it for E. coli."

Her head jerked back as if deflecting a blow. In a shredded voice, she asked, "You found that in there?"

"In the back of your son's drawer."

Michael froze at the porch steps, and Cathy met his eyes. "The smoking gun," he said. "Good work, Max."

Max didn't look at him. "So you've never seen this?" he asked Mrs. Haughton.

Mrs. Haughton dissolved in a coughing fit, and Cathy went to her, wishing she could help her. The oxygen attached to her nose did little good.

Finally, laboring to breathe, she said, "It was him, wasn't it? My son . . ."

As she broke into tears, her skeletal face drawn up in pain, they all waited quietly. Holly, sitting next to the old woman, put her arms around her.

Mrs. Haughton shook out of Holly's embrace and got to her feet, took a wobbly step . . . then collapsed. Holly and Juliet caught her going down.

"Help!" Holly shouted. "Somebody call an ambulance!"

Max took her pulse as they got her back in the chair. "She's breathing, but it's shallow." As he radioed for an ambulance, Michael helped them lay Mrs. Haughton down.

Moments later, Cathy watched as they loaded her onto a gurney and into an ambulance and rushed her to the hospital. She hoped the search hadn't killed her. But it wasn't the police's actions that had hurt her. It was the actions of her own son.

CHAPTER 41

Warren sat inside the ICU, wishing for a place he could lie down. This vigil was getting old, but he couldn't leave Jackson's side. If he could somehow interrupt the IV fluids, or impede Jackson's breathing, or interfere with dialysis . . .

But the nurses were too diligent, and over his bed was a camera that broadcast every move he made on the screens at the nurses' station. He doubted it was recording. It was probably just a live feed to help them monitor patients. But it was possible at any given time that one of the nurses at the station was watching them on that feed. He couldn't take a chance, not yet.

Jackson still lay limp on the hospital bed, sleeping deeply most of the time. If only Warren's mother hadn't interfered last night when Jackson got so sick. If she hadn't seen the bloody diarrhea, he could have waited longer to get Jackson to a doctor . . . long enough to be past the point of recovery.

His phone vibrated in his pocket, and he pulled it out. His mother's neighbor was calling.

Had something happened to his mother already? He

hoped not. If she died before Jackson, then Jackson's share of the inheritance would pass to Jay when the kid died. Then it would be lost to Warren forever.

His pulse quickened as he picked up the phone. "Hello?"

"Warren, this is Mildred, across the street from your mother."

"Yes ma'am," he said.

"I didn't think you were home, so I wanted to tell you that your mother was just taken to the hospital in an ambulance."

"When?"

"Just a few minutes ago. I came out when I heard the siren, and there were police cars there too."

Police cars? Warren's heart jolted. What would police cars be doing at his house? He tried not to panic. Maybe they were simply updating his mother about the investigation.

"I tried to find out what was going on, but nobody would talk to me. They were just coming and going from your house, bringing stuff out. They're still there. Your poor mama. I hope she's all right."

Warren felt the blood draining from his face. "I'm at the hospital now. I'll go down and see if they're bringing Mom here."

"Oh, good. I would come if you needed me."

"No ma'am. I'll take care of her."

He cut the phone off, got up, and looked out into the area where the ICU nurses went from one partitioned area to another. He glanced at Jackson. The kid was on oxygen and had an IV running antibiotics and other drugs into his veins. His chest was covered with leads monitoring his heart, and he wore a catheter.

Police cars. What did this mean? His mother in an ambulance. He paced back and forth next to the bed, trying to think. If there were police cars at his house, was it possible they'd figured out his involvement? Had his assault on Jackson been overreaching?

Was it possible they'd gotten a warrant to search his house? He racked his brain, trying to think of what he might have there that they could find.

He'd destroyed the clown suit and the tainted food.

It was the perfect crime. No, they couldn't have figured it out.

Sweat dripped down his face, though the air conditioning was probably set in the sixties. What might they find? His copy of his mother's will in his drawer, along with all the bank statements he'd managed to get from her account. Evidence that he had a more than passing interest in her financial condition.

Then it hit him. The petri dish in his drawer. He hadn't wanted to throw it in the trash. He'd meant to dispose of it in the incinerator at work, but he hadn't been back.

Suddenly he realized how much trouble he was in. They were on to him. Had they told his mother? Had that killed her? Were they going to come for him now?

Panicked, he looked toward the doors. He could walk out of here right now, leave and not look back, before they ever came for him. But if they were about to make an arrest, they could stop him before he made his escape.

No, he wasn't going to prison. He would never survive there. He couldn't let that happen.

His chest tightened, his heart pounding in his rib cage. He had to do something.

Think, Warren, think! He looked down at the boy. As much as he wanted to take Jackson out of the equation, it was too late now. If they'd figured it out, if they knew what was going on, then he wasn't going to get any inheritance at all, because he'd be sitting in a prison cell, maybe on death row.

An alarm clanged throughout the ICU, startling him. The man across the unit was coding again. Nurses abandoned their duties and rushed toward the patient in a frantic attempt to revive him.

Warren turned to Jackson.

The boy could be a hostage. If he took him out of here right now while they were all distracted, would they stop him?

Warren stepped to Jackson's bed, pulled the IV from his hand. Jackson's eyes fluttered open.

"Shhh," Warren warned him. "Don't say anything."

The little boy gazed up at him.

"Go back to sleep." Jackson closed his eyes again.

Quickly, Warren took Jackson's oxygen mask off, peeled the leads for the heart monitor from his chest, pulled his catheter out, untangled him.

The kid reacted with grunts and gasps, but before he could say anything, Warren had bundled him in a sheet and lifted him up off the bed. "Where are we going?" Jackson asked.

"We're going to see your daddy. He's downstairs. I'm taking you to him."

Jackson's groggy eyes rounded. "Okay. Does he know I'm sick?"

"Yes. Your dad's gonna take real good care of you. I need for you to duck your head under the sheet. I don't want anyone to see you."

"Why?"

"Because they don't want your dad to see you. They won't let us go if they see you. Just do it. He's waiting."

The kid seemed lighter than he had before. Had he already lost more weight?

Quickly, Warren slipped through the door into the hallway, knowing they hadn't yet noticed he was gone since they were all distracted by the code. He headed for the stairwell and started down it.

"Uncle Warren?"

"Shhh," he said. "Just be quiet. Daddy's in the lobby."

He got to the bottom of the stairs. Nobody had come after him. He couldn't believe it.

Out of breath, he reached the first floor. Keeping the boy covered up, he raced through the lobby out to his car. Where had he parked?

He remembered putting the car back in the wheelchair parking in front of the ER. He raced around the hospital, found the Cadillac, popped the lock.

As he put Jackson in the passenger seat, the boy looked out of the sheet. "Thought you said Daddy was here," he said weakly. "I thought—"

"He's not here. I'm going to take you to him."

"But you said . . ."

"Lay down. I need you to hide," he said. "Get down and be still!"

He backed out into the parking lot, pulled around, headed for the exit. Perfect, he thought. They'd never be able to take him now. He could figure out how to move his mother's money to a foreign bank. He could get out of the country.

He'd keep Jackson until he was sure he was home free. Then he wouldn't need him anymore.

CHAPTER 42

Michael followed the convoy of sisters to the hospital. As doctors worked on Mrs. Haughton, the four headed back up to the ICU waiting room. Max was working on getting the arrest warrant. Any minute now, Michael expected uniformed cops to show up to make the arrest. Michael couldn't wait to see the killer escorted out in handcuffs.

But when they arrived on the ICU floor, there were two nurses in the hall, talking rapid-fire to two security guards.

"He just took him! Unhooked his heart monitor and took out his cath. Jackson's kidneys have failed. We were about to start dialysis. He could die."

Michael pushed through the guards. "What's going on?"

"Warren Haughton took the boy out of here while we were working on a code," the charge nurse said. "He got out of the hospital before anyone could stop him. We have every security officer looking for him."

"What?" Cathy cried. "You just let him walk out of here with Jackson?"

"I'm sorry," the nurse cried. "We were all working the code."

Michael's mind raced. "He must have gotten warning that they were going to arrest him."

"But why would he take Jackson?" Juliet cried.

"Because he needed a hostage to get away," Cathy said. "He's probably trying to leave town."

Michael speed-dialed Max's phone, told him the situation. As he hung up, he said, "Max is putting out an APB and Amber Alert. The police need a description of his car. And someone who recognizes it should come with me to see if it's in the parking lot."

"I know where it was parked," Holly said. They hurried down to the parking lot while Cathy called Max with a description of Warren's car. Holly led them to the wheelchair parking spot where she'd seen the car the last few times she'd been here. Just as Michael expected, it was gone. Jackson was out there with a murderer who placed more value on his death than his life.

"We need to split up," Michael said. "If I were him, the first thing I would do would be to get rid of that car, so we'll need to check all the rental car places in town."

Holly went to her cab and got the phone book from under the seat. Michael grabbed it and opened it to the rental cars. Quickly, he assigned several to each of them.

"The minute you find out that he rented from one of these, call all of us and let us know," he instructed. "At least then we'll know what kind of car we're looking for. He'll be anticipating road blocks and Amber Alerts, so he might wait it out in a hotel, unless he can get out of town in a chartered plane."

Juliet covered her face. "Maybe he'll leave Jackson somewhere, now that he's escaped. Maybe someone will call us. Maybe he'll be okay."

But even as she said the words, Michael knew she didn't believe them. The little boy was in grave danger.

. . .

Cathy went to each of the rental car companies on her list—the ones closest to the hospital—and on the third one she hit pay dirt. Yes, a man had come in and rented a blue Grand Cherokee. The owner had seen him transferring a little boy who appeared to be sleeping from his silver Cadillac, which now sat abandoned in the parking lot. Armed with that information, Cathy called Max, then ran back to her car and texted Michael, Juliet, and Holly.

"Blue Grand Cherokee," she wrote, and typed in the tag number. "Heading north on State Street."

Michael wrote back immediately: "I'll start with hotels south of 15th Street. Holly—Lynn Haven Parkway area. Juliet—near the mall. Cathy, go to private airport & see if he's tried to charter a plane."

"What do we do if we find his car?" Holly texted.

"We call Max & let him take it from there. And call each one of us to let us know."

As Cathy set down the phone, she headed to Sandy Creek Airport. If Warren had chartered a plane, would he take Jackson with him? Surely he wouldn't want to be saddled with a sick child when he was on the lam.

Wishful thinking, she told herself. She reached the airport, pulled in, and scanned the few cars in the parking lot for a blue Grand Cherokee. There wasn't one. She ran to the door that said GULF AIR SERVICE. A man with a baseball cap sat at a desk with his feet up.

"Hi," she said.

The man dropped his feet. "Hey there, pretty lady. Do I know you?"

"No," she said. "Listen, I'm looking for a man who may have rented a charter plane today. He had a little boy with him. His name is Warren Haughton, but he might have used another name."

The man shook his head. "Nope, not here. We haven't had anybody come in today. It's been really slow."

Her heart sank. "Are you sure? Have you been here all day?"

"Yes ma'am, I have."

"Well, has anyone rented a plane for tomorrow?"

"No, the weather's not going to be that great. Right now there's a pretty fierce wind surge, so nobody's flying much today."

She couldn't give up. "Is there any other service here?"

"Yeah, the one next door. You could check with them."

"Thanks."

She pushed out through the exit, went to the business next door. A woman sat at a desk, watching a Spanish soap opera.

"Hi," Cathy said, out of breath. "Listen, I need your help . . . Could you tell me if a man came in today wanting to rent a charter plane for some time this week?"

"No, it's been slow," the woman said. "A guy called,

though. Asked about prices to Grand Cayman. Said he'd call back."

Her heart jolted. "Did you get his name?"

"No, he didn't leave it."

"What about your caller ID?"

The woman checked. "No name. Must have been a wireless number. I'll read it out to you."

Cathy wrote the number on her hand. "If he comes in or calls back, would you let me know?" She told her what Warren and Jackson looked like. "It's life or death for the boy, and the man is fleeing the police," she said. "Please, I need to know if he tries to get out of town."

After securing the woman's promise, she went back to her car. So he hadn't rented a plane . . . not yet.

What else might he do? Surely he wouldn't fly commercially. Security would be too tight. That would be too much of a risk. He could drive out of town, but if he knew there'd be an Amber Alert, he might not try it.

The most logical thing would be to hole up in a hotel room somewhere, trying to figure out his next move.

She checked with the hotels, striking out at each of them. No blue Grand Cherokee, and none of the clerks at the front desks had seen a man fitting Warren's description.

As Cathy drove, desperation brought tears to her eyes. "Lord . . ." she said as she drove. "I know you don't owe me anything, as mad as I've been at you."

The tears spilled out and rolled down her face. "You may be mad at me too. I wouldn't blame you, after how I've acted. But if you could just put that aside for Jackson's sake . . .

"That little boy is so sick. He's suffering, and now he's in the hands of a murderer. God, please show us where he is. And send angels to surround him and take care of him. I'm begging you."

Suddenly her phone rang. Michael. She picked it up. "Any luck?"

"Yep. His rental car is sitting right here in the parking lot at the Holiday Inn on Frane Street. Same tag number you gave us."

Her heart leapt. "Did you call the police?"

"Yes. Max is getting the SWAT team together."

A SWAT team. Dread crushed her. What if Jackson got hurt?

"I'm on my way over," she said.

CHAPTER 43

The smell of Jackson's soiled clothes was getting to Warren. The child hadn't had anything to eat since going into the hospital, yet his diarrhea continued to flow. Jackson had vomited twice since checking into the hotel—mostly bloody liquid. Warren hadn't taken time to get Jackson's clothes out of the hospital locker, so the boy lay on the bed in the rancid hospital gown. The stench made Warren gag.

Maybe he should just abandon him, launch out on his own, and hope he made it across the state line. If he could just get out of town, maybe he could get to one of the private airports in another town, rent a charter flight to Mexico. But if he did it that way, he'd have to leave the money behind. If he hid out here, there might be a little time to transfer his mother's funds.

On his iPhone, he went to her bank's website and tried out different passwords to get into her bank account. He knew she had online access because he had set it up for her. She apparently had changed her password since he did it—probably at his sister's prompting—but it shouldn't be too hard to figure out. He typed in her birthday . . . Annalee's birthday . . . his own . . .

He tried Jackson's, but that didn't work either. He wiped the sweat from his forehead, went to the window and opened it, trying to let out some of the stale, puke-laden air. His mother was simple. She wouldn't choose a password she would have trouble remembering. It would be something easy like 12345 or the word *password* itself.

He went back to the computer. Maybe it was something as simple as her grandson's name—Jackson.

He typed that in, and suddenly the ball began to spin. Access! After a few seconds, up came her account information.

Now what?

He could make a payment to his own account, as if he were paying a bill. She did have that capability, didn't she, to pay bills online? He checked her balance. She had $50,000 in her checking account, $200,000 in savings. The lion's share of her money was tied up in stocks and bonds, municipal funds, and of course, her house. Warren supposed that was lost to him, since he'd been found out. He could only get away with what he could grab now.

Quickly, he set the account up to pay a bill, then wrote himself a check for $49,000. It wasn't much, but it was something. It would be enough to get out of town and get set up somewhere south of the border. But it didn't sit well with him, not when there was $200,000 more sitting in her savings account. How could he get that out?

He heard Jackson's labored breathing, and he turned. The boy's eyes were closed and he seemed to be sleeping. He was burning with fever. The E. coli was advancing.

He turned back to the computer. Maybe if he transferred her funds from savings to checking, then wrote himself another payment . . . but would it raise red flags at the bank? Would they alert the police and put a hold on the account?

He didn't have much time. He had to hurry. He opened another browser window, found a bank in Grand Cayman. Was it possible to open an account online? He quickly scanned their website, found a screen where he could do that.

Typing as fast as he could, he filled in the information, using his alias, Doug Streep, opened the account, got the number. Yes, this was perfect. He could transfer the money from her savings account to her checking account, then "pay a bill" to his account in Grand Cayman. He could get out of here tomorrow by driving over to Mobile, taking a charter flight down to the Cayman Islands, getting the money out, then fleeing to Mexico. He already had a fake driver's license and passport in the name of Doug Streep. He'd taken care of that in case things went wrong with Annalee.

It could all work, but should he keep Jackson with him in case he needed a hostage? No, the boy would hold him back. No pilot would want to fly with a kid who was throwing up and soiling his clothes, especially one who was so clearly critically ill. They might notify the police.

If they'd issued an Amber Alert, the kid would raise red flags. If he went alone . . .

He could dye his hair, put on glasses, disguise himself somehow. Maybe he could even leave an anonymous call that the boy was in the hotel room, so somebody would come get him and they'd quit looking for him as if he were a kidnapper.

Kidnapper . . . murderer . . .

The labels didn't fit. He wasn't a bad person. He just needed money. His sister hadn't deserved any of it. She was a narcissist who was willing to rip her child's father out of his life for her own fickle appetite. That should have disqualified her as an heir under his mother's strict moral code. And Jay . . . Warren had owed him since he exposed his joblessness to Warren's mother a couple of years ago. She'd been all too happy to help him financially while he was working, but then Jay discovered that he had never been employed where he claimed to work. Because of Jay, Warren's mother saw him as a liar. It had taken two years and a stupid janitorial job before she trusted him again. He'd been waiting to get even ever since. With Annalee's death, he'd killed two birds with one stone.

He wondered if his mother was dead yet or if she lay in the hospital believing the things they were telling her about him. He did feel bad for her. She was the only one who'd ever supported him, the only one who believed in him. She would want him to be happy, want him to be free, want him to have the money he needed to start a normal life. That was her dream for him, wasn't it?

But how had it gone so terribly wrong? He had set it up so perfectly, figuring out exactly what would make Jay's story unbelievable, so he would be the main suspect. It had seemed hilarious at first. Dressing up like a clown, murdering his sister, emailing "Jay's" note to his sisters and then emailing Jay to come over and work things out. He'd enjoyed every moment of it. He'd imagined Jay telling the story of how the clown had bounced out of Annalee's house before he found her body.

Since he knew it would be harder to get away with it once Cathy got involved—and he knew she would— he'd added a red herring to lead her on a wild goose chase. She'd been so suspicious since her fiancé's death, she had gotten famous with her skepticism. She was too smart for her own good, so he had to throw her off his trail. But his notes pointing to Leonard Miller hadn't worked.

Now Jay would be released and the police force would be after Warren. And Cathy would be blogging about his guilt, and people would leave their nasty little comments about him on her page, and people all over the country would recognize him.

He had no choice. He had to risk transferring the money and get out of the country. He arranged the transaction, transferred $199,000 into his mother's checking account, waited to make sure it had gone through. Then he wrote his alias another payment from her checking account to the Grand Cayman bank.

Quickly, he signed off, signed back on in his own name, went to his own account. If only he could get some cash—but that was impossible right now. He'd just have to do the best he could with what he had in his pocket—about $800, which he'd been carrying for getaway money in case his plan with Annalee went south. That would have to pay for the first part of the charter flight. Maybe he could get the pilot to take him to Grand Cayman and wait for payment until he could get the money out of the bank.

It wasn't ideal, wasn't what he had wanted to happen, but he should've known Cathy and her sisters would figure things out.

Jackson's breath was louder now, more labored. Was the E. coli affecting his lungs? He thought of putting a pillow over the kid's face and being done with it. Jackson had served his purpose to help him escape. Now he was a liability.

Ending his suffering would be the kindest thing.

CHAPTER 44

Where were the police? Cathy sat in the passenger seat of Michael's car. Juliet and Holly had gotten in the back, and they all waited with anticipation for the police to come and make an arrest at Warren's hotel. Time was ticking away for Jackson.

Michael had gotten the hotel manager to tell him which room Warren was in. He'd checked in as Doug Streep. But the SWAT team was taking too long. They should be here by now.

"Maybe we can't wait for them," Cathy said. "Maybe one of us needs to go to the door."

"No," Michael said. "We're not equipped for this. We have to wait."

"I'm equipped," Cathy said. "I have a .38 in my purse."

"Are you crazy?" Juliet countered. "You're dealing with a maniac. What are you gonna do? Shoot your way in?"

"All I have to do is aim it."

"Cathy, listen to yourself! This isn't a game!"

"Nobody's going," Michael said, checking his watch. "We're sitting right here."

"Jackson could be dying in there," Holly muttered.

They got quiet, and Cathy looked up and down the street, wishing she could hear a siren or see lights flashing. *Where were they?*

"Okay, I'm gonna be sick," Holly blurted. Before anyone could respond, she opened the door, leaned out, and heaved onto the pavement.

Juliet stared at her. "What's wrong with you? You threw up the other day at my house. You almost did earlier today. Are you getting it too?"

Holly straightened, wiping her mouth. "No. It's probably just nerves."

"You've never thrown up before when you're nervous," Juliet said.

"Well, I just did, okay?"

"Are you sure you're not sick?"

"No, but even if I were, I can't do anything about it now. Can we get back to catching the murderer?"

Cathy stared out the windshield, thinking. This wasn't like Holly. She was the type who embraced sickness, wanting attention and empathy. All her life, she'd milked her ailments for all they were worth. Maybe she was just growing up. This wasn't a normal moment, and Holly was focused on Jackson. But wouldn't her nausea at least make her wonder if she might have E. coli too?

Suddenly it hit her. Her breath caught in her throat. Cathy turned around. "Holly, you're not pregnant, are you?"

Juliet sucked in a breath and looked at Holly.

Their younger sister's mouth dropped open. "Why would you . . . Just because . . . I would tell you if . . ."

"Whoa, he's coming out!" Michael cut in.

They all looked to the door on the side of the hotel. Warren was carrying Jackson, wrapped in a blanket, hurrying toward his rental car.

"Block his car!" Cathy said, grabbing her gun out of her purse. "Make sure he doesn't get out."

Michael started his car, threw it into DRIVE, and lunged toward Warren's rented Cherokee. Warren froze at the sight of them.

Cathy jumped out of the car, clutching her revolver with both hands. "Warren, stop! Put Jackson down carefully. Lay him in the grass!"

Warren didn't move as Michael got out of the car. "Do what she says, Warren! Put him down!"

Ignoring them, Warren turned and ran back into the hotel, Jackson jostling limply in his arms.

Cathy couldn't shoot for fear of hitting Jackson. She aimed the gun at the ground and ran after Warren. Behind her, she heard Michael shouting, "Wait, Cathy!"

Cathy didn't listen. She burst into the building, looked up and down the hall. Warren was gone. His room was on the fourth floor. He wouldn't have taken the elevator.

The stairwell!

As Michael raced through the door behind her, Cathy burst into the stairwell. Suddenly, a blow came from her left—Warren's fist smashed her cheekbone, knocking her back. Warren had Jackson slung over his shoulder, but he jerked the revolver out of her hand.

The door flew open, and Warren backed up the stairs and turned the gun on Michael. "Get out of here, Hogan, or I'll kill all of you."

Michael put his hands up. "Warren, there's a SWAT team on its way. It's over. Put Jackson down and give me the gun."

Cathy held her breath and froze. Warren's face twisted with panic. Jackson was limp, his head and arms hanging down behind Warren's back. Was he breathing?

The smell of diseased waste filled the room.

Suddenly the gun fired, and Michael jumped back. Cathy screamed as ceiling plaster crumbled down. Thankfully, he hadn't hit Michael. Warren stepped closer to Michael, threatening to fire again.

"Michael, get out!" Cathy cried.

Michael opened the door, backed away, his hands still up. "Warren, you don't want to make this worse."

Warren's hand was shaking, his finger over the trigger again. "Out!" he yelled, his voice echoing up the stairwell. Michael inched a little farther out the door. Keeping the gun aimed at Michael, Warren crouched and lay Jackson on the landing.

Cathy lunged at him and went for the gun, but Warren managed to grab her wrist and twist her around. As her back arched in pain, he let her wrist go, and his arm came up to clamp around her neck. He shoved the barrel of the gun against her head. Her neck strained as she tried to lean her head away. She saw the fear on Michael's face.

"Don't!" Michael said. "Warren, I'll go. I'm backing away. You can take off, up the stairs, make an escape. I won't come after you. Just leave her and Jackson here."

Warren's hold on Cathy loosened, then just as

quickly tightened again. He was compressing her windpipe, and she struggled to breathe.

"I . . . told you . . . to leave. Out . . . now!"

She felt the gun shaking in his hand, vibrating against her head as his arm clamped tighter. Her vision grew blotchy . . . black . . . He was going to kill her right here, without firing the gun.

Her body grew weak, her knees buckled. She sagged, the weight of her body making his arm tighten even more.

"Okay, I'm going," Michael said in a desperate whisper. "I'll back out into the hall. Just . . . let her breathe."

She heard Michael stepping out, and the exit door slammed shut. Finally, mercifully, Warren dropped his arm, and Cathy fell to her knees, clutching her throat and gasping for breath as if she'd been drowning.

CHAPTER 45

Jay had spent most of the day lying on his bunk and praying, trying to avoid the other inmates spoiling for a fight. He hadn't been able to reach Michael again since talking to him this morning.

If Jackson had died, they would have come to tell him, wouldn't they?

But he couldn't be sure about anything.

"Cramer, you might want to see this."

Jay sat up. An older inmate who went by the name of Horace stood in his doorway. "What is it?"

"The news. There's an Amber Alert, and the kid's name is Cramer."

Jay sprang off the bed and followed Horace into his cell. It looked like he'd been here for a long time. He had pictures taped up on the wall and a number of paperback books on his table. A Bible sat on his bed table and the small TV he was allowed sat in the corner.

Jay walked closer to the set and read the crawl under the *Dr. Phil* show:

An Amber Alert has been issued for five-year-
old Jackson Cramer, abducted from the Bay Medical
Center ICU.

Jay brought his hands to his head and stumbled
back. "No. It can't be."

"That your son, man?"

"Yes!" He got down on his knees and locked onto
the screen again.

Police are looking for the boy's uncle, Warren
Haughton, who is believed to have taken him. He's
described as a white male, five-foot ten inches . . .

Warren? Why would Warren abduct Jackson? What
would he want with him?

Tears assaulted him, and he sat back on his haunches
and began to weep. Horace stooped down next to him.
"You okay, man?"

"My son . . ."

Horace nodded. "Bad stretch of luck, huh?"

Jay couldn't speak.

"You can keep watching it, man. I'll go out there and
make sure they leave you be."

Jay just sat on the floor, his eyes glued to the screen,
as he read the crawl over and over.

CHAPTER 46

Outside, Holly and Juliet got out of the car. "What is Cathy doing?" Juliet cried. "That was a gunshot!"

Holly ran back to her taxi and pulled her .22 revolver out of her glove box as she heard distant sirens. Running back to Juliet, she brandished the gun.

"What are you doing with that?"

"I carry it for protection. I'm going in."

"No!" Juliet said. "Wait here for the police. I mean it, Holly!"

"Sorry, Sis." She took off toward the door the others had gone in. "Tell the police where we are."

"Holly!"

Holly pushed through the heavy door and found Michael standing at the door to the stairwell. She heard Warren's voice on the other side of the door, then Cathy . . .

Michael saw her. "Give me the gun," he said.

Holly hesitated. "But you can't!" she whispered. "You'll go to jail."

"He's got Cathy!" He jerked the gun out of Holly's hand, pulled out the chamber. "Holly, it's not loaded!"

"Really?" she said. "I haven't used it since I practiced at the shooting range. I forgot to put more bullets in."

He closed the chamber and looked through the narrow panel of glass to see what Warren was doing. Maybe he could use the gun to scare him. It was better than nothing.

. . .

"Get up!" Warren said, pulling Cathy up by her hair. "Pick the kid up. Now!"

Cathy kept gasping for breath, but she stumbled for her nephew. Was he alive? *Oh God, please!*

She went the few steps up to the landing, grabbed Jackson. He was burning with fever, but she could see his chest rising and falling with wheezing breath.

He was still alive! "Jackson," she managed to rasp out. "Honey, are you okay?"

He seemed unconscious, his eyes sunken, and vomit and diarrhea crusted on his hospital gown.

"Warren, please . . . just let me take him to the hospital. He's dying!"

"Go up the stairs to the fourth floor and open the door," Warren said through his teeth.

She hesitated.

"Do it!" he shouted, and she feared the gun would go off. Adrenaline propelled her as she hurried up four flights, opened the door, and stumbled out into the hall, holding Jackson close.

Warren prodded them to his door, shoved his key card in, and threw it open. "Go in!" he said.

Cathy went into the small hotel room, and Warren locked the door behind them. He hurried across the floor and looked out the balcony window.

"Warren, there's no way out. Your best bet is not to hurt Jackson, to just cut your losses and give it up. Maybe they can't prove you killed Annalee. But there are witnesses if you kill Jackson."

"I'm not going to prison!" he bit out.

"You can still get away. Run, now. Just go before the police get here!"

"I can't get out of this without a hostage," he said.

"Fine. I'll be your hostage. Just let Jackson go. We can leave him in the hallway. They can get him into an ambulance, take him to the hospital. With me you could get out of the country. I could help you. We could pretend to be newlyweds on our honeymoon."

For a moment, she thought Warren might be considering it. Then his head jerked toward the sound of sirens.

CHAPTER 47

Michael reached the fourth floor, but they had already gone into Warren's room. His mind raced. He could kick the door in, but Warren could kill both Cathy and Jackson before he could get to them. And with an unloaded gun, Michael could only bluff.

He looked up the hall, saw a maid peering out of a room with terrified eyes. He took off toward that room, moved the woman aside, and went in.

"You cannot come into here," the woman shouted. "I call manager!"

Michael ignored her and went to the balcony door, threw it open. He heard Holly behind him. "Michael, what are you doing?"

"Going to their balcony," he said, stepping over the railing to the balcony next door.

The sound of sirens rose over the hum of the air conditioners. Wind whipped up, blowing Holly's pink hair into her face. "Holly, when the police get up here, tell them where I am."

"I'm coming with you," she said, stepping over the rail herself.

"Holly, so help me . . . Go back! I need for you to tell the police."

She finally acquiesced and went back into the hotel room. Michael stepped over two more balconies, the unloaded gun in his hand.

He reached Warren's balcony. The curtains were closed. Michael heard Cathy's voice inside, Warren shouting back at her. He sounded panicked. Surely he heard the sirens. Would he kill Cathy and Jackson now and try to run for it?

Michael prayed that fear would keep him from doing further harm.

CHAPTER 48

Inside the room, Cathy tried to take care of Jackson. He was weak and limp, and his hospital gown was filthy. She pulled it off of him, then headed for the bathroom to get a washcloth.

"Stay there," Warren said. "Don't move out of my sight."

She threw up her chin and kept walking. "You know what, Warren? Just shoot me. I'm going to get a wet washcloth to clean up my nephew. If you want to kill me for it and bring the entire Panama City police department down on your head, you go ahead."

She went into the bathroom, snatched a hand towel off the towel bar, and turned the faucet on. Rage pulsed through her. For him to take Jackson out of the hospital like this, leave him limp and sick, wrapped in his own vomit . . . It was cruel. But everything about this was cruel. Poisoning Jackson with E. coli was cruel. Murdering his own sister . . .

She squeezed out the towel, shut off the faucet. She saw herself in the mirror. Her neck was red where Warren had tried to strangle her, and a red splotch marked where he'd hit her.

He stood in the bathroom doorway behind her, watching her in the mirror.

He didn't shoot her. Instead, he let her stalk back to their nephew. "Come here, honey," she said, lifting Jackson's head, though he was still not conscious. She wiped his face, his chest, scrubbing him down the best she could. If he would just wake up, she could make him drink. He was probably drastically dehydrated.

"Warren, he's on fire with fever. He's dying. He's your nephew . . . your own blood!"

But she knew blood relations didn't matter to Warren. She didn't wait for an answer. She wrapped the boy in one of the clean bed sheets, lifted him, marveling at how light the five-year-old was in her arms.

"What are you doing?" Warren asked, clutching the gun.

"I'm putting him outside," she said, daring him to stop her. Her heart pounded with uncommon courage as she carried Jackson to the door.

Suddenly, he fired. She jumped and screamed, almost dropping Jackson. Warren stood with the gun smoking, and his thumb cocked it again. "Back away from the door, Cathy," he said. "I'm not playing."

She drew in a long breath. "Warren, you can do just as much with me as a hostage as you can with him. Probably more, and you know it. I'm not going to raise red flags like a sick boy in a hospital gown would. We can go wherever you want and you can get on a plane or get a car—"

The room phone rang. Warren looked at it but didn't answer. Then they heard a bull-horned voice from the hallway. "Warren, this is Detective Max Hogan of the Panama City Police Department. Leave your hostages and come out with your hands over your head."

"Max Hogan," he said bitterly. "Of course. That's perfect. Another one of your dead boyfriend's brothers."

Cathy had the sense he was feeling powerless . . . that it might lead to his killing them both. "Warren, it's not too late," she said. "We could leave Jackson on the bed. We could go out the back, over the balcony. I'll go with you. They won't shoot you if I'm with you."

Warren's eyes shifted from the front door to the back.

"We can climb down . . . It's only four flights."

"And then what? I can't get to my car."

"I have a car here," she said. "We could get to it, and I could drive us to the airport."

She held her breath as he seemed to weigh his options. Sweat glistened on his face and wet his armpits in huge rings. The phone kept ringing, and in the hall, Max made another plea.

"Warren, let the hostages go. You don't need a child's death on your head. Pick up the phone so we can talk."

Finally, Warren made a decision.

"Okay, we'll do it. Leave Jackson on the bed."

CHAPTER 49

It got quiet inside the hotel room. Michael stood on the outside of the sliding glass door. Warren had surely heard the sirens. If Michael were Warren, he would try to come out this back way.

Then he heard a clicking sound, heard the door unlocking, sliding back. He mashed himself against the bricks, raised the gun.

Warren opened the door, his arm around Cathy's neck, the gun against her head. Slowly, the two of them stepped out.

Suddenly Michael was on him, knocking both Warren and Cathy to the balcony floor. Warren dropped the gun, reached for it, almost grabbing it.

Cathy rolled out of the way as Michael cocked Holly's pistol and rammed the barrel into Warren's temple.

Warren froze. Cathy grabbed the loaded gun. She got to her feet, chambered around, and pointed it at Warren's face. "I'd freeze if I were you, you rodent slime, because I have every reason to kill you!"

The front door crashed open and police filled the room. SWAT team members appeared on the roof across the parking lot and in balconies above them and below them.

Cathy backed away and stepped over the railing to the next balcony to give them a wide berth. But suddenly Warren flipped Michael over, got on top of him, wrestled Holly's gun out of his hand. Michael managed to get on top again, this time pulling Warren to his feet, butting his mouth with his head, knocking him back against the rail. Warren aimed the gun up at Michael's chin . . . pulled the trigger.

It only clicked.

Cursing, Warren threw it over the rail, then flipped Michael around, bending him backward over the rail. Stationed on the roof across the parking lot and behind cars on the ground, the police couldn't fire; the men were too close together.

"Michael!" Cathy screamed. Taking careful aim, she fired at Warren's leg.

The bullet grazed his calf. He screamed out and disengaged from Michael, clutching his wound.

Michael slid to the side, giving the police and Cathy a clear shot. Suddenly, Warren stepped up on the rail . . . and leapt.

SWAT team members beneath them held their fire as Warren hit the ground.

CHAPTER 50

Cathy went back over the balcony rail and threw herself into Michael's arms. Her body trembled as she clung to him.

"Are you okay?" he asked. "Did he hurt you? Did I hurt you?"

She ignored the question and touched a gash on his face. "You're bleeding."

"I'm fine," he said. "It's over."

They didn't let go as they watched the activity below. Neither seemed able to move. Cathy had no desire to stand on her own, so she allowed Michael's embrace to hold her up.

They watched as the SWAT team surrounded Warren with rifles. He moved an arm, tried to turn himself over.

The fall from the fourth floor hadn't killed him; paramedics rushed to the scene.

Now if they could just get Jackson help. Pulling out of Michael's embrace, Cathy hurried back into the hotel room.

CHAPTER 51

They needed one more miracle. Holly struggled to see through her tears as she followed the ambulances in her taxi. Warren's leap had left him broken but not dead. It wasn't fair, since Jackson lingered so near death.

Why did God let cruel men live and innocent boys die?

Please, God . . . Jackson needs you!

At least Jay would be released this afternoon and could be at the hospital with his son. Maybe his presence would help Jackson's recovery.

But dread of a death vigil crushed Holly. She lost Jackson's ambulance as it raced through a red light, cars pulling to the side of the road to let it pass. She waited at the light as sobs overtook her.

Annalee dead . . . Jay arrested . . . Jackson's illness . . . Warren's jump. In her heart, the traumatic events got tangled up with her pregnancy. Hormones didn't help matters.

She turned off the highway, looking for a place to pull over until she could stop crying enough to see. She cut through a residential area with cars lining the road. Nowhere to stop, so she kept driving.

Before she knew it, she was at the post office again. She pulled into the parking lot, once again facing the abortion clinic.

No, this was not where she wanted to be. But she couldn't seem to make herself leave.

Most of the protesters were gone for the day, but two women still stood across the street, their huge posters of an unborn fetus leaning against their car. She couldn't help staring at those posters.

One of them had Six Weeks written at the top.

Her hand went to her stomach. Was that what her baby looked like now? Were there tiny little fingers and toes? Eyes? A nose?

Her gaze strayed to the door of the clinic. Would she be able to actually call and make that appointment? Would she manage to walk up that sidewalk and go in? Would she get the words out to tell the receptionist that she wanted an abortion? Would she be able to go into that examining room?

And after it was over . . . how would she walk out and go home, as if nothing had ever happened?

She'd just risked her life to save her nephew. Couldn't she risk her convenience to save her own baby?

She wanted to be noble, someone others might want to be like. But so far, her life was a study in failure. What not to do. She hadn't succeeded at one thing.

No, she told herself quickly. That wasn't quite true. She had succeeded today. She had helped in the search for Jackson. Even though her gun wasn't loaded, she'd been part of the team that had solved the murder and led to Jackson's rescue. If they'd waited for the police, Warren would have gotten away.

So maybe she did have the potential to succeed. Maybe she could change. Maybe she could even parent a child.

But that was ridiculous. She wasn't fit to be a parent. She could almost hear Juliet now, ranting about how irresponsible and immoral she was, reminding her that she always made the wrong choices.

But she couldn't make the wrong one now. The stakes were too high. Her baby's life was more important than a thoughtless whim.

Adoption was a possibility . . . a much better one than abortion. But if she gave the baby up, she had no doubt that Juliet would want him. Holly would never be able to stand seeing her child growing up in her sister's home. As good a parent as Juliet was, this was Holly's child. God had given this baby to her.

So how could she consider destroying it?

Unable to look at that building any longer, she pulled her car back out of the parking lot and headed to the hospital.

When she got to the ER, they had already taken Jackson in. He was still alive, and the doctors assured them that with IVs and drugs, his prognosis could still be hopeful. She couldn't see him for a while, she was told, since only one person could be with him while they admitted him back to the ICU.

Cathy and Michael left to go pick Jay up when he was released from the jail, and Juliet stayed in the room with Jackson. Holly sat alone in the waiting room for a few minutes, fidgeting and helpless. Adrenaline still pulsed through her, making it hard to sit still. Finally, she decided to check on Mrs. Haughton. If she were still alive, she probably didn't know that Warren had been injured. Who would tell her?

Holly found out what room they'd admitted her to on the third floor. She rode up in the elevator, then went to the nurses' station. "Excuse me. I want to see Doris Haughton."

"Room 318," the nurse said without looking up from her charts.

Holly just stood there for a moment. "Can I ask why you didn't put her in intensive care? She seemed really sick."

The nurse looked up then. "She has a DNR order in her file, so we're trying to keep her comfortable here."

"DNR?" Holly asked.

"Do not resuscitate."

Holly's heart jolted. "Can I see her?"

"Yes. Are you family?"

"No, just a friend."

Holly went to her door, knocked softly, pushed it open.

Mrs. Haughton lay limp on the bed, an oxygen mask on her face. She was asleep or unconscious; Holly couldn't tell which.

She leaned over the bed, touched the thin skin of Mrs. Haughton's cold hand. The limp woman didn't flinch.

"Mrs. Haughton?" Holly whispered. "It's me, Holly.

I just wanted to come by and make sure you're all right."

Mrs. Haughton didn't move or react. Holly looked around, saw a blanket in a chair. She went to get it, unfolded it, and spread it over the bed. "Is that better?" she asked.

Still . . . silence.

"Mrs. Haughton," she said, "I'm so sorry for everything that's happened. Annalee, Jackson . . . Warren. I know your heart is broken."

Mrs. Haughton probably didn't know that Warren had kidnapped Jackson and almost killed him. She didn't know he had tried to hurl himself to his death.

She pushed the gray, coarse hair out of the woman's wrinkled face. "Life just doesn't turn out like we expect, does it?" She sat down in the chair next to the bed, stroked Mrs. Haughton's hand again. "If Juliet were here, she'd tell you that there's more on the other side. That all things become new again. That there's healing and life. But I don't know if I believe that." Her voice trailed off, and her gaze settled on the window beyond the bed.

What, exactly, did she believe? She wasn't an atheist. She cried out too much to God to claim she didn't believe. Faith had molded Juliet, and to some extent, Cathy. But Holly's spiritual core was tainted with cynicism. How could she believe in the things her father preached, when he'd been proven a fraud?

And the church that had been such a family to them when she was little had abandoned them so easily. Her mother never sought another one. Oh, she'd attended one now and then and dragged the kids along, but she'd never put her trust in the people again.

To Holly, the body of Christ was as sick and broken as Warren and his mother.

But now, as she sat with this woman hovering on the brink of death, she found herself wondering if her impressions were true. Did it really matter that the world was full of hypocrites, when it came right down to it? Would God give her a pass because she'd been hurt by his people?

"I take that back," she told Mrs. Haughton. "The truth is, I do believe that there's more. And if I didn't believe in forgiveness, I guess I'd just give up. It wouldn't be worth going on." The words caught in her throat, and tears sprang to her eyes. "I know it all sounds far-fetched. I've thought that too. That my mistakes . . . and there are an awful lot of them . . . couldn't possibly be erased clean. That Jesus couldn't possibly forgive them. But I think that's the whole point of why he came."

The words were cathartic, infusing her with peace, though they were meant for Mrs. Haughton. Holly swallowed and squeezed Mrs. Haughton's hand. "I hope you can hear me."

. . .

Juliet waited with Jackson until they moved him up to the ICU. It would be an hour or so before they got him set up and she could see him. By then, she hoped that Jay would be here.

She couldn't imagine what her little brother had

been going through. Had he somehow heard about the Amber Alert and the search for his kidnapped son? It must have been torture.

She decided to take a few minutes to check on Mrs. Haughton. The woman had been brought to the hospital without any fanfare. There had been no one from her family to receive her and stay with her. No one who cared whether she lived or died.

Juliet's heart ached for Annalee's mother. If she found out how evil her son really was . . . what would it do to her? She could hear it on TV or read it in the paper tomorrow.

Maybe Juliet could break it to her gently, without telling her everything he'd done.

She got Mrs. Haughton's room number and went up to her floor. She went to the door, found it partially open. Quietly, she stepped inside.

Holly was already there, her back to the door, sitting close to the woman's bed. "I know it all sounds far-fetched. I've thought that too. That my mistakes . . . and there are an awful lot of them . . . couldn't possibly be erased clean. That Jesus couldn't possibly forgive them. But I think that's the whole point of why he came . . . I hope you can hear me."

Juliet touched her chest as tears came to her eyes. She started to step forward and stand beside her sister, but she hesitated when Holly spoke again.

"I've done so many things wrong. Things that are life-changing. I haven't told anybody this yet . . ."

Juliet's hand dropped, and she took a step back, out of sight.

"Juliet would have a heart attack. She would tell me how stupid I've been. That I have terrible judgment. She'd be right. She would tell me that I'm not fit to be a mother."

Juliet almost gasped, but she threw her hand over her mouth. What? A *mother*?

Had Cathy been right in the car?

"I'm pregnant, Mrs. Haughton," Holly said. "And I was thinking about an abortion, but I can't go through with it." She paused, looked down at the wrinkled gray face. "I don't know why I'm telling you this. I haven't really had anyone else I could tell. You probably can't hear me anyway."

Juliet slipped out and walked down to the nurses' station, stunned. She leaned back against the wall, looked up at the ceiling. Holly pregnant? No wonder she'd been throwing up. No wonder she cried so much.

She tried to imagine what her baby sister was going through . . . considering abortion . . . wondering what to do. She'd been carrying this alone. Suffering and angry at herself.

After a few minutes, Holly came out of the room, wiping her face. When Holly saw Juliet, she stopped walking. Juliet pushed off from the wall and went toward her.

"Juliet," Holly said. "Did they move Jackson to this floor?"

"No," Juliet said. "I came to see Mrs. Haughton."

Holly's face tightened. "Oh. She's in there, but she's not conscious."

Juliet's face twisted, and she thought of pretending

she hadn't heard. But then Holly would have to keep enduring her situation alone. Suddenly, Juliet pulled her sister into a hug, held her as if she were her own child.

"What is it?" Holly asked on a whisper.

Juliet began to cry. "You're a beautiful girl, Holly. Inside and out. And you'll be a wonderful mother."

Holly pulled back suddenly, and stared, stricken, at her sister. Her wet face turned crimson, and her jaw dropped open. Then she began to laugh. Juliet laughed with her and pulled her back into the hug.

CHAPTER 52

Darkness was beginning to set in as Cathy and Michael reached the jail. Jay's attorney was just pulling up. He went in to process Jay's release while Cathy and Michael waited outside.

The temperature had dropped, and a cool wind whispered across the parking lot, ruffling Cathy's hair. The moon hung low, full.

"The moon looks like it's closer to the earth than usual," she said. "Weird to think it's just an illusion."

"Not just an illusion," Michael said. "It's a reminder."

"Of what?" she asked with a smile.

"Of God's having control over everything. The moon . . . Jackson's life . . . our lives."

Cathy smiled. "Something happened to me during all this. I realized some things."

"About God?" he asked.

He always seemed to read her thoughts. "Yes. About his listening to me when I pray. I found out that he does. He even answers."

"You knew that already."

She looked into the wind, squinting. "Yeah, I knew.

You've reminded me enough. But I didn't want to admit it. I blamed God for everything. For my father's betrayal . . . for my mother's cancer . . . for Joe's murder."

"And you don't anymore?"

She thought about that for a moment. "I'm still grappling with all of this. But I do know one thing. God's love trumps evil. Jesus is the evidence of that."

Michael looked at her, moonlight glistening in his eyes. "I knew you'd come around."

"And another thing happened. When I was trying to figure out if the killer was one of the people I'd blogged about, I realized how what I do impacts lives."

"It does, Cathy. You do good work."

"No, I mean that it impacts them in a negative way. I'm not sure I've always been that careful. If someone looks guilty, I tell the world."

"But you have great instincts. And you dig for the truth."

"But I never pray about it. What if there are people like Jay, who are completely innocent, whose lives have been ruined because of what I've written?"

Michael considered that for a moment. "I hope you're not planning to quit blogging. It's too important, what you do."

She met his eyes. "Really? You think so?"

"You know it is. For some reason, God took me out of the police force and put me where I am. For some reason, he's given you a blog that people like to read. Think of how many dangerous people you've helped get off the street."

"Maybe I won't quit. Maybe I just won't draw

conclusions before I should. I'll pray about these things before I sink my teeth into them."

"Sounds like a good plan."

She met his eyes, mirrored his smile. "Thank you, Michael."

"For what?"

"For encouraging me. And for being there. I knew when Warren opened that balcony door that you'd be there. You're always there. You're my hero."

She couldn't manage to look away as he gazed at her, and she felt her heart hammering against her chest just as it had done when she was in danger.

She wondered if she was in danger now.

His face moved close to hers, and she didn't back away. Suddenly his lips touched hers, sweet, soft . . . just the way she'd imagined. The kiss deepened, lingered . . .

His hand came up to touch her face. She melted to his touch. She had known he would taste like this . . .

Too soon, he pulled back and met her eyes. She drew in a deep breath . . . held it.

"I'm sorry," he whispered.

She hadn't expected that. She looked down at her feet, sudden guilt assaulting her. "For what?"

"For . . . that. I shouldn't have been so bold. You're Joe's girl."

"I *was* Joe's girl."

"But my brother loved you."

"He loved you too."

He let his eyes linger on her face. "It feels wrong . . . doesn't it?"

She didn't know what she felt. Was it wrong or

right? If Joe knew, would he be devastated or delighted? Would he have chosen Michael for her or declared him off limits?

She didn't know. Unable to speak, she touched his face, pulled him back to her, and kissed him again. This time she lost herself in his kiss, touching the stubble on his jaw, the silkiness of his hair, the texture of his skin. His fingers buried themselves in her hair, gently tilting her head.

The door opened suddenly and light spilled out, startling them apart.

"Cathy?"

She turned to see her brother standing in the light. "Jay?"

He ran toward her, and she threw her arms around him. "Are you all right?"

"Yes," he said. "How is Jackson?"

"He's back in the hospital."

Jay's eyes filled with tears. "They said on TV Warren kidnapped him. They said he was dying."

"He'll be better now with you there. Come on, we'll take you to him."

Michael pulled Jay into a hug. "Glad to see you out, man."

As they drove Jay to the hospital, Cathy didn't look at Michael again. The air seemed charged with enough voltage to power her heart for years.

But guilt still had its own current.

CHAPTER 53

"So you're having a baby before I am." Cathy's gut reaction to Holly's news disturbed her. Why couldn't she just empathize with her sister? This wasn't about her, of course. But it reminded her . . . if she'd married Joe, by now she'd probably be shopping for maternity clothes and cribs.

Holly sat on the sand in front of her, the ocean at her back. She looked so small and pretty with the wind whipping her long pink hair into her face. Her skin had more color now, and those dark circles that often marked the morning after a night of clubbing had disappeared. Though it wasn't ideal for her to be pregnant and unmarried, maybe it was pushing her toward being more healthy.

"I know. It's crazy."

The end of day sun burned on Cathy's face and shoulders. She dusted the sand off her feet and slipped them back into her sandals. "Are you going to tell the father?"

Holly breathed a mirthless laugh. "No. I don't even know his last name. I'll never see him again. And that's just as well, because I hardly knew him. I was just drunk."

Cathy sighed. "Holly . . ."

"I know. You don't have to say it." She looked down at the sand and drew a circle, finished it off with two eyes and a smile.

"Say what?"

"All the things I've done wrong. All these years I should have listened to you and Juliet. You've always been right. You warn me of where I'm heading, but I race there anyway."

"So maybe this time you'll slow down. Think it through. Raising a child can't be done by the seat of your pants. It takes thought, planning, commitment."

"I know. It scares me to death."

Cathy looked into the breeze. A family was sitting on the packed wet sand at the edge of the waves. A little toddler was piling sand in a tower with a plastic shovel. His father stood in the water with a baby on his shoulders, frothy tongues of sea water nipping at his feet. The mother dug through a sack and pulled out a baggie of crackers.

Cathy had experienced that as a child, but in so many ways that scenario had been lost to Holly.

Cathy turned back to Holly. "I think you're going to do fine. I see changes in you."

Holly's eyebrows lifted. "Really?"

"Yes. You've been more caring lately. You've done things to help. You've taken responsibility."

"Probably because I'm not going out drinking every night. Can't really do that when you're pregnant."

"Oh, you can. Lots of people do. You choose not to. And that speaks volumes about your putting your baby's needs before your own. You'll do fine, Sis. You had a rough start, with Dad and everything."

Holly shook her head. "No, I can't blame him. Not anymore. I make my own choices." She wiped away the sandy happy face she'd drawn, dusted off her hands. "I saw him, you know."

"Saw who?"

"Dad."

Cathy squinted to study her face. "You went there?"

"Yes. To the nursing home. I sat with him, saw how helpless he is. This cranky nurse's aide was feeding him, and I made her give me the spoon so I could do it."

Cathy was stunned. "Did he know you?"

"No. I was a stranger to him."

Cathy felt the pain rising in her throat. "Did he say anything?"

"Not a word. I could have been anybody off the street. He's not really in there. But I guess it helped me in some way just . . . to see him. Just to know that he can never redeem himself. I have to stop living my life as if I'm waiting for him to pay back his debt to me."

Cathy stared at her, amazed at the bravery of her sister. Since they'd learned their father was in a nursing home here, they'd all dealt with it in their own way. Cathy didn't know if Juliet ever visited him. Juliet hadn't ever mentioned it. But for Holly, the weak one, to go there and serve him . . .

Holly's phone buzzed, and she looked down at the text. "It's from Jay. He says the doctor came by and they're releasing Jackson tomorrow."

"Very cool," Holly said. "So that whole prayer thing. It really does work."

"Yeah, it does. Go figure."

When Holly went back to her taxi, Cathy sat alone for a moment, trying to shake the conversation about their dad from her mind. But it wouldn't leave her.

Did her father still look the way he had years ago? Was his hair more gray? Was his face more wrinkled? Had he put on weight?

He'd been so animated and charming as a preacher, and his flock had adored him. Did he still have that twinkle in his eye?

There was a way to find out.

She knew where the nursing home was. She had passed it many times, since it sat on Highway 98 along the beach. At least his wife had chosen a nice place for him.

She dusted off the sand and crossed the street to her house, wondering if she had the courage to go to that place and dredge up all those memories. But had she really ever escaped them?

Not sure what she would say to him if she saw him, she drove to the nursing home and went in, feeling incompetent and awkward, which she deplored. But she found her way to the Alzheimer's wing.

She walked slowly down the empty hallway, looking at the names on the doors. Rogers, Wright, Gonzales . . .

Finally she heard a voice inside a large room up ahead. A man's gentle voice, reading. "For His anger is but for a moment, His favor is for a lifetime; weeping may last for the night, but joy comes in the morning."

She stopped outside the door and saw that many of the residents were in there, some seated on chairs, others in wheelchairs. A young man stood at the front, an open Bible in his hand. Was today Sunday? Had she come during church?

She turned to walk away, but the preacher stopped her. "Ma'am? You're welcome to join us."

Embarrassed, she shook her head. "No, that's okay. I was just . . . looking for someone. I'm sorry to interrupt."

"You aren't interrupting. Come on in."

She hesitated, scanning faces . . . mostly women . . . and settled on two old men.

There he was. Her father, a little grayer than he'd been in the last picture she had with him, when he'd escorted her to the father-daughter banquet at her school. He didn't seem aware of her or the man at the front. He merely stared at the air, unengaged with his surroundings.

A lady sitting at the piano followed Cathy's gaze. "Is Mr. Cramer your relative?"

She cleared her throat. "Yes . . . my father."

"Well, come on in, honey."

One of the aides in scrubs brought a chair up beside him, and realizing she couldn't escape now, Cathy crossed through the residents and sat down. Her father didn't look at her.

As the preacher resumed his sermon, Cathy only stared at her dad, a million emotions flipping like a slideshow through her mind. The shock of his infidelity. The pain of his abandonment. All the phone calls she'd made that he hadn't returned. Birthdays coming and going without a notice. Christmases changed forever.

In fact, they rarely ever saw him again after he ran off with the woman. It was as if he'd gutted the family from his life.

And now, here he was, unable to have the epiphany about how wrong he'd been, unable to repent and beg for forgiveness. Unable to start over fresh and be the father she needed.

Her bitterness seemed such a waste, over an empty shell of a man who didn't even know he'd done anything wrong. What good was it?

It was her own prison, one of the things that held her back. In some ways, his failures challenged her to be better, do better, in hopes of showing him that she had become somebody even without him. That she didn't need him. That her own human spirit had risen above his indifference.

But now that didn't even matter. Her father was a broken, empty old man who didn't even know where he was.

The preacher talked about David's plight during the writing of the Psalms . . . words that revived memories of her dad waxing poetic in his own pulpit. But then the preacher read again.

"As for me, I said in my alarm, 'I am cut off from before Thine eyes; nevertheless Thou did hear the voice of my supplications when I cried to Thee.'"

Yes, Cathy thought as the preacher read on from Psalm 31. God had heard her supplication. He hadn't cut her off or forgotten her.

I see you. Those words filled her spirit, reviving her soul, bringing tears of pain and joy to her eyes. Then her father turned his warm familiar eyes to her. For a miraculous moment they connected, and she would have sworn he recognized her. A gentle smile lifted the sides of his lips.

"Daddy," she whispered.

He lifted his shaky hand, and put it over hers.

Tears shimmered in her eyes as she sat there with him, taking in the sustenance of the sermon like a starving orphan, as that recognition faded to vacancy.

EPILOGUE

A week later, the gravesite swarmed with mourners, some friends of the family, others well-wishers who'd prayed for them. A couple of TV reporters hung on the outskirts of the crowd, their cameramen anything but discreet.

Cathy got out of her car and walked across the spongy grass. Several of the mourners saw her and stepped aside, allowing her to pass through. She saw Holly and Juliet standing near the tent. Michael turned as she came closer. She met his eyes.

Then she saw Jay, sitting on the front row of the folding chairs near the caskets. Little Jackson leaned into him. He was still pale, but he'd come through his illness with no lasting effects, and the doctors assured them that he would have a full recovery.

They'd delayed Annalee's funeral until he was well enough to attend. Mrs. Haughton had passed peacefully in the hospital. She never woke up after finding out her son was her daughter's killer. Now they celebrated both mother and daughter's lives together, and would bury them side by side. Jackson would only have to endure one funeral.

"Is he okay?" Cathy whispered to Juliet.

"Yes, he seems fine. Jay did a good job of preparing him."

They got quiet as the short service began. As the preacher spoke, Cathy's mind wandered to Warren. He had broken his back in the fall, and was paralyzed from his waist down. He lay in a rehab hospital now with a guard at the door. Though he'd pled guilty to Annalee's death and the other charges against him, she knew his personal prison would be worse than the state could inflict on him.

When the funeral was over, Jay gave Jackson a bundle of balloons and allowed him to set them free into the sky. He waved to them, a soft, poignant smile on his little face as the balloons drifted out of sight.

Despite Annalee's behavior over the last year, Cathy hoped that in the last few moments of her life, she'd called out to Jesus. Maybe she hadn't died with guilt and shame crushing her. Maybe she had been washed clean as she bled out in the bathtub. Cathy hoped so. Jackson would be expecting to see his mother someday when he made his own walk into heaven.

Later, they all met at Jay's house—the house he'd built with Annalee, the house she'd died in. Jackson would be allowed to continue living in his own home, sleeping in his own bed, playing in his own yard. Jay was no longer banished to a bare apartment.

But the grief would be with them for a long time to come.

Mrs. Haughton's entire estate went to Jackson, and Jay had assigned it all to a trust fund that Jackson could access when he was older. Until then, he'd support his son himself.

Relatives and friends brought food and lingered, talking of their memories of Annalee and her mother. The sisters worked tirelessly in the kitchen, making sure that everyone felt welcome.

But Cathy wondered what had happened to Michael. He'd disappeared shortly after they'd arrived at the house. Though their relief was profound after solving Annalee's murder, Cathy knew that Michael's thoughts had returned to Leonard Miller. His appearance back in town had reignited Michael's desire to catch him committing another crime. He'd spent much of the last few days following the man around town. She knew he wouldn't rest until his brother's killer was off the streets. So far, Miller had stayed within the law.

When she could get away, she walked out of the kitchen and looked around. Michael wasn't inside, so she glanced out the window. His Trailblazer was still parked on the street.

He must be out back. She crossed through the big house and stepped out the back door. There he was, sitting on the porch swing with Jackson, their backs to her.

"Can Mommy see me?" Jackson asked him, looking up at the clouds.

"I'm not sure," Michael said. "But I do know that Jesus can see you. And he probably keeps her updated about all the cool things you do."

"Someday we'll be together again," Jackson said wistfully "Me and Mommy and Daddy and Grandma."

Michael patted his knee. "That's right, buddy."

"And your brother will be there too. What was his name?"

"Joe."

"Yeah, Joe. He's probably bowling with my mom." Jackson smiled at the thought.

Michael chuckled. "Bowling? You think they have bowling alleys in heaven?"

"Probably," Jackson said. "Mommy likes to bowl."

Cathy stood quietly near the door. Michael would make a wonderful father . . . a great husband . . . to someone.

That guilt rose inside her again, reminding her that it shouldn't be her. She stepped back inside and saw Juliet watching her.

"You're wrong, you know."

"Wrong about what?"

"About Michael. You were Joe's two favorite people. Why wouldn't he want you together?"

"Because he was the jealous type."

"He's in heaven now. He's not struggling with that anymore."

Cathy looked at the floor. Juliet came closer, put her hand on Cathy's shoulder. "I think it's okay."

As Juliet walked away, Cathy went back to the door. She looked out and saw that Jackson was on his swing set now. Michael stood in the middle of the yard. He turned and saw her . . . and a smile overtook his face.

For that moment, Cathy let herself be happy.

A NOTE FROM THE AUTHOR

Recently, as I was stressing about my writing process, God showed me that He understands, because He is a writer too. As the Author and Perfecter of our faith (Hebrews 12:2), He is writing each of our stories.

Did you know that? Do you understand that you're the leading character in your story? That your story has a theme and a purpose, and a conflict and a resolution?

You are the character—God's masterpiece. Ephesians 2:10 (NLT) says that we are "God's masterpiece. He has created us anew in Christ Jesus, so we can do the good things He planned for us long ago."

When I begin writing a book, I approach it in a number of different ways. Sometimes I start with a plot, and the characters are designed to serve that plot. Other times, I start with the characters. But in either case, the stories and each of the characters have a purpose and a character arc. I plan for them to grow, so I give them challenges they aren't expecting. As they deal with those challenges, some of them catastrophic, I show them growing until, at the end, they aren't the same people they started out to be.

I know it isn't easy to imagine God writing your story, because a lot of us see ourselves as extras in the broad scope of His-story. But you do have your own story. God did design your character for a purpose. He did give you a character arc. He made you a certain way, and He will give you challenges to help you grow. As He's writing this character growth in you, He wants you to learn something. He wants you to change somehow. He wants you to do something. He wants you to impact someone.

So much of what happens to us can't be explained. Sometimes we never understand it. We don't always come to the end of our lives and have a light bulb come on and some grand epiphany where everything suddenly makes sense. But God knows the story. He knows the purpose. He knows how it will fit into His broader plan, because He wrote it.

But every good story has conflict. If I had a story without any conflict, no one would read it. It would be boring. Our conflicts are the things that build us, strengthen us, make us more useful. Without them, we are one-dimensional. And God doesn't write one-dimensional characters.

When I'm writing a character, I love them as if they were real people. I cry over them and pray over them. Remember when Jesus wept when Lazarus died, even though He knew He was going to raise him from the dead? It recently occurred to me that it's the same thing I do when I have to kill a character I've spent chapters developing, and I literally weep over it. I only let a character die if I know that it advances my plot and my purpose in telling this story, but it hurts me when I do it, even though I know the end of the story.

When I killed off a child in one of my books, it threw a lot of my readers for a loop. I can't tell you all the letters I got from people who were still wiping tears as they wrote to me. But almost all of those people said that they understood why I did it, and it was the only right choice for that story. I let that child die to teach a principle that would help many people. Sometimes God does the same thing. As the Author of our Faith, He writes things into our story that are hard to take. But He has a plan and a purpose for that pain, and He promises that it will turn out well for those who love Him and are called according to His purpose (Romans 8:28).

Some of you are thinking, *God couldn't have written my story, because I've done so many things wrong. I've made mistakes that make God gasp.* But guess what? God can't be shocked. He isn't surprised at the mistakes you've made; He plans to use them. He already knows the purpose of all those mistakes, and He already knows how they work into your redemption story.

I love writing characters who are a mess because there's so much I can do with them throughout a series. In the case of Holly in the Moonlighter Series, do you think I'm looking at her and thinking, *Wow, I hate this character. She's such a loser. She's a failure at everything.* No! I absolutely love her. I cry with her, I laugh with her, and I have big plans for her. I hate to see her hurting, but I'm letting her hurt, because I have a purpose for that pain.

Some of you may remember my character Issie from my Newpointe 911 Series. Issie was the same kind of character. She was a mess. The first time we see her, she's trying to break up someone's marriage. But as the series progressed, I took her through a growth arc, and when I featured her in the final book, I was able to show her growth. I loved her from that first day I conceived of her.

In the same way, God is not surprised by your mistakes. If you're a mess, if you've had failures, if you've done every single thing in your life wrong, God can use it in your story. He has a plan for it. No matter what you've been, God still loves you. If I can love Holly and Issie as I'm writing their stories, God can love you while He's writing yours. I'm not more compassionate than He is.

He knows you. He wired you that way. He gave you the background that would lead to that. He understands why you wound up here. He wants to see you learn and grow and change. He knows just what obstacles to put in your path, when to lighten up on you and give some comic relief, when to tighten the screws to get you out of your comfort zone, when to pull your security out from under you so you'll reach for Him. He wants your character arc to be the kind of story that impacts others when the last page is written.

I have a friend named Jeff Gerke, and a few years ago he adopted a little girl named Sophie from China. Sophie had a cleft palate, so a few months after they got her, they took her for surgery. Jeff blogged about that difficult day and Sophie's fear and the pain afterward, and I was particularly touched by this. He wrote, "Sophie couldn't see that she needed this surgery. She couldn't understand why people she loved and trusted would allow her to go through such fear and pain for no apparent reason. Of course, we could see she needed it and that this was all for her benefit through the rest of her life, but all she could see was the fear and pain."

I think we go through things like that sometimes. I think God allows us to undergo pain and fear for no reason we can see. He knows we need it and that it will help us in the long run, but all we feel is afraid, hurt, and maybe even a little betrayed and abandoned. As Jeff's son told Sophie, "You're going to be scared and it's going to hurt, but we're going to be here after, and we're not leaving you."

That's exactly what God says to us when He's taking us through a trial we don't understand. Because He knows the resolution. He knows the beauty that will come from it.

In Jesus' story, His suffering was catastrophic. Hebrews 2:10 says, "For it was fitting for Him, for whom are all things, and through whom are all things, in bringing many sons to glory, to perfect the author of their salvation through sufferings."

Jesus suffered because His character arc included a sacrificial death to take our punishment—the greatest act of love in all of history. Remember all those mistakes and failures I mentioned earlier? The ones you and I have done? Jesus' story was all about those sins. It was all about taking the punishment that we deserved. He suffered so that we wouldn't be burdened with sin and shame, but we'd be set free with redemption and grace and an eternity with Him. That can be how our story ends.

Or it can end differently. Some of us decide to get angry at God for the story arc He's given us. Some of us would rather raise our fists to God than open hands reaching for Him. Some waste all of it. Some of us miss the whole point of our story.

But it doesn't have to be that way.

Can you trust God with your story arc? Can you trust that, as the Author of your life, He is writing in it what needs to be there, and that however it turns out, it's for your good? Like Jeff's baby Sophie suffering through the fear of surgeons and abandonment and pain, without knowing they're just trying to fix her birth defect and heal her, God is doing something in us that we might not be able to see.

God has an eternal future in mind for you. It can be yours if you surrender to His redemption in your life. Whatever regrets you have can be turned into something beautiful . . . something impactful. Something meaningful. There can be a happily ever after for you if you trust Him no matter what.

I pray that everyone reading this will grasp that, and that when the last pages of our lives are written, we'll each embrace the happily-ever-after that Christ was dying to write into our lives.

Terri Blackstock

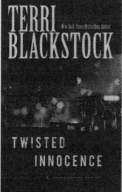

THE RESTORATION SERIES

In the face of a crisis that sweeps an entire high-tech planet back to the age before electricity, the Brannings face a choice. Will they hoard their possessions to survive—or trust God to provide as they offer their resources to others? Terri Blackstock weaves a masterful what-if series in which global catastrophe reveals the darkness in human hearts— and lights the way to restoration for a self-centered world.

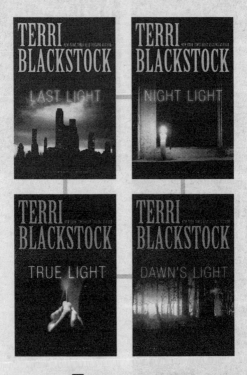

THE INTERVENTION SERIES

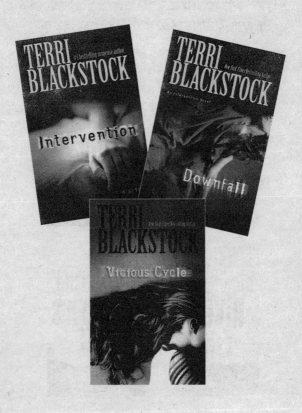

ABOUT THE AUTHOR

Terri Blackstock has sold over seven million books worldwide and is a *New York Times* bestselling author. She is the award-winning author of *Intervention*, *Vicious Cycle*, and *Downfall*, as well as such series as Cape Refuge, Newpointe 911, the SunCoast Chronicles, and Restoration.

. . .

Visit her website at www.terriblackstock.com
Facebook: tblackstock
Twitter: @terriblackstock